# CRAVING A HERO

## St. John Sibling Series, Book 3

## by Barbara Raffin

---

*Craving A Hero* © 2014 by Barbara Raffin.

All rights reserved by author. The reproduction or other use of any part of this publication without the prior written consent of the rights holder is an infringement of the copyright law.

Cover Art/Design: Covers by Rogenna.
All rights reserved.

This is a work of fiction. People and locations, even those with real names, have been fictionalized for the purposes of this story.

---

*From award-winning author of the St. John Sibling series, another St. John Sibling contemporary romance, Craving a Hero by Barbara Raffin:*

Kelly Jackson always said heroes were just ordinary people who did extraordinary things. Unfortunately, she didn't believe there was any man out there who would do anything extraordinary for her. Not that she was looking for a mate. She was a woman focused on proving herself as a Conservation Officer to the world and her father.

Then Dane St. John showed up in her little corner of the world with the looks, the ego, and the charm to take him to the top as an up and coming movie action hero. He paid attention to her. He made her feel like a woman. He was the perfect fantasy tryst.

Too bad he turned out to be a whole lot more substantial than some airhead hunk and Kelly fell in love. Too bad because, in spite of his strong family values, his idea of having a family fell into the *someday* category; and history had taught Kelly, when a man isn't ready for a family, he can't be counted on. So, when she discovers their affair produced a baby, she doesn't tell him because there are no heroes...not for her.

## WHAT THE CRITICS ARE SAYING:

"Barbara has created a love story that manages to keep you in suspense throughout. There's just no way to know beforehand whether or not there will be a happy ending. Kelly and Dane come across as real life individuals with real life concerns and insecurities. And the internal dynamics of Kelly's family add an additional reminder...that sometimes events outside ourselves can greatly affect our...choices." *Rick Roberts, platinum-recording artist and author of* Song Stories and Other Left-Handed Recollections


"In *Craving a Hero,* Raffin delivers another sexy love story laced with humor, but it's also a heartfelt book, involving the complex entanglements when what seems like a lusty attraction rapidly turns into something deeper, not to mention consequential.

Raffin is so good at taking readers inside a dilemma and then letting us wonder if these characters will walk away or solve the problems. Now I'm waiting the next St. John book to come out!" *Reviewed by Virginia McCullough, award winning author of* Greta's Grace

# Also by Barbara Raffin

*Contemporary Works*

Taming Tess: St. John Sibling Series: book 1
Finding Home: St. John Sibling Series: book 2
The Mating Game
The Sting of Love (short story)

*Paranormal/Suspense Works*

The Scarecrow & Ms. Moon (novella)
Jaded (novella)
The Visitor
Time Out of Mind
Wolfsong

*Historical Works*

The Indentured Heart

LINK TO MY WEB SITE:

http://barbararaffin.com/

LINK TO MY BLOG:

http://barbararaffin.com/barbsblog/

# CRAVING A HERO

St. John Sibling Series, Book 3

by Barbara Raffin

### CHAPTER ONE

"OMG, you're Dane St. John," squealed a teenage girl from the boat's bow seat, letting the tip of her fishing rod dip into the lake.

"Holy crap," hooted the younger boy on the middle seat of the small craft. "You're *the* Hawke!"

"Watch your language, boy," the father said from the rear of the boat as Conservation Officer Kelly Jackson took the fishing license he held out for her.

She noticed the father's gaze sharpen on the man seated in the bow of her boat. From the corner of her eye she could see her passenger sitting sprawled out, muscled arms draped over the gunwale, legs so long he'd propped them on the center seat. He'd assumed that pose from the moment she'd refused to allow him to help her launch the craft from shore. She was, after all, as capable of handling a boat by herself as any other Conservation Officer.

Still, the puckish grin of the newest action star to come out of Hollywood had taunted her all morning. If she didn't know better, she'd swear he'd chosen the remote Upper Peninsula of Michigan to research his next movie role just to torment her.

"You that actor all the kids are crazed about?" the father asked.

"Mom likes him, too," said the boy through the wide grin he'd fixed on *the Hawke* a.k.a. Dane St. John.

No doubt St. John was flashing his pearly whites for his *fans*. He'd done so at every boat they'd stopped. And if their passengers weren't fans already, a wink from his brook-blue eyes won them over.

Somehow, she'd managed to remain immune to his charms. Maybe it was his longish hair or the smug way he watched her through his Ray Bans...which he removed whenever they pulled up to another boat. Couldn't pass up an opportunity to show off those famous blue eyes. Though, judging by *Daddy's* frown, maybe she wasn't alone in that immunity.

"OMG," the girl squealed again, this time dropping her fishing pole into the bottom of the aluminum boat and producing a cell phone from the purse on the seat beside her. "No one's going to believe this! I have to get a picture!"

"Me, too," said the boy, likewise discarding his pole and lurching to his feet.

Their boat rocked and Kelly shifted her attention from the license to the overall situation. "Sit," she commanded. "You'll tip your boat."

The boy obeyed and the father added, "And mind your poles. What if you get a bite?"

The boy had plopped his backside down off center of his bench seat, causing the small fishing boat to list toward the DNR craft.

"OMG! OMG!" the girl kept repeating, raising her phone in front of her face, and twisting to get herself and Dane in the same frame, her movement adding to the already precarious tilt of their boat.

Dane grabbed the neighboring bow and tucked it in close to the larger DNR craft, holding it steady...all the while posing practically cheek to cheek with the girl while she snapped pictures with her phone.

"Teenagers," the father grumbled.

Kelly smiled at him. "Bet she's bugging you for the car keys all the time."

"Not a chance of that for another couple years," the

father said through a sigh of relief.

Kelly ticked off any necessity to check for further licenses. A good CO didn't always have to ask direct questions to gain information…like whether or not the teenage girl in the boat was old enough to need a license herself.

Having given the father's fishing license a cursory once-over, Kelly handed it back to the man. "I see you've got one of Sven Maki's boats."

"Renting a cabin from him, too," the father said.

"My turn," the boy said, rocking the boat again as he leaned from his seat toward Dane.

A muscle popped in Dane's arm and a vein bulged in his neck. He was one-handedly keeping that boat from swamping…or showing off big time. She didn't know whether to be impressed or annoyed.

"Settle down there, champ," Kelly said to the boy.

"Use your own phone," the girl groused.

"I left it at the cabin."

"Take a picture for your brother," the father said, mumbling under his breath about how the boy had at least the courtesy not to bring his phone on their fishing trip.

"Your sister will take a picture of you and me together, won't you little lady?" Dane said in his deep, slightly raspy *Hawke* voice that females were swooning over ever since his first movie's recent release. But not Kelly. Definitely not. She had more sense than that.

Dane had a hand on the boy's shoulder and was bathing the girl in his high wattage smile. She was blushing, her fingers flying over the phone's keyboard.

"I'll just finish this twee—" She glanced into Dane's blinding smile and her fingers went still.

"So," Kelly said, turning her attention back to the father, mentally ticking off her script of Conservation Officer's questions. "Catch anything yet?"

The father eyed his kids huddled in the bow of the boat getting their pictures taken with Dane St. John. "Just a movie star."

#

Kelly knew how the father felt. A double major in conservation and criminal justice and trained alongside Michigan State Police candidates, yet she was still being handed fluff jobs like babysitting an actor. Boat stowed, morning duties behind her, and still stewing over the fact she yet had to prove she was more than the token minority hire, she led her charge along a trail on a ridge through the woods.

"Nice family back there," her charge said, dogging her heels, so close she swore she could feel his breath slipping past the braid hanging down her back. "But since you scoped them out with your binoculars, why'd you still check on them?"

"I could see the girl was giving her dad grief about her life-preserver. Didn't want to buckle it up. That's something we can't ignore."

"So you'd have given him a ticket because *she* refused to buckle up?"

"I could have if she hadn't by the time I got to their boat," she said.

"But you wouldn't have, right?"

There was something in the tone of his question—something almost pleading—as if he would have found her lacking if she admitted she would have written a ticket. And damn, it made her want to tell him what he wanted to hear.

"A true law and order CO—" *Like my father.* "—would have written a ticket."

"But there's room to give a person a break, right?"

"Kids and life-preservers, that's black and white—life and death," she said, avoiding giving him a straight answer.

"But the dad was trying to do the right thing and teenagers can be contrary."

She peered over her shoulder at Dane. "What do you know about teenagers?"

He grinned back at her. "I had seven years' experience as one."

Before she could stop herself, she rolled her eyes. One corner of his mouth twitched. She stifled a groan and turned her attention back to the trail in front of them.

"You wouldn't have ticketed him," Dane said, sounding way too sure of his assumption.

"It's a moot point. By the time we caught up to them, the dad had gotten the daughter to buckle up."

"Yeah," he said, still sounding like he didn't believe she'd have ticketed the father.

Maybe she wouldn't have. Maybe the threat would have been enough to make an impression on the girl about how serious her lack of compliance was. Kelly did see things more in shades of gray than black and white like her father did. That was one of *her failings* as her father saw it.

"I heard you tell that dad where to take his kids for some fishing action this evening. That was nice of you." Dane's voice ruffled past her braid, his nearness causing each strand of hair on the back of her neck to stand up as though a raw nerve.

"Just spreading a little good will," she returned. "Good for the tourist trade."

"Is that part of the job?"

"As a matter of fact, it is."

"So, I learned another aspect of the job," he said.

"And what else did you learn today?" she asked before she remembered she didn't really care what he learned, if anything.

"There're no shades of gray when it comes to safety laws, and binoculars are a CO's best friend."

Surprised he had even extracted that much from her morning duties, she gave him a cursory glance. His grin stretched.

"Surveilling the boaters on the lake before we launched—" he started.

*"We?"* she cast over her shoulder, quick to remind him

that she hadn't allowed him to help her in any aspect of *her* job.

"Correction," he said, giving her a conceding nod. "Surveilling the boaters on the lake before *you* launched the boat saved a lot of unnecessary stops once we were on the water."

"That's why binoculars are a good tool of the job," she said.

"That's what I said."

She huffed and trudged off along the trail, sweat trickling down her spine. Ordinarily, she'd have taken the afternoon off after a morning of marine surveillance, then gone back out when the boaters came off the lake when she could check their catches…or waited to check on the night fishing crowd. July afternoons were generally too hot for field work unless there was a fishing tournament or another such event happening.

But she was in no mood to make things easy for *Joe Hollywood*. So, she'd taken him hiking through a dense, mosquito-filled woods. And they were quickly sweating off their insect repellent. Good thing they each carried a fresh supply in their backpacks. Oh yeah, she'd made him don a backpack under the guise of *you wanted the full experience.*

"So," he said still way too close behind her. "Just what are we out here looking for?"

*Your breaking point.* "Any sign of poaching."

"And what would that look like?"

"Animal carcasses. Make-shift hunting blinds. Worn patches where someone might have been squatting— waiting for deer to pass." *Mostly the sort of poaching evidence left over from the winter that I look for in spring rather than hot mid-summer because poachers generally use the same spots to illegally hunt from winter to winter.* Not that she was about to inform him of that fact.

"Circling crows overhead mean there's a carcass on the ground, right?" he asked.

In her peripheral vision she caught the upward sweep

of his arm and glanced up. *Damn*. Just her luck, *Joe Hollywood* was some sort of Boy Scout. She exhaled.

"Looks like they're over the highway. Probably just road kill."

"So, is this all you do, wander around the woods looking for signs of something illegal?" he asked, all but tripping on her heels.

"Yup," she said without so much as a backward glance. "Nice and mundane."

"Is that another reference to how my portrayal of field work in my last movie missed the mark?"

She stopped short and wheeled around at him. "Listen, I may not have been on this job very long, but I'm the daughter of a CO and not once in his thirty-year career did he come home sooty and singed from an explosion."

"That's because he never played a Game Warden—a CO in an action movie."

"No, that's because none of that over-the-top crap happens in real life."

He shoved his hands in his pockets and grinned down at her. "Reality doesn't make for interesting action films. Besides, I portray a Game Warden along the Tex-Mex border. Things get a little more heated when the bad guys carry Oozies rather than fishing poles."

"So your Game Warden character stumbles across drug mules for a drug cartel and winds up in an all-out war. Does *that* even happen in Texas?"

He shrugged, his grin oozing charm. "Wouldn't know. I didn't write the script."

"Yet you came all the way to the Upper Peninsula of Michigan to *research* the next installment of your gung-ho game warden movies?"

"Figured if they were going to create a series around my character, I had an obligation to learn a little more about him and what he'd encounter in the second movie."

"And you think the Texas Department of Natural Resources would send one of their Game Wardens to the northern most reaches of Michigan?"

"Actually," he said, "my character's supposed to be taking a vacation after all the mayhem he encountered in the first movie."

"And they thought nice, boring Upper Michigan was just the place for him to recuperate from…how many shots did you duck and explosions did you narrowly miss?"

His grin widened and he hovered closer. "You really hate all that action crap, don't you?"

"Tell me they aren't going to blow up my woods for the sake of a movie."

His grin turned into a grimace. "Wouldn't be much of an action film if there weren't some fireworks. Besides, where the Hawke goes trouble follows."

She groaned at the reference to one of the tag lines hyping his movie character, turned, and trudged off, calling back to him, "Just stay on the trail and watch your step. I'm responsible for your safety."

"Yes, ma'aaaam."

The humorous note in his voice turned into a wail. Kelly spun around to see her charge somersaulting down the slope the ridge bordered. She cursed and skidded the forested hill after him. If the man broke a body part, the production company backing his latest movie was sure to blame her. They'd probably take the entire production budget of his up-coming movie out of her salary, which meant she could kiss good-bye any plan to move out her parent's house let alone a new truck. She'd be lucky if she even kept her job as a CO after this…not to mention any chance of getting her father's approval.

"This isn't my fault," she shouted, skidding down the hill toward where St. John had come to a stop against a stump.

Dane St. John's screams and the angry buzz of ground hornets swarming up around him were the only responses she got as he scrambled to his feet.

"Dammit!" She shrugged off her backpack, dug out a spray can of wasp stopper, and blitzed the swarm, dropping them in midair.

But her movie action-hero star kept running, flapping his arms like some giant bird trying to get air born, one of those long-legged sorts. He was truly a man-sized action hero...whom she, *a mere female*, had just saved from a swarm of angry ground hornets. The fans of his high-octane action movie, soon to be plural, should see him now.

A smile tugged at her lips as she watched him race off through the trees, trying to outrun hornets that currently lay stunned at the bottom of the gulley he'd fallen into. *Some hero.*

Though she had to admit, ground hornets had a nasty sting and he probably didn't know she'd rendered them helpless.

Not that the Michigan Department of Natural Resources was likely to see it her way, either. Even if tall, buffed, and handsome admitted it was his own fault he'd gotten stung by hornets, she was in deep doo-doo. Never mind that she'd told him to watch his step on the narrow path.

A flurry of irritated buzzes hummed from the leaf-covered forest floor near where she stood. The hornets fought the effects of the stunning spray. It wouldn't keep them down much longer, and when they came out of it, they would be angry. If ever there was a cue to exit...

She grunted at how easily she'd slipped into stage direction terms as she climbed the ridge St. John had fled. This is what babysitting a movie star got her, thinking in movie slang terms when all Kelly wanted was to be taken seriously as a Conservation Officer and given real assignments that got her outside the office. Not just fluff jobs like escorting a pampered movie star on what was essentially a nature hike.

She caught up to her charge on the two rut road where they'd left her company truck. St. John was bent over at the waist, hands on his thighs, breathing hard.

"Take your backpack and shirt off," she ordered.

He grumbled but complied. It was the first order of hers he'd obeyed without question.

"The backpack saved your back," she said, surveying his broad, sun-kissed shoulders and the expanse of skin tapering to the waist of a pair of jeans that hugged trim hips and a firm butt. She'd never stopped to explore what about a man's backside intrigued her, but his was the best she'd seen fill out a pair of well-worn jeans.

What'd he do, scavenge from some movie wardrobe the right *in-character* look? Or was it possible the man whose paycheck for one starring role no doubt exceeded her annual income times ten actually owned a pair of faded jeans with one corner of a back pocket tattered.

"Of all the damn stupid things—"

"Excuse me?" Kelly demanded in no mood to be dressed down by some actor. "But if you'd stayed on the path behind me like I told you to do—"

One look at his welted arms and face, though, and she stopped her lecture in mid I-told-you-so. "You're not allergic to wasps, are you?"

"I'm not allergic." He kept his head down, refusing to meet her gaze.

"You sure?"

"Yes," he snapped, his knuckles white around the shirt gripped in his fist.

"Because, if you are, we had better head back to civilization right now."

"I'm fine," he growled, giving her a lethal glance.

*What a jerk.* She was the one who should be angry. He'd gotten himself into this fix, one she'd likely be blamed for.

Taking in the extent of damage done to his face, noting at least his lips had been spared—his luscious lips…

*Stop it*, she silently ordered and dumped her backpack on the lowered tailgate of the truck and dug a Benadryl from her first aid kit. "You better take one of these."

"I'm fine," he all but howled.

"Look here St. John, you've got multiple bites. If your airway swells, you die just like us plain folk. Take this pill while you still have an opening to swallow through." *And I still have a job, Mr. Hot-Hunk-Out-of-Hollywood.*

The set of his mouth shifted and the eyes that turned millions of women into quivering puddles of hormones narrowed at her. But he took the capsule from her hand, the scrape of his callused fingers over hers leaving a strange itch in her palm. Mesmerizing eyes she expected from a movie star, but not callused fingers.

"This'll ease the sting," she said, breaking open a tube of topical antihistamine, trying to ignore the tingling sensation where his fingers had touched her.

She dabbed at the bites on his arm and tried not to notice his Adam's apple bobbing up and down with every swallow as he washed down the Benadryl with water from his canteen.

Or the jagged little scar on the underside of his chiseled chin. So Dane St. John didn't run to a plastic surgeon to correct his every little defect.

The scarred jaw lowered and he nodded at the arm she dabbed. "Is something wrong there?"

"No. Why?" she asked.

"You've been dabbing the same spot for an awful long time."

"Oh." She started, and let go of his arm. "Tube's empty."

Kelly broke open a fresh vial and went to work on his other arm, noticing a wide scar slashed across his forearm. Maybe the guy wasn't as pampered as she'd first thought. "Not as many bites on this one."

"I'm sorry," he said without a hint of sarcasm.

Dabbing at the bites on his shoulder, she peeked up at him. The squint lines framing the famous blue eyes lent his face an apologetic expression. Add the puppy-dog look in his eyes to the sincere note in his voice that framed his apology and maybe...

*No way.* She was *not* falling under the spell of his charms. He was an actor, albeit one of those who quipped out witty lines in the midst of flying bullets and fiery explosions.

Still, curiosity got the best of her. She lowered the sting-kill swab from his broad shoulder, and scrutinized him through narrowed eyes. "What are you sorry for?"

"I shouldn't have snapped at you. None of this is your fault."

"It wasn't? I mean, I know it wasn't."

The corner of his mouth twitched.

Sunlight cut through the trees and across his face, his considerably welted face. She winced. "When are you supposed to start shooting your next movie?"

He grunted. "Judging by your reaction to my face, it better not be any time soon."

"Sorry," she said, retrieving a fresh tube from her kit.

"Not the kind of face that would make magazine covers now, huh?"

She cocked her chin and offered him an impish smile. "Oh, I don't know. I can think of a tabloid or three that would jump at the chance to feature *this* face on their front page."

"That good, huh?" He smiled the trademark smile that sent most women swooning.

*Most women.* Not her.

Yeah, right. Three mornings ago, when they'd met face-to-face and he'd turned that smile on her, she'd very nearly melted at his feet. It'd taken every ounce of control to retain her professional persona. She was, above all else, a woman trying to prove herself at a man's job. She had no time for infatuations, especially with any man as superficial as an actor. So, she'd pasted on her best CO face and shook his hand...which had left hers tingling far longer than was healthy for a career woman.

She nodded at a stump on the side of the road. "Sit and I'll dab your face."

He frowned at the stump. "Think I'll just stoop down for you, if you don't mind."

"Leary of stumps now, are you?" she teased and dabbed the welts dotting his forehead, trying to ignore how he smelled more of pine needles and rich, loamy soil than of fancy aftershave.

"Something like that," he murmured. His smile faded and his eyes angled at the ground.

So Mr. Macho Movie Star didn't want to admit he'd been taken down by a hornet laden stump. Fine, she wouldn't blow his image.

Straightening, she said, "Now let's see the part of your backside the backpack didn't protect."

His gaze widened at her. "Surely you aren't serious."

"Surely I am. Drop the pants, Buster."

"I'll have you know I get big bucks for baring my butt," he said as he turned away from her and unzipped his jeans.

"Well, whether administering first aid to your butt or the butt of somebody less famous, I get the same bucks, and not many of them I might add."

He looked over his shoulder at her. "So why'd you become a Conservation Officer?"

"It's all I've ever wanted to be."

He hitched a questioning eyebrow at her.

"My dad was a CO," she added, "a very dedicated one."

"And you idolize him."

"Something like that," she said, using the same line he'd used when he'd hedged about the true reason he hadn't wanted to sit on any stump. Before he asked any more questions that might force her to admit she was out to prove something to her father and the local group of all male, old-timer COs, she prompted, "Enough talk. Drop the shorts and bend over."

The sight of screen star Dane St. John's bare backside covered in angry welts made Kelly laugh.

"That's not the reaction I usually get," he muttered, but there was a good-natured undertone to his voice.

"I imagine not," she replied, more serious now, breaking open a fresh vial of sting kill. "Lean over the tailgate."

He complied but not without a groaned, "You'd get big bucks for the kind of shot I'm giving you." He glanced back at her. "You don't have a camera in that pack of yours, do you?"

"As a matter of fact, I do," she chirped, continuing to dab at his welted behind. "Big bucks, huh?"

He peered over his shoulder at her. "You wouldn't."

"A picture like this could help pay for the damages your production company is sure to charge me for getting you hurt."

He shook his head. "The production company won't sue you."

She glanced up, hope surging through her. "They won't?"

He grinned back at her. "They'll sue your DNR."

She frowned. "Then I can kiss my job good-bye."

"A job you clearly like." His grin faded. "I was just kidding about the production company suing the DNR. Besides, you didn't get me hurt. I did it myself trying to impress you."

She paused in her dabbing. "Impress *me*?"

"Yeah," he said, still looking back at her. "You're the real deal. Law enforcement in the field and I'm just—"

She all but choked. "Did you just call me the *real deal*?"

He pulled up his pants, zipped them, and faced her. "That's what you are, right?"

She gazed up into his earnest eyes. "But-but, nobody takes me seriously."

He shrugged. "Nobody takes me seriously, either." He pointed at his face. "You thought I was a male bimbo. Right?"

She felt herself blush. "Sorry."

He smiled at her, not the big screen smile the world got to see. This one was smaller, a little sheepish, and a whole lot more endearing.

"I'm the one who should be sorry," he said. "I was so busy showing off for you I didn't even think about how my screwing up could affect your job."

"Yeah, right. Dane St. John showing off for me." But, in spite of her words, her heart was doing a two-step against her ribs.

"Why not? You're not impressed by my Hollywood image. That's quite a turn on." He fingered the crisp collar of her khaki shirt, his knuckles just one thin layer of cloth away from her skin. "Besides, you're damn cute in your CO uniform," he finished.

"Cute?" she countered, her bluster hiding that she liked that he liked what he saw. "Is that all it comes down to?"

He shook his head, his gaze locked on hers. "Mostly it's because you're the real thing."

"Real thing, huh?" she retorted, not feeling anywhere near as defensive as she had earlier.

"Yeah," he said, leaning close. "Now give me one of those sting kill swabs."

"Did I miss a bite?" she asked, trying to stifle a grin.

He took the swab she held up to him, cupped her chin, leaned in closer, and dabbed at her forehead. "Yeah. You missed one all right. But that's okay because I didn't."

There was a husky tone lacing his words, something that implied he meant more than he was saying. It was in the way his dazzling blue eyes met hers and in how his less-than-Hollywood polished fingertips held her chin. It was in the way he smelled of the woods rather than pricey aftershave and the way his broad shoulders blocked out the sun as he hovered over her. Damn, but was she finally falling for his charm?

"Has anyone ever told you how amazingly bright your eyes are?" he asked.

"They're brown," she murmured, still caught up in his gaze, his touch, his smell.

"Pale with a hint of green and oh so bright," he returned, his face lowering towards hers.

Instinctively, she lowered her eyelids and tilted her mouth up to meet his. His kiss was gentle, warm, just a hint of tongue testing the line of her lips. Then his lips were gone and she was left with hers slightly parted, expecting—wanting more.

She opened her eyes to find him frowning down at her. All at once, the words rushed from both of them at the same time.

"Why aren't you slugging me?" he asked.

"Why'd you stop?" she asked.

"You didn't want me to stop?"

"You expected me to slug you?"

Their words tangling, they laughed together.

She noticed he no longer held her chin. Instead his hands filled the space between them, one still holding the used sting stop stick, the swab looked dwarfed between his long fingers, fingers in perfect symmetry to his large, masculine hands. Why was she noticing such stuff about him *now*. She better change the mood here real quick.

She side-stepped him and gathered up the used swabs.

"I still can't believe you didn't slug me," he said, propping a lean hip against the lowered tailgate of the truck where she dumped the used swabs into a waste bag.

"Why?" she asked, pleased her voice sounded reasonably normal.

"To say you haven't been receptive to my charms would be an understatement. You've been downright prickly toward me."

She shrugged. "You were a job."

"Babysitting job, I seem to recall overhearing you say."

As if her cheeks weren't already warm enough, a fresh

flush of heat flooded them. "I didn't mean for you to hear that."

"Even if I hadn't, you made it pretty clear I wasn't welcome."

"It wasn't personal," she said, putting her emergency kit in order.

"Glad to hear it."

"Being the token minority hire, I get all the jobs nobody else wants."

"Didn't know I was such a bother."

She closed the lid on her kit and gave him a chastening look. "You could listen better—follow instructions better. If you had, you wouldn't have fallen into that ground hornets' nest."

"At least I got your attention…finally."

She studied him for some sign he was making fun of her, that what he'd said earlier about trying to impress her was just some ploy to charm her. But *damn*, the man looked so blasted sheepish. Or maybe he looked vulnerable because his Hollywood face was studded with welts.

"You didn't want me to stop kissing you?" he asked, this time with less astonishment and far more wonder.

"It was a nice kiss," she said, stowing her kit—keeping her voice as neutral as she could manage.

The cocky, movie star smile stretched across his lips. "Just nice?"

Good grief, of course not! The kiss had been wonderful, but much too brief, she wanted to say.

Instead, she cleared her throat, back to business. "I better get you to where a doctor can look at those bites."

"I'm fine," he said, adding the swab he'd used on her to the bag she was about to tie up.

"Sure you are," she said, closing the tailgate he still leaned against and making him jump away. "But I'm not taking any chances."

She headed for the driver's side door. He headed for the

passenger side but stopped dead, eyeing himself in the oversized side mirror.

"That doesn't look good," he said.

"Maybe now you'll listen to reason—understand why I want you to see a doctor."

He climbed into the truck. "I don't need a doctor. But I'd sure like to avoid being seen by the paparazzi booked into the motel room next to mine."

"Isn't that just typical of you Hollywood types, more concerned about your looks than your health," she said, inserting the key in the ignition.

One man-sized hand covered hers, stopping her from starting the truck. "Kelly—"

It was the first time he'd called her by her given name and it made her stomach do flip-flops. Or maybe it was his touch, or the quietness, the sincerity with which he spoke her name. Or maybe he was a better actor than she had expected him to be.

"What?" she snapped.

"This business I'm in, it's focused on looks way more than I like. But, worse, it feeds on gossip. One front page tabloid picture of me looking like this, and it'll set off a firestorm of outrageous stories."

She thought of the tabloid papers her mother religiously read, of how they filled the racks at every checkout in the grocery store and gas station in little Copper Falls—how, whenever she picked her mother up at the beauty shop, the content of those rags was all anyone was talking about. She'd always thought it better than their gossiping about their neighbors. But, now, with one of the popular subjects of the tabloids sitting next to her in her truck, she had to wonder.

"The headlines will read everything from Action Star Brought Down By Hornets to Action Star Struck With Career Ending Virus," he said.

She settled back in her seat, pulling her hand out from beneath his. "You sure you feel okay?"

"Yes," he said.

Still, she took one more shot at convincing him to let her take him to a doctor. "I thought the saying was better any notice rather than no notice."

He motioned to his welted face. "I know this is hardly a career ending story. I'm just not accustomed to being in the spotlight so much."

She gave him a you-chose-the-career look. "Comes with the territory, no?"

"Yeah. I just never expected that every little move I made, every little mistake I make would be front page news."

"So you admit you made a mistake in not listening to me."

He threw his head back and laughed. "Didn't I already say I did?"

She smiled. "How badly do you want to avoid that paparazzi?"

He sobered and settled his head against the headrest. "Real bad."

"Bad enough to rough it for a day or two until those welts disappear?"

He tipped a roguish grin at her. "I can rough it with the best."

She snorted and started the truck. "We'll see about that."

His grin stretched. "Guess not everything I did today was a mistake."

## CHAPTER TWO

What had he meant by, *not everything I did today was a mistake?*

More to the point, what did she want his words to mean? That kissing her *wasn't* a mistake?

Those were the questions haunting Kelly as she'd driven Dane St. John deeper into the woods to her family's camp, as she'd unlocked the cabin for him, and muttered apologies for the sparse accommodations.

"It's a great place," he'd said, not a hint of mocking in his tone or his eyes, as they'd taken in the one room cabin with double-wide bunks built-in on one end and kitchen and living area on the other.

"Outhouse is out back," she said, almost challenging him.

He didn't gasp in horror, just nodded.

"I'll prime the pump for you before I leave and show you how to do it in case it loses its prime," she'd said.

"I know how to prime a pump," he'd said, increasing her curiosity of the man. She was beginning to realize she knew very little about him beyond the tabloid gossip.

"If you want to wash up, you can heat water in the kettle on the gas stove." She turned a knob on the stove and the burner flamed to life. "Stove's good to go." She turned off the burner and found him peering out the back window between the cook stove and free-standing wood stove.

"Is that a shower set-up?" he asked.

She didn't need to join him at the window to know what he'd spotted out by the wood shed.

"Yeah. It's pretty basic," she said. "Just a cistern to collect rainwater and four slab-wood walls."

His long legs took him across the room and out the door before she'd taken two steps after him. By the time she cleared the door, he had disappeared around the corner. She caught up to him out back examining the rustic enclosure.

"I'd love to shower off all this sweat and bug juice," he nodded and peered up at the cistern. "Think there's enough water in there for a shower?"

"Probably, but it'll be cold."

"Wouldn't be the first cold shower I've taken," he said, giving her a wink.

What was that supposed to mean?

He climbed onto the frame of the wall and tapped his way up the cistern. "There's plenty of water in there."

"It *has* rained a lot lately," she said.

He hopped down.

"If you're seriously considering showering," she said, taking hold of a rope draped over a nail on one wall, "you pull this to open the spout. I suggest you use just enough water to wet yourself down, soap up, and save the rest for rinsing."

"Got it," he said, looking at her through eyes that suggested he already knew how to take a field shower. Who was this man?

"Soap's on the back of the kitchen sink and towels are on the shelf opposite the bunks."

He nodded. She headed back into the cabin. He followed and, snagging the soap and a towel, headed back out to the cistern.

What possessed her to peek out the back window she hadn't a clue.

*Wrong.* She knew exactly why she did it. Dane St. John peeling his t-shirt up his trim six-pack abs and off over his broad shoulders was a sight any woman would enjoy. She wanted another look at that manly back she'd seen as she'd applied sting stop to his body. And such a fine back it was. Then, in one fluid movement, he pushed his jeans and shorts down his long legs.

Her jaw dropped and she stepped away from the window. Spying on people was normal for a CO, but *this* was not CO business. Better she survey the cupboards for supplies.

But, even as she declared the non-perishables adequately stocked, she couldn't erase the image of Dane St. John's naked body from her mind.

A yowl from the back of the cabin told her he'd doused himself in cistern water and was safely hidden from view by the shower's slab walls. She took quick note of the contents of the gas powered refrigerator. A few condiments, some cheese, and a questionable carton of eggs. She wrote up a grocery list in record time and exited the cabin.

As she stepped around the back corner of the cabin, a second yowl warned her he was rinsing.

"Warned you it would be cold," she said as she neared the makeshift shower.

"Bracing," he called back as though he'd enjoyed the shock of cold water against his heated skin. At least she assumed all that tan, muscle-stretched skin she glimpsed between the ill-fitting wood slabs of the shower stall was hot. Wouldn't she just love to step around those boards and find out? Wouldn't she just love to check out where the tan lines ended on Dane St. John's fine body?

But he was no doubt the add-another-notch-to-his-belt *Joe Hollywood* type; and she called, "I'm heading into to town to get you some groceries. Be back in a couple hours."

#

So, here she was, three hours later, bouncing along the two rut road through the woods to the cabin, the back of her personal SUV loaded with grocery bags and still thinking about Dane St. John's bare butt. Worse, his, *not everything I did today was a mistake* comment still nagged her, mostly because she knew what she wanted it to mean—still wanting there to be more to that whisper of a kiss he'd given her behind her DNR truck.

But she was a plain-Jane, boondock living, Conservation Officer, who'd taken the time to shuck her company gear, shower every hint of insect repellent from her body and brush out her hair...which had looked like a frizzed out bird's nest so she'd re-braided it. She'd even added lip gloss before she'd headed back to the camp. Lot of good it did, since she'd eaten it off halfway into the thirty minute drive.

She powered her SUV up the final incline to where the camp sat atop the bluff, thinking she could reapply the lip gloss before she hauled the groceries inside and came face-to-face with *him*. But he was outside when she arrived, sitting atop the picnic table on the point beyond the cabin, feet on the attached bench overlooking the valley and woods beyond. All she saw, though, was that he hadn't put his t-shirt back on.

She braked to a halt, licked her lips, and stepped down from the truck.

He hopped off the table, gait loose as he approached. "That's a helluva view."

"It's the highest point around," she said, fixated on the view she was getting of his bare, broad shoulders, tapering hips, and everything in between.

He stopped in front of her and peered over his shoulder as though he couldn't get enough of the view behind him. "Is there a name for this place?"

"Angel Point," she said, staring at his muscle-sculpted chest well within her reach.

He nodded. "Someone got the name right."

She blinked and lifted her gaze just as he faced her.

"Must be spectacular when fall colors peak," he said.

"You know about the leaves turning color here in the fall?" she asked, partly surprised, partly frazzled she'd even fleetingly thought about touching his naked chest.

He smiled that smile Kelly was beginning to recognize as a mix of amusement and scolding. "I wasn't cloned full grown in Hollywood. I've seen a fair share of the world, and long before I ever set foot in LaLa Land."

Flushing with embarrassment, she turned toward the

SUV. "I have the groceries."

He was instantly at her side, crowding her as he reached past her into the vehicle to grab a couple of large paper bags. His naked shoulder brushed her thinly-shirted one, making her fingers fumble on the plastic handles of the smaller bags, and her stomach feel as if butterflies had just taken flight.

*Bad, bad, bad.* No matter his reference to his past life, he was still *Joe Hollywood*, a babysitting job…a mere annoyance.

"Do you have any idea how great the air smells here in comparison to L.A.?" he stated more than asked as he led the way into the cabin. "God's country," he said as he put the bags on the countertop. "Isn't that what the locals call it up here?"

She nodded dumbly, still reeling from those butterfly wings inside her stomach. He unthreaded the plastic bags from her fingers, leaving her yearning for more contact.

"So, what'd you get me?" he said, digging through the bags. "I'm so hungry I could eat a bear."

"Not bear," she said through a weak chuckle, her attempt at levity.

"Looks like you bought enough to last a week."

"I didn't know what you liked. Beef, pork, chicken." A horrible thought struck her. "I didn't think to ask you if you were vegetarian."

"So many of us Hollywood types are, is that it?"

She blinked at him, not sure if she should be offended or amused by his mocking.

He laughed, breaking the tension. "My first morning in the DNR office I brought in a bag of *sausage* and egg biscuits for everyone. Maybe you remembered that."

"Maybe I did…subconsciously."

His smile stretched—that perpetual smile that gave him the boyish looks that belied his reported thirty-something age. "I think you notice everything."

She all but dropped the gallon of milk into the fridge. "What do you know about what I notice?"

"Those of us who play-act characters find it useful to pay attention to the mannerisms and speech patterns of people around us, especially those who we might emulate, or we won't get the details right."

She turned within the open fridge door so she faced him. But whatever she was about to say was lost as he leaned in and set a carton of eggs on the shelf behind her. He lingered, his body inches from hers, peering down at her with that enigmatic smile she couldn't seem to ignore. She should be trying to read whether he mocked her, not recalling how those lips had touched hers and awakened something in her she wasn't sure she was ready to explore.

"Maybe you should have kept the eggs out," she managed in a voice that sounded reasonably level...at least in her ears. "Hungry as you are, nothing cooks up quicker than a couple eggs."

"A couple eggs aren't going to satisfy the hunger I have," he said, still standing too close. Then he winked and turned back to the bags on the counter.

There he went again, implying something...or not. But his words as much as his tone was thick with innuendo.

"Steak," he said.

"Huh?"

"If that grill outside has gas in its tank, it'll make quick work of a steak. Add a salad, throw a little garlic on this crusty bread—" He lifted a loaf of bread from one of the bags. "—brown it on the grill, and we've got a meal."

"We?" The word came out as a squeak. "I wasn't planning to stick around and—"

He handed her the packages of chicken and chops to put in the fridge. "You bought me a big sirloin. More than I can eat on my own. Besides, I owe you for hiding me out and grocery shopping."

"You can repay me for the groceries and the cabin is sitting here empty," she said, busying herself with stowing the extra meat. "No sweat."

"I'd like the company."

She straightened, her heart skipping a beat. He wanted *her* company?

*No. No. No.* Determined to remain immune to the man, she shot back, "What's the matter? Lost without your entourage?"

"Did you see me arrive in town with an entourage?"

"I wasn't among the bevy of fans welcoming you to town," she said, closing the fridge to find he'd taken the sirloin from its package and placed the slab on a plate.

"There was no *bevy* of fans gathered to greet me," he said, taking a garlic powder shaker from the cupboard. "There wasn't a crowd at all. I just drove into town in my rental and registered at the hotel all by myself…except for that paparazzi who trailed me here."

She sliced the crusty bread lengthways and buttered it. "We're pretty grounded here in the Upper Peninsula."

He handed her the garlic powder. "So *movie stars* don't turn heads much around here, huh?"

She thought of the plethora of local tabloid-gazing inhabitants, her mother included, as she seasoned the bread, but knew better than to bring it up.

"In small towns, everybody knows everybody and half the populace is related to the other half. We've learned discretion…or at least to keep our gossip close."

"Sounds like my kind of town," he said, flipping the steak over for a second round of seasoning.

Okay, a lot of guys knew how to season and grill a steak. That didn't surprise her. But what was this *'my kind of town'* remark supposed to mean? And why did she want it to mean Copper Falls was a place he'd like to live? He was a movie star for heaven's sake. Probably lived in a Hollywood mansion with servants.

She shook off the thought and headed outside to turn on the grill before she said…or did something stupid in front of him.

#

His shorts were on the picnic table, spread out like he'd put them there to dry. Boxer-briefs, the kind that she doubted any store within fifties miles of Copper Falls kept in stock. She lived in boxers *or* briefs country. No fancy hybrids in this neck of the woods. And his were blue, navy blue, but still blue. Her father definitely didn't wear colored underwear. He was black and white from undies to attitude.

She switched on the grill and high-tailed it back into the cabin, belatedly realizing if his shorts were out on the picnic table, that meant beneath his jeans he was... Her gaze dropped to his crotch the minute she walked into the cabin...and ricocheted away about as fast. She wasn't the kind of girl who checked out men's crotches, especially that of a man she knew had gone commando.

"Those are quite some mounts," he said.

"W-what?" She blushed, certain he'd caught her staring at his crotch. But, he wasn't looking at her. He was gazing in the direction of the trophy heads mounted above the fireplace that seemed to define the living room area between kitchen and beds.

He strode over to a ten-pointer with a near perfect spread. "Nice," he said, read the name on the placard beneath the mount, and added, "Hey, it's yours."

He grinned at her. "So you're a hunter, too."

"Pretty much goes with being the daughter of a CO," she said, turning to the kitchen counter, picking up a fork, and poking the steak he'd seasoned; doing pretty much anything so she didn't have to face him. She was certain her cheeks were still pink.

"Here's another one of yours," he said from further back in the cabin. "And a bunch of those little antlers stuck up around the top of the walls have your name on them, too."

"I've been hunting with my dad for as long as I can remember. Started me plinking tin cans with a bb gun as soon as I was old enough to understand how to handle a gun safely."

He nodded. "Gun safety."

Was there a hint of anti-gun sentiment in his tone? There was a lot of that in Hollywood.

She tossed down the fork and faced him, arms folded over her chest. "Yeah. There isn't a kid who grows up in these parts that doesn't know not to touch a gun until someone teaches you how to handle it safely."

He nodded, still studying the deer mounts. "There were guns all over the place where I grew up, too. We all knew they weren't anything to play with."

The fold of her arms loosened. So he wasn't one of those ultra-liberal, tree-hugging Hollywood types. Then again, there were a number of card carrying NRA actors, too. She should have noted he hadn't freaked over the dead deer heads mounted on her walls. More importantly, he'd just made another reference to a less than ordinary youth.

"Just where did you grow up?" she asked.

He faced her and gave her that maddening, winning smile that made a person want to smack him in the head at the same time as melt into a puddle at his feet.

#

Even with her arms crossed over her chest, Kelly looked like she wanted to deck him. Dane didn't blame her. He'd been giving her a hard time ever since she gave him her hand to shake upon first meeting rather than returning his smile. She'd worked so hard at being all business he couldn't help but take up the challenge to break through her façade. Besides, he'd sensed a spark of the woman behind the CO uniform.

Hell, he'd heard her chuckle when she'd teased him about taking a photo of his hornet-bitten ass. He'd also gotten a taste of *the woman* behind the job when he'd kissed her. Damn, if he didn't want to know her all the more now, and that presented an even bigger challenge.

"You really aren't a fan of mine," he said, unable to keep from giving her a verbal poke.

She huffed. "I guess with an ego like yours you expect everybody in the world to be a fan."

One corner of his mouth twitched. "I'm not *that* big a

star...yet."

She groaned, grabbed the plate of meat off the counter and headed for the door. "The grill should be hot by now."

Balancing plates and silverware on top of the salad bowl, he followed her out to the picnic table, where she nodded at his shorts.

"And what are those things doing on the table?"

"Drying. Since they're the only pair I have here, I washed them out."

From the side of the grill, she blinked at him, her expression wavering somewhere between astonishment and approval before finally matching up with her frown and her grousing command. "Whatever, just get them off the table."

"Yes, ma'am," he said through a grin and stuffed them into his pocket.

She flipped up the grill cover and slapped the steak onto the rack. In spite of the progress he'd been making in getting past her stiff demeanor, she was still angry about something, and he'd bet his last dollar there was a lot more to it than her being stuck babysitting him.

He straddled the end of the nearest bench. "You still want to know where I grew up?"

"Sure. Why not?" she said, arranging the slab of sirloin on the grill as if she was more interested in the food than whether he told her anything about himself or not.

"Admit it," he said. "You're dying to know my background."

Her shoulders came up with a deeply drawn breath then slowly sank back to their normal squared position. Why did she work so hard to contain herself? Because she was trying to perfect the persona of a hard-ass law and order CO? Or because she *was* attracted to him and fought it?

That last was reason enough to keep nettling her. But more so, she intrigued him in a way no woman, officer of the law or not, had ever done and he wanted to find out why.

She peered over her shoulder at him, a forced smile on her lips as she responded to his challenge about dying to know his background. "Can't help it," she said. "Curiosity comes with being a CO."

She faced him, arms crossed over her chest and barbecue tongs spearing the air like some weapon. "So spill, St. John. Where did you grow up?"

Her defensive pose sliced away some of his swagger. "Mostly Europe. Eastern Block."

"Military brat?" she asked, her tone softening a tad.

He shook his head, the truth likely to chase off whatever sympathy she'd just found for him. "My parents were in the foreign service. Support staff. Mostly embassies."

And there it was, the upward sweep of the chin—the hint she was about to tell him he was full of bull. "I can't imagine embassies are all that rustic that you'd know about hand pumping water and cistern showers."

"True. The embassies weren't rustic," he said. "But, in some places, things beyond the embassy walls weren't quite up to western standards."

She narrowed her eyes at him. "You telling me you hobnobbed with the locals?"

Memories of his childhood flashed through his brain. "My parents encouraged it. They believed us kids should learn about different cultures and make friends with all kinds of people."

She arched an eyebrow at him. "You didn't find variety enough at your private embassy schools?"

"You are one suspicious woman, Kelly Jackson."

"Comes with being a CO."

He laughed and shook his head. "Yeah, I met a lot of different kinds of kids in those well-appointed schools set up for the children of ex-patriots. I'm still friends with some of them."

He sobered. "But the friends who made the biggest impact on me are the ones I played street soccer with, pumped water with, and—" For a split second, his mind went back to a certain Lithuanian field. "—learned which fields were best not to play in because they might still contain old landmines from World War II."

The dubious slant of her mouth fell away and concern pinched a line between her eyes. "I've heard about there still being old landmines buried out there."

"So, you don't think I'm giving you a line of bull? You actually believe me?"

"I'm pretty good at reading people. Comes with the job."

"You haven't read *me* all that well."

The pale brown eyes narrowed on him again. "Jury's still out on you."

"You're a hard sell, CO Kelly."

"Just cautious."

He was about to comment that being too cautious sometimes got in the way of discovering something new when flames shot up behind her. His gaze shifted past her to the grill. "How's that steak coming?"

She wheeled about, a squeal of distress escaping her. An uncontrolled reaction from a woman who was far too controlled. Oh yes. He wanted to know *that* woman.

#

When she'd served the blackened steak, she'd apologized…and then they'd laughed, cut the steak in half and eaten the charred beef with the salad and garlic bread. She'd gotten him to tell her more stories about being raised as an embassy kid. Damn she was easy to talk to. Easy to be quiet with as well. Later, side-by-side at the sink doing dishes, they'd hardly spoken, yet he'd found silence with her equally comfortable.

It was getting dark when she folded the towel over the towel rack and asked, "Do you want me to drive you into town to get your car?"

"Do I look presentable enough to chance it?"

She tipped his face into the light of a ceiling-mounted gas lamp, her fingers soft yet firm against his chin.

"Maybe not," she said, releasing him. "Besides, now that I think of it, I doubt your rental has four-wheel drive and you need all-wheel drive to navigate these back roads. Is your cell charged up?"

He pulled the phone from his pocket. "Yeah, it's charged but there's not much for bars."

"Even though we're on a bluff, we're in a kind of a dead zone. Has to do with where the towers are. You should be able to get enough bars outside. Before the DNR issued us satellite phones I sometimes had to stand on the picnic table to get service."

An image of her in her CO fatigues standing on the picnic table made him laugh out loud.

"What?" she asked.

He shook his head. "Nothing. Just a silly thought."

She nodded as though she understood, or was distracted by something bigger on her mind. "You sure you'll be okay alone here?"

"You brought me extra antihistamines and that pink stuff for the itching," he said. "Besides, it's been hours since I was stung and I'm still breathing. I'll be fine."

Instantly, he regretted his words. He didn't want her to leave.

"Then again," he said, "maybe you should stay the night. Keep an eye on me."

She snorted, all concern slipping from her features. "In your dreams."

"You're the one who's concerned. And now that I think about it, my throat does feel a little scratchy." He added a couple dry coughs for effect.

She frowned at him.

He shrugged, sure he'd over-acted, but hoping she'd take pity on him.

She looked at the door, her brow creasing.

"There's plenty of sleeping space," he said.

She glanced toward the double wide set of bunks built into the back corner of the cabin, still frowning. "You better not be playing me."

He grinned. "And if I am?"

Something flitted across her eyes. Hope or abject fear?

He sobered. "I'm not playing you, Kelly. But I wouldn't mind more of your company. It's been a long time since I had anyone other than family around that I could talk so candidly with."

There went that dubious eyebrow lift again.

"I'm not kidding. You *are* easy to talk to," he said.

The eyebrow settled back into place.

"Besides," he added, "I'm not all that happy about you driving out to the highway on these back-roads."

She stiffened. "I'm a highly-trained CO, not to mention I grew up traveling these woods. I can take care of myself in the woods."

He gave himself a mental head slap. He should have stopped while he was ahead. Conceding, he shook his head. "I have no doubt you can, Bright Eyes, in the woods and just about any other place. But please stay."

#

Kelly had given in to Dane's request and now couldn't sleep, not with him just one bunk below her. She wasn't even sure he was breathing. He'd stopped snoring, not that he'd been all that loud. The sounds he made as he slept were more like heavy breathing. Not the kind that comes from the other end of a creepy phone call, either. Dane's heavy breathing had a quality to it that drew her in, not chased her away.

*What the hell was she thinking?*

She muttered a curse, crawled out from her tangled sheets, dropped barefoot to the floor, and tugged her camisole down over her belly. Snagging the flashlight off the nightstand, she knelt on the edge of the lower bunk and shined the light on him.

He was on his side facing the wall, the sheets dipping low over his hips revealing an expanse of bare, well-muscled back, reminding her the last time she'd seen his shorts he was stuffing them into his pants pocket. She reined in her wayward thoughts and focused on what she'd come to the lower bunk to check. Dane's breathing. His lack of movement made her uneasy.

She crawled across the double wide mattress toward him.

No movement from him.

She played the flashlight beam over his shoulders and along his jawline…and a strong jawline it was. His lips were slightly parted, but…

She peered over his muscled arm at his sculpted chest looking for any rise and fall to it. She listened for the telltale whisper of breath, leaned closer when she heard none, her braid slipping over her shoulder and brushing his shoulder.

The next thing she knew, he'd rolled onto his back, hauling her over him so she wound up straddling him.

"Hey," she protested.

"Hey yourself," he said, holding a hand up against the beam from the flashlight she'd managed to hang onto. "Don't you know better than to creep up on a guy while he's sleeping?"

"I was checking to see if you were breathing."

He grinned and settled his head back on his pillow. "Check for swelling while you're at it."

Considering her crotch hovered somewhere just north of his, her mouth dropped open and her cheeks flamed. "Ummm…"

He motioned to his face and shoulders. "The wasp bites."

"Of course," she said, sweeping the light beam across his lips, his square chin, and his chest. The swelling was down.

*So why didn't she climb off him?*

"What's this?" he asked, flicking the bottom hem of her camisole.

"*Joe Hollywood* doesn't know what a camisole is?"

"I know a camisole when I see one. I've just never felt one that was a cotton blend." The backs of his fingers brushed her belly as they slid along the hem of her camisole. "It's like a little spaghetti strap t-shirt."

"What do you know about spaghetti straps," she said, more breathless than she meant to be.

"You're the one calling me *Joe Hollywood* and implying all us Hollywood types know about fashion."

She had nothing to say to that, not when a certain part his anatomy seemed to have grown closer to where the apex of her legs lingered, a part she found herself drawn to. She'd die of mortification if he was just toying with her.

"I feel like I'm being interrogated," he said, pushing the light away so it reflected off the wall between the upper and lower bunks. His grin faded in the softened light and his fingers flattened over her stomach beneath the camisole.

She sucked in a breath and his eyes darkened.

"You like that?" he asked.

"What woman wouldn't?" she asked in a shaky breath.

"You might be surprised at the answer to that."

He drew his legs up behind her, nestling her backside and erasing any doubt about what was going on in his crotch region. "You turn me on, Bright Eyes."

She squelched the impulse to remind him that just about any woman probably turned him on because she'd just discovered something about herself. For this moment, for this one night, she wanted to live the fantasy and Dane St. John was that fantasy.

His fingers spread across her skin beneath the cotton blend camisole, his voice as tender as his touch, his tone as hoarse as her need. "Just say no and it stops here."

She dropped the flashlight on the mattress beside them and leaned in. His palm found her breast and his mouth met hers. Then he rolled her, placing her beneath him, peeling off the camisole, and freeing himself from the sheets and her from her panties.

He touched her gently and kissed her in places no other man had. She arched for him, crying out as he played her body, lost in mindless pleasure. By the time he entered her, she was ready to explode with need. And explode she did. Seconds later he followed, flooding her with new sensations.

Braced over her on his elbows and knees, he kissed Kelly's eyes and nipped her earlobes. "I think I just died and went to heaven."

She'd have shushed him if she'd had the breath. She didn't want to hear any bull from him, not now, not in this glorious aftermath. But damn, he'd said just the right thing to add to the fantasy. Indeed, if she died at this moment, she'd go having known heaven.

#

Come the false dawn of a new day, though, Kelly wasn't so sure abandoning herself to the whims of her hormones had been the smartest thing to do. She'd found her panties among the sheets and donned them, but gave up on her chemise when she spied an edge of it peeking out from beneath Dane's still sleeping form. Jeans and shirt were where she'd left them, neatly folded on the foot of the upper bunk. She now sat on the bench at the foot of the double bunks tugging on one of her cross-trainers when her wayward camisole slipped over her shoulder along with a deep, nerve-ruffling voice.

"You forgot something."

She snatched the camisole from him, muttering, "You were sleeping on it. I didn't want to disturb you."

"Not even going to wake me to tell me you were leaving?" he asked, stretching out on his side by her hip.

She tugged on her shoelaces. "I have to get to work. I didn't think it would matter to you."

He ratcheted himself up onto one elbow. "You didn't think I'd care whether or not you were here when I woke?"

"I thought it might be easier if I wasn't."

"Easier?"

"Yeah. I hear guys aren't always the happiest to wake up to find the night's conquest still in their bed."

"Conquest? You think you're some metaphorical notch

on my bedpost?"

She shrugged, going for nonchalance. "Maybe you're a notch on *my* bedpost."

"Maybe I am. You wouldn't be the first to bag herself this bad boy. Heck, you can even add movie star to your resume of conquests."

She went still. She'd thought to put him in his place when she'd said what she had about him being her conquest. And now, he sounded like she would have had the shoe been on the other foot. Exactly how she had felt when she was trying to escape before he woke.

He tugged on her braid. "But I'm hoping I'm not just a conquest to you, Kelly."

If only he hadn't tugged on her braid—made that teasing gesture.

She twisted around on the bench, tearing her braid free, and faced him. "And me? What am I to you?"

She regretted the words—their neediness—as soon as they left her lips. But, before she could turn away and hide how pitiful she was, he cupped her cheek in his free palm and brushed his thumb across her lips. Helplessly, she gave into his touch.

"I don't exactly know yet," he said.

He sounded sincere. Even those damn, bottomless blue eyes of his looked sincere.

Then, he smiled. In the dim gray of false dawn, his pearly whites glinted as he added, "But I am sure I'm not done carving out that notch yet."

She swatted him. "You are such a little shit."

"Little?" He sat up, the bed sheet slipping off his lap.

She groaned and snagged her other shoe off the floor. He laughed and reached for her, but she slapped his hand away.

"I have to go to work," she said. "I think it's best you lay low for another day."

He saluted. "Whatever you say, ma'am."

"If you'd been this obedient out on the trail yesterday,"

she said, pulling on her shoe, "you wouldn't be in this fix today."

And I wouldn't be in this fix either, Kelly thought. As glorious as their lovemaking was, she was nervous, apprehensive. What did this entanglement mean for him? For her? Her job?

"Kelly?"

"Yeah."

"I want to wake up and watch you sleeping beside me."

"Nice line," she said, lacing her shoe.

He took her braid between his fingers and twitched it at her nose. "I want to make love to you while running my hands through your hair."

She tugged her braid from his fingers even though she didn't want him to stop saying things that made her feel wanted. "In your dreams, St. John."

The next thing she knew, a strong arm was around her waist, dragging her back onto the mattress where she'd experienced the most glorious sex of her life. Braced over her, Dane's voice took on a less playful tone.

"I know we haven't known each other long, Kelly, but I think I want more than dreams where you're concerned."

There he went again, sounding so damn honest. She appreciated honesty, but she still wasn't hearing the reassurances she needed.

"I know this much," murmured Dane, his voice lowering, the humor in his tone fading. "I haven't heard nearly enough of the little sounds you make when I touch you."

He plucked at the top button of her shirt. "I know I want to experience unwrapping you myself."

She mewed.

"That's one of those sounds," he said, lowering his mouth toward hers.

She flattened a hand between them to ward off the kiss. "I have morning breath."

"So do I," he said, gently pushing her hand aside and completing the circuit between their mouths.

His kiss was so warm, so sweet, so tender she easily gave into its intoxication...for the briefest of moments.

"I have to get to work," she said, scrambling out from under him, a misguided hand confirming how fully naked he was...and ready to repeat last night's performance.

*Performance. Just a Performance.*

The word dogged her heels all the way to the door. He was an actor after all. This could all be nothing more than a performance—words and actions meant to seduce.

Was that her problem with him, that he was like a certain man who'd come before him long on seduction but short on commitment?

And just what kind of commitment did she want? She was a woman focused on her career. She wanted to be a career CO. She wanted to follow in her father's footsteps, prove herself worthy.

And Dane was an actor who lived in a world far removed from any she knew.

Her fingers closed on the doorknob and turned. But a large, masculine hand reached over her shoulder and flattened against the door, holding it shut.

"You are coming back tonight, aren't you?" Dane asked, his mouth so near his breath stirred against the back of her ear. She wanted to sink back into the warmth—the strength of his body, to give in to her desire for him. How easy it would be.

"You are my only means in or out of here."

*Of course.* He was talking about transportation, not her, and certainly not another passionate night.

"—unless I want to hike out to the highway and hitchhike. But, I don't think I'm yet ready for any close-ups."

She glanced over her shoulder at his face, not really noting the remnants of the wasp stings but agreeing nonetheless.

He slid a hand over her hip, possessive. She shouldn't like that, but she did. Or maybe it was the heat of his breath blowing across her ear when he spoke that jumbled her thoughts.

"I'll make supper. Chicken?"

"Sure," she said, even when she meant to say no.

His fingers tightened on her hip and his lips nipped at her earlobe. "And Kelly."

"Yeah."

"Tell whoever you called last night that you won't be home tonight, either."

She tried to twist out of reach of the deft play of his tongue and lips against the back of her ear. "I don't think my staying is a good idea."

"Why not?" He slid his arm around her and spread his hand across her stomach, pulling her back against his hard, muscled…naked body. "Didn't I do a good enough job last night to merit a repeat performance?"

There was that word again. *Performance.*

"Let's just not mess with perfection," she said, plucking at his fingers.

"Perfection?" he asked against her neck. "You thought what I did last night was perfect?"

For her it had been, not that she was about to admit any such thing to a man with Dane St. John's ego.

"It was unprotected," she said. "Let's not tempt fate."

"You're right," he said. "We should protect each other."

"Fine. It's settled then."

"Yeah," he said, easing back from her. "When you come back tonight, bring a big box of protection."

## CHAPTER THREE

Her father followed her into the kitchen, his cane tapping across the tiles. "You're part of the DNR, Girl. You have responsibilities now."

Kelly dropped her duffle by the back door, her work truck out in the driveway already packed with the purchases she'd made after her morning shift. She thought she'd made her mind up about what she was doing by the time she'd walked into the drug store over in Watersmeet. But her father had her rethinking her decision. She sighed and faced him.

"I know, Dad. You taught me well."

Her father leaned over his cane at her. "You have duties."

She almost shot back that her current duties were little more than babysitting an actor, but given the circumstances… "I can do my job from the camp just as well as I can do it from home."

"Being part of the Department of Natural Resources isn't just a job, it's—"

"A vocation," her mother chorused from where she stirred a pot of soup at the stove.

Her father scowled. "That *vocation* put food on our table and a roof over your head for the past twenty-two years, Alma."

"And a bullet in your leg, Frank," her mother returned, setting a bowl on the counter next to the stove.

"A poacher put that bullet in my leg," he fired back.

Her mother didn't respond, but not because of Dad's shouting. Kelly had witnessed enough such exchanges to know her mother knew when arguing with Dad was pointless. The incident that ended his DNR career, and still prevented him from enjoying the woods as he once had, ranked among the touchiest of topics.

Turning back to Kelly, he demanded more than asked, "What if the DNR needs to get a hold of you?"

"I have my company phone."

"Service is sketchy at the camp."

"Not for the satellite phone. Besides, I doubt they'd be calling me for any real emergencies," she said, stuffing a light jacket into her duffel.

"You're a rooky. You've yet to earn your way."

"Frank," her mother said, filling a glass with water. "It's time for a pain pill."

"I'm not in pain."

"Yes, you are," she said, holding the glass and a tablet out to him. "You get cranky when you're hurting."

He grumbled, but popped the pill and drank the water. But as soon as he swallowed his pill, he offered up another argument. "Your mother has enough to do without dealing with Max, too."

"I'll take the dog with me," Kelly said.

Her father's eyes softened. "He'll like getting out in the woods."

Every bit as much as her father would have. She knew. He'd lived his entire life in the Upper Peninsula. He lived and breathed the out-of-doors. He'd taught her everything she knew about the woods—taught her to love and respect nature. Their entire relationship as father and daughter had grown from their mutual love of the woods. And a poacher's bullet had taken away his mobility and what he loved most.

Her mother scrubbed a hand up and down her father's arm. "Let Kelly live her life, Frank. Right now she needs a little time to herself."

Her father frowned, but said nothing more as he limped off into the living room.

"Thanks, Mom," Kelly said, picking up her gear and taking Max's leash from a hook by the door.

As she stepped into the fenced backyard, Max came bounding up to her, leaping in the air like a pup in spite of his eight years of age. So was the nature of Golden

Retrievers, and this one had been her father's constant companion on and off the job until last year when he'd been shot.

She held the gate open, knowing the truck's open door hinting of a ride to the woods would suck Max in. As expected, Max leapt into the back of the extended cab, she tossed her duffle in after him, and climbed in behind the wheel.

Her mother appeared on the back stoop, a covered carton in hand. "Take this."

"That's a lot of soup, Mom," Kelly said, taking the container from her mother. "You expecting me to stay at camp a long time?"

Her mother stroked her cheek and looked her in the eye. "I expect you'll stay at camp as long as you need to."

There was something knowing in her mother's eyes that suggested she understood more about why her daughter had decided to spend the night at camp.

"Thanks," Kelly said.

*Mental note: Appreciate Mom more.*

#

Kelly braked to a halt in front of the cabin, Max leaping over her as she opened the driver's side door. She smiled as his bushy golden tail disappeared around the corner of the cabin. She understood his enthusiasm. She felt much the same way.

Gathering up her purchases, she entered the cabin only to find it empty. Instantly, the old feelings of abandonment cut through her. She should have known. *Joe Hollywood* was gone. He'd gotten his jollies and run for the hills.

She set the bottles of wine she'd bought on the countertop and dropped the bag from the drug store next to them.

*Pathetic girl.*

Outside, Max barked. Better see what he was into.

She stepped around the corner of the building and found Max jumping in the air for the stick Dane held over his head. Her heart skipped a beat, and not because he looked so natural playing with a dog; not even because he looked so gorgeous with his head thrown back and his cheeks dimpled with laughter. Her heart skipped a beat because...

"You're still here," she said, her voice sounding breathless in her ears.

He threw the stick, sending Max bounding off into the woods, and turned toward her. "Where'd you think I'd be?"

She shrugged, embarrassed she'd voiced her fears aloud. His grin widened and he strode toward her. Had he figured it out?

"Did you think I'd climbed up on the picnic table to get a cell phone signal and sent out an SOS?" he asked.

"I wouldn't have blamed you if you had. It can get pretty boring out here."

He stopped in front of her, so near her breath caught in her chest, his enigmatic blue eyes capturing—holding hers—as he spoke. "I'd never get bored here."

She nodded, wanting to believe he truly believed his own words.

*Stop thinking so much.*

She stroked his hair back from his face, letting her fingers get lost in his shaggy locks—letting herself get lost.

"Something wrong?" he asked.

She pulled her hand back, his words having jerked her back to reality; and she masked her anxiety. "The bumps are almost gone."

"Guess that means I'm back shadowing you tomorrow."

Her heart sank at the thought of having to share him with the rest of the world again.

*Where did that come from?*

"Guess so," she said, satisfied she at least didn't sound pathetic.

His smile twitched. "We still have tonight."

"Yeah," she said, the suggestion he intended there to be just one more night with her twisting through her chest.

He wagged his eyebrows at her. "Did you bring *us* something?"

She blinked, thrown by the sudden change of topic. Or maybe it wasn't a change of subject at all.

*We still have tonight.*

Of course he expected her return to be all about another romp in the sack. When they went into the cabin and he saw what was in the drug store bag, he'd see just how pathetically easy she was...at least for him.

She started to back away. Max, with stick in mouth, bounded out of the woods and jumped on her, knocking her flat against Dane. Dane enveloped her in his arms.

She wanted to melt into his embrace—melt into him. She *was* pathetic.

He laughed, settled her on her feet as Max bounded about them, stick still in his mouth.

Dane grinned. "I think your dog is playing matchmaker."

Kelly straightened herself. "I think Max just wants someone to throw the stick for him."

Dane took the stick from the dog and flung it deep into the woods. Then he stepped past her toward the cabin.

She swayed in his wake for one mesmerized moment before reality broke through. She wanted to know where he stood regarding their *relationship* before he found the bag of condoms. But he was already through the door and halfway to the sink where she'd left the goodies she'd bought.

"You brought wine," he said, picking up the bottles and giving their labels a look. "Red *and* white."

"I didn't know which you preferred," she said.

"White with chicken," he said, returning the bottles to the countertop.

Maybe if she was lucky he wouldn't notice the other bag.

"And what's this?" he stated more than asked, picking up the package beside the wine bottles. "A bag from the pharmacy. A *big* bag."

He wagged his eyebrows wolfishly at her, dangling the bag from a finger.

"Just what you think it is," she said, reaching for the bag, hoping to regain possession of it before he saw *all* it contained.

He held the bag out of her reach. "What's in here you don't want me to see?"

Her cheeks flamed.

He opened the bag and peered inside.

She cringed.

"You make me randy as a teenage boy, Bright Eyes," he said, peeking over the rim of the bag at her and grinning. But I doubt I'll be able to use up four boxes of condoms in one night."

"I didn't know what kind you preferred," she muttered.

He laughed. "So you bought every kind they had?"

"Not all of them," she cut in, hating that she sounded petulant.

His laughter faded, but the twinkle remained in his eyes as he held up one of the boxes. "I'd like to try the ribbed ones with you."

The innuendo in his tone all but brought her to her knees. When he slid a hand around her neck and kissed her, she sagged into him, her hands somehow finding their way under his t-shirt. His groan vibrated inside her mouth. She spread her fingers across the hot, hard skin of his chest. His hand slid down her back, settled on her butt, and pressed her against him. His chest wasn't the only hard thing about him.

"How hungry are you?" he murmured against her lips.

"Famished," she said, letting him back her toward the double bunks.

The edge of the bottom bunk nudged the backs of her knees. She slipped her fingers into his waistband. The box in his hand exploded, spilling packages of condoms onto the bed and floor. He lifted his mouth a millimeter from hers.

"Tell me you aren't talking about food."

"I'm not talking about food," she said, peeling the t-shirt off over his head.

His fingers tore at the buttons of her shirt and the snap on her jeans. Hers parted the zipper on his jeans, and she fell back on the bed, parting her legs with invitation. He snatched up a condom package, tore away the wrapper with his teeth, sheathed himself in the lambskin then, kneeling between her thighs, sheathed himself inside her.

"So wet, so ready," he murmured.

"More than ready," she whispered in return, lifting her pelvis to meet his thrust.

*More than ready.*

#

When they were sated, he rolled her with him onto their sides, still linked. She lie in his arms in mindless bliss.

So this was what lust felt like. Delicious, mind-blowing, escape. She never wanted to leave Dane's arms, never wanted him to move out from between her legs. Just the thought made her muscles contract.

He stirred, still inside her. She shifted, moving around him.

"I'll need more than a couple minutes to recover after *that*, Bright Eyes, even as hot and wet and inviting as you are."

He pulled her closer and nuzzled her neck. She hooked a leg over his hip, hugging his pelvis to hers. He pulsed inside her.

"Maybe it won't take as long as I thought…to recover," Dane said, wagging his eyebrows.

But, just as he rolled her back under him, Max jumped against the screen door, barking his head off. Dane frowned down at her. "He's not going to go away, is he?"

She shrugged. "It takes a lot of stick throwing to wear out Max."

He groaned and rolled off of her.

Kelly began to get up, but he stopped her. "I'll go throw

the stick for him."

"Aren't you the gentleman," she said.

He brushed a kiss across her cheek as he sat up. "My mama raised me to be a gentlemen."

"Good for your mother," she said, watching him pull his jeans up his long, muscular legs, noting he hadn't put his boxer-briefs on yet. Hunky, handsome, and free-spirited enough to run around commando. No wonder she lusted after him?

It was just *lust*, right?

#

Kelly had dressed and joined Dane outside, taking turns throwing the stick for Max until the dog finally tired out and stretched out under the picnic table to nap in its shade. They'd eaten his roasted chicken dinner, which she'd declared delicious…though not without a note of surprise.

"Just about any guy can grill a steak," she said as they washed dishes after the meal. "But where'd you learn to roast chicken?"

"My mother," he said, drying the rinsed plate she handed him. "She always said no boy of hers was going out into the world to starve. She insisted we each learn the basics and how to cook a special dish or two."

"A *special* dish or two?"

"She told us being able to cook something special would impress the girls."

A shy smile flexed across Kelly's lips as she scrubbed the roasting pan. "She was right."

He grinned more inwardly than outwardly, pleased he'd impressed her. "Yeah, my mom's a smart lady."

Rinsing the roaster, she said, "I notice you said *'no boy of hers'*. No sisters?"

"My sister was a natural in the kitchen. Mom didn't have to force cooking lessons on her."

"Force?" Kelly chuckled, a light, sweet sound that he knew he wanted to hear a lot more of.

"Some of us weren't the most willing students," Dane said, as she wrung out her dishrag and he wiped the pan.

She lifted one of her mink-brown eyebrows at him and pinned him with her see-all, translucent eyes. "Some? Or just you?"

Through a twitchy grin, he replied, "Guilty."

She dried her hands, nodding at the dishtowel he held. "Hang that thing up and come with me."

He folded the towel over a towel bar and followed her out of the cabin. "Where're we going?"

"For a walk," she said, leading him around to the back of the cabin towards the woods, Max already bounding past them. She peeked over her shoulder at Dane and gave him a poke in the midsection. "Gotta walk off all that chicken we just ate. I hear the camera adds ten pounds."

She sprinted off beyond the shed after Max.

"Hey," he called, following them onto the two rut path carved out by years of four-wheeling. "The protein isn't the problem. It's that potato salad you brought. All those carbs."

She kept them moving at a steady lope for what he guessed was about a quarter of a mile before slowing to a walk. She wasn't even perspiring.

"Don't you know you're supposed to stretch before running?" he asked, sucking breath but keeping stride with her in the parallel tire rut.

"That wasn't a run," she said, the near corner of her mouth quirking upwards.

"Are you showing off for me?" he asked.

Her cheeks pinkened though she huffed as though he'd said the most ridiculous thing. "Why on earth would I want to show off for you?"

"Because you like me."

"I do not. I mean, I do. But..."

He stepped over the grassy median, joining her in her rut, and looped an arm around her shoulders. "It's okay. I like you, too."

For a moment, she frowned. Then she laughed. "Yeah. That was pretty sophomoric of me."

"No more so than me. At least you didn't fall into a ground hornets' nest in the process."

She stopped, caught his chin between her fingers, and studied his face. "You're looking good."

He grinned. "I hear that a lot."

She smacked him in the chest. "You are so full of yourself."

He pulled her close. "Not nearly as much as you think." And he bent his head and kissed her. He kissed her hard and deep, but not nearly as long as he'd liked to.

#

Not nearly as long as Kelly would have liked either as Max jumped against them with a stick in his mouth, jolting them apart.

"Does he never get tired of chasing sticks?" groaned Dane.

"He's a retriever. Retrieving things is what he does."

He ruffled the dog's ears. That he didn't hold Max's interruption against the dog was one more thing she liked about Dane.

They continued along the path, Dane throwing sticks, Max retrieving them.

"You hunt with him?" Dane asked.

"My dad did."

"He's your dad's dog then."

"They were inseparable until..." She hesitated, struck by how easily he drew her out and wondering if that was a good thing or not. After all, a good CO *chatted* people up to get information from them.

Dane flung a stick, sending Max into the woods, before prodding, "Until what?"

She inhaled, giving herself another few seconds to decide giving him some family history wouldn't do any harm. "He got shot in the leg by a poacher, which forced him into early retirement. It put an end to him and Max hunting together."

Max bounded up to them and Dane asked, "He can still throw a stick for the dog, can't he?"

"Sure," she said, as Dane accepted the stick from Max. "He just can't take him out in the woods any more to do it."

Dane flung the stick deep into the woods. "Must have been a bad injury to keep him away from all this."

"It wasn't really *that* bad. Dad's more hurt he can't function the way he used to."

"Then he must not have loved the woods all that much, 'cause nothing would keep me away from something or someone I truly loved."

She gaped at Dane, stunned he had put into words something she'd often thought herself.

"We better head back before it gets dark," she said, finding a comforting kinship in Dane thinking the same way she did.

#

Back at the cabin, they sat side-by-side on the picnic table bench watching the sun set, backs braced to the table edge and Max stretched out underneath, finally having chased enough sticks.

"Some people say the best sunsets are on the ocean," Dane said. "Have you ever seen a sunset on the ocean?"

"I've never seen an ocean, let alone a sunset on one," she said, thinking how limited a life she'd led compared to his.

"Against all that horizon," he said, "it seems...small."

Surprised by his comment and curious, she studied his profile as he stared out over the forested landscape at the distant range of trees behind where the sun sank.

"This—" He waved a hand that encompassed the full range of a sky view framed by forest. "—is majestic."

Following the sweep of his hand, she gazed across the valley—gazed at the oranges and purples and pinks with which the slipping sun painted sky and clouds.

"I always liked our sunsets," she said.

He slung an arm around her and hugged her to his side. "And well you should. They're among the most beautiful

I've seen from anywhere in the world."

"Really?"

His face caught in the last golden ray of sunlight, he looked her in the eye and smiled. "Really."

Then he kissed her forehead and rested his temple against hers as they sat together in amiable silence watching the oranges and purples and pinks sharpen in their final glory before fading toward night. Kelly had told herself what was between them was just lust. It would be over soon. But now, hugged against Dane's side sharing a sunset, it didn't feel like *just* lust. It felt more like something she didn't want to give up, something she wanted worse than breath.

## CHAPTER FOUR

They were back on the job the next morning, the previous night's rain and the nearby swamp of the lowland they patrolled spongy beneath Dane's feet. He was struggling through a thicket of brush when her arm came up against his chest, stopping him.

"What?" he asked.

She nodded at the ground in front of them. "Rabbit guts."

"And you were afraid I'd step in them?" he asked, even though he sensed there was more to her stopping him than preventing him from gooing up the soles of his boots.

"Animal predators don't leave behind the guts."

"So this rabbit was killed by a human?"

"You got it, Sherlock." She squatted, studying the ground around the remains.

"Given your interest, I would venture to say rabbits aren't in season?"

"Another good deduction." Carefully, she swept back the underbrush. "Aha," she said. "The remnants of a snare."

"Is that illegal, too?"

"Yeah. Falls under the realm of trapping, and traps require identification."

He squatted and peered over her shoulder. "It looks like a string. How do you put identification on a string?"

"You don't," she said, standing and shrugging off her backpack. Retrieving her field camera from the pack, she ordered, "Hold that brush back so I can get a shot."

"Got yourself a poacher, huh?"

"Looks that way," she said, snapping shots of the snare and the rabbit guts.

"So now what do we do?" he asked.

"We track him," she said, shooting the imprint of a boot

in the damp soil.

"Hot damn. Some real action." He took one step toward the footprint and she stopped him.

"Behind me."

"Yes, ma'am."

"You never track *on* the trail," she said. "You track alongside it. Preserve the trail in case you lose it and need to backtrack."

"Handy bit of information for The Hawke."

"Glad to be of service in your research," she said, stowing the camera. "And here's something else *The Hawke* should know. Stay behind me and keep quiet."

They'd gone about a quarter mile, the terrain gradually rising—getting drier. But even when the footprints disappeared, she didn't lose the trail. Pointing out broken twigs and bent branches, they tracked in silence.

"There's an excitement to this," he said in a lowered voice.

"Don't expect too much," she said in an equally quiet voice. "It's only rabbit poaching. Hardly big time."

Shortly, she stopped him again. "Smell that?"

He sniffed the air. "Smoke."

"Campfire, and this isn't a designated camping area."

"The offenses mount," he said.

She cocked her head at him. "And what was the fire danger designation yesterday?"

"High risk," he answered.

"Good boy."

"So you can get this poacher on making a campfire during a high risk fire danger as well?"

"Yup. Though, since we had a good soaking rain last night, I'll probably just give him a warning on that count...provided he doesn't give me any trouble. Giving them a break on something minor is good public relations."

When the trail dipped over an outcrop of rocks, she raised a finger to her lips and motioned him toward the rocks. At the top, on their bellies, they looked down on a campsite. It wasn't quite what he'd expected to find.

Beside an older car with a decrepit open trailer attached to it, a man worked the illegally gained rabbit carcass onto a stick while a woman sat beside the illegal campfire hugging a crying toddler with a hollow-eyed girl squatted beside her. He swore he heard Kelly curse before she motioned him back from the crest of the outcrop.

"They're just a hungry family," he said once they were beyond earshot.

She stared at the ground, frowning.

"That trailer looks like it's packed with all their belongings," Dane said. "And the little girl beside her mother—"

"I saw," Kelly snapped.

"You can't ticket them."

"He broke more than one law," she said, frowning.

"Can't you just make like you didn't see them? Pretend you didn't find the rabbit guts and snare?"

"Dammit, Dane. I'm law enforcement and the law in this case is clearly spelled out."

He frowned. "I don't know how you can do this job."

"If you can't handle the reality of it, stay here while I go down there."

"I'm coming with you."

"Then be quiet. Not a sound."

Much as he wanted to step on a twig or trip and send some rocks tumbling to warn the family, he respected Kelly too much to sabotage her. This was her job, her domain, her life. And sometimes reality sucked. He'd learned that a dozen times over in his years of growing up in Eastern Europe.

So he followed her, careful to avoid brittle sticks. Then, incredibly, she slipped, sending a cascade of small rocks clattering off the outcrop.

Dane glanced down into the campsite in time to see the man fling the skewered rabbit carcass under the car. Had Kelly also seen? Would she drag out the evidence and still nail the guy for poaching?

"Morning," she called. "How you folks doing?" she asked as they strode into the campsite.

"Fine," the man said, shoving his hands into his pockets. If they got a good look at them, Dane was sure they'd find dried blood.

The toddler whimpered and the mother looked up at them with wide eyes. Only the girl who couldn't be more than five years old rose and came toward them, hope in her eyes. He'd seen eyes like those before. He squatted and smiled at her. "What's your name, little lady?"

"Janey," she said, those big eyes looking at him as if he was some sort of hero come to rescue her and her family.

Behind him, Kelly was doing her CO thing. "Looks like you're doing some long distance traveling."

The man he assumed to be Janey's father nodded. "Headed to North Dakota. Heard there's work there."

"So they say," she said. "You folks Yoopers?"

Dane had observed her enough to know she was testing the guy to see if he knew the nickname for residents of the Upper Peninsula—the U.P.—testing to see if he was local.

"Nah. We come up from just below the bridge." The dad forced a short laugh. "What you folks up here call trolls."

"I'm Officer Jackson with the DNR and this fellow, Dane, is job shadowing me."

"Ah," the father responded, giving Dane a passing glance.

"Been camping here long?" she asked.

"Just since last night. We were all pretty tired of the road and thought this looked like a good place to stop."

"May I see some identification, sir?"

Dane winced. The man was going to have to remove at least one bloody hand from his pocket to give Kelly his ID. He held his breath as the father offered her his driver's license with a shaking hand.

Kelly accepted it without comment and wrote the man's information in her notepad, Kelly who never missed anything.

She handed the license back to the man. "Do you folks know this isn't a designated camping area?"

"We'll move on," the father said, stuffing his ID into his pocket.

Kelly nodded toward the fire pit. "We're posted for high fire danger, too."

"We dug the pit nice and deep," the mother said. "Put rocks around it."

"I can see you're being real careful about the fire. But you can't have a fire here."

"Needed a fire to boil the water from the creek," the father said.

Dane looked at the kettle hanging over the fire.

"We ran out of drinking water," the mother said.

Kelly nodded. "Good thinking to boil the water. But you can't have a fire here."

Kelly removed her backpack and retrieved two bottles of water from it and handed them to the mother. "Drink this. Use that creek water to douse the fire when you leave."

"You can have my water, too," Dane said, removing his pack and digging out his water bottles.

The baby cried and the mother stuck a knuckle in his mouth for him to chew on.

"When did that baby last eat?" Kelly asked, her tone soft.

"We ate the last of the crackers last night for supper," Janey said.

"I've got a couple power bars," Dane said, digging them out and handing them to Janey. There was that hero worship look again that would have brought him to his knees if he wasn't already on the ground.

Kelly unzipped a side pocket on the pack and took out an individually wrapped peanut butter cracker snack and handed it to the mother who immediately opened the package and handed a cracker to the baby. Kelly placed another cracker pack and power bar on the ground next to where the mother had set the water bottles. Then she turned back to the father.

"There's a designated rustic camping area about two miles further along this road. Fire pit's metal lined. Given the drenching we got last night, nobody should give you trouble about building a fire there. If they do, you just tell them I said it was okay."

She wrote on a back page of her notepad and handed it and her card to the father. "Here's the address of a shelter in Marquette. When you get that far, they can get you set up with some supplies."

The father blinked from the paper to her.

"You move to that designated campsite. I'll stop by later and check to see how you folks are doing."

Numbly, the father nodded.

"You folks take care," she said, tapping the brim of her hat and heading back up the trail.

Dane jumped to his feet, shook the father's hand, grabbed his pack and followed Kelly. When they were out of earshot, he said, "You knocked those rocks over on purpose, didn't you?"

"After all the fuss I made of telling you to be quiet, do you think I'd really give us away like that?"

He grinned. "Yes. And I also think you saw him throw that rabbit carcass—"

She whirled about at him and stuck a finger in his face. "Don't say another word, St. John."

He closed his hand around her pointing finger. "I knew you didn't have it in you to ticket them."

"You tell anybody I went soft on those people and I'll put out the word to everyone with a hard luck story that you're a soft touch."

"What do you mean?"

"You gave the dad money, didn't you?"

"Not much. Just what I had in my wallet. Couldn't have been more than eighty bucks. Enough for a tank of gas and some groceries."

"Sap," she said, pulling her finger free and heading off along the trail.

"Like they say, a fool and his money is quickly parted."

"Then you're a fool, St. John."

He caught her by the arm, stopped her. "Kel, I just got a huge advance against this next movie. If I'd had this kind of money a month ago, I could have helped my sister big time. But I didn't, and now that I've got it, she doesn't need it. But those people back there do need it. If helping them with a few bucks makes me a fool, then I'm a happy fool."

Her brow furrowed as she seemed to study him through those clear, bright eyes of hers. "You're a good man, Dane St. John."

Then she turned and stepped out of his grip, heading off through the woods like a hungry mama bear on the scent of a honey comb.

"Why are we in such a hurry?" he called, darting after her.

"Can't run his license until I get back to the truck."

"You're going to check them out?" he asked, catching up to her.

"Of course. They could be fugitives."

"And if they are, what's going to happen to those kids?"

Her pace slowed. "Child Protective Services will take custody and those kids will have full tummies and a bed to sleep in tonight."

"That's the real reason you're checking up on the father, to protect those kids," he said.

She tossed him a hard look and picked up her pace. "I'm law enforcement, Dane. Checking out people is what I do."

"Watching out for those kids is what you're doing."

"And the residents of my district. If the mom or dad have outstanding warrants—"

"Yeah, they looked like they were a real threat." He said, scrambling to keep up with her.

"People aren't always what they seem to be."

"I know that, Bright Eyes."

Her step faltered and she glanced back at him. "Sorry. I keep forgetting how you grew up. Of course you'd know you can't judge a book by its cover. Now quit slowing me down. I've got groceries to buy."

"We don't need any more gro—" What she meant dawned on him. "You're buying groceries for *them.*"

"I'm going to have to check up on them later, make sure they moved to a designated campsite. Might as well see to it the kids get something wholesome to eat."

He laughed. "Now who's the sap?"

"Just because I'm law enforcement doesn't mean I'm heartless," she grumbled.

He caught up to her, hugged her against his side, and kissed her cheek. "I already figured that out about you, Bright Eyes."

She brushed him off and hurried off ahead of him. "Don't get carried away, St. John."

"You think the grocery store has an ATM?" he called after her.

She shook her head, her braid swishing across her back. "You're going to give them more money, aren't you?"

"Can't help it. I'm a sap for the underdog."

"That's for sure."

"And you love that about me, admit it."

"Don't get a swelled head over it, St. John."

"Oh no. My head's getting so big, I don't think I can carry it. Look, I can't fit it between the trees.

She kept trucking. But her shoulders shook with silent laughter.

Damn, if he didn't like making her laugh.

#

It was more than the beauty of the valley stretching for as far as the eye could see from Angel Point—more even than the natural beauty of the woman sitting across the picnic table from Dane distracting him as he shuffled the playing cards. He'd seen how Kelly had soothed the homeless couple's toddler quiet while the mother and father stowed the groceries he handed out to them from the back of the truck later that afternoon. The little girl may have latched onto him, but there was no denying a nurturer lie beneath the uniform of CO Kelly Jackson.

"You did a nice thing for that family today," he said, setting the card stack in front of her.

"You implying I'm a soft touch, St. John? Because, if you are, I would remind you you're the one who gave them all the cash in your pocket then went to the ATM and got more."

She cut the deck. He turned up an Ace. She grunted, a dissatisfied sound. Because of the card or because he'd given the homeless couple money?

"That wasn't being a soft touch," he said, dealing them each the seven cards required for a cribbage hand. "That was being compassionate."

"Gotta' use compassion judiciously, or the world will take advantage of you," she said, gathering up her cards.

"My sister operates mainly on compassion," he said, picking up his own cards.

"And how's that working for her?" she asked, studying the cards in her hand.

"Quite well, actually."

She raised one eyebrow at him. He palmed his cards and watched her as he elaborated.

"Dixie's been through a lot in the last couple years, what with her husband getting killed in an accident and her father-in-law fighting her for custody of her son to the point she lost her home and means of income. But, because of her compassion, she found a new home and even fell in love again."

She frowned at him. "Must have been hard for you, watching your sister lose her home."

He grimaced, suffering a pang of guilt over that period in his life. "I was still pretty much the stereotypical starving actor back then. My first movie hadn't come out, yet, and I hadn't been paid all that much for it. I'm just now commanding that big salary most people think all us actors get."

She flicked two cards from her hand facedown into his crib for counting later. "You can help her now."

"Except she doesn't need my help now," he said, discarding two cards from his into his crib.

"How do you mean?" she asked, rearranging her cards.

"She's got Sam now."

She glanced at Dane just long enough for him to see the dubious glint in her eye. "The man she fell in love with out of compassion?"

"Compassion wasn't the reason she fell in love with Sam," he said, knowing she was going to jump all over what he was about to tell her. "Dixie invited him into her home because of her compassion."

She folded her cards, braced her forearms to the table edge, and gave him a full on I-told-you-so look. "And you're certain this guy isn't just looking for a roof over his head?"

He chuckled. "You *are* a cynic."

"Comes with the job," she said.

*Which seemed to be her excuse for the hardline persona that hid the compassionate woman he knew lurked inside her.*

He gave her a consoling smile. "Sam's a trust fund baby. He doesn't need any roof Dixie offers him."

She grunted.

"But I will admit," he added, "until last week, I had my reservations about Sam."

"What happened last week?"

"He showed up at our Fourth of July family reunion and faced the whole family."

This time, her eyebrows slanted an impressed angle. "Walked into the lion's den for her, huh?"

"Yup."

"Brave guy," she said, a hint of wistfulness to her voice.

"He looked terrified." Dane all but chuckled, then he

sobered. "But the important thing is he loves my sister enough to fight *for* her...and *on* her behalf."

Both her eyebrows lifted. "*On* her behalf?"

"The short of it is he risked that cushy trust fund of his to make life right for Dixie and her son."

She gave an impressed huff. "Way to go, Sam." Adding as she fanned out her cards, "Not many men would risk everything for the woman they love, become their hero."

He smiled across the table at her. "That's a romantic way of putting what Sam did. I wouldn't have thought you had such idealism in you, Kel."

She shrugged, studying and rearranging her cards. "Heroes are just ordinary people who do extraordinary things. Risking his own security for the woman he loved was extraordinary."

His comment had been meant to prod the romantic he believed lurked deep inside her. He hadn't expected her to come back with such a rational explanation for heroism. There was almost a note of cynicism to her reasoning. Something she got from her family?

"So," he ventured, "is it just you and your little sister?"

Her fingers stilled on her cards. "How do you know I have a younger sister?"

"In the pictures in the cabin. Little blond girl and bigger—"

"Non-blond girl," she cut in and slapped a six of hearts face-up on the table.

*Non-blond girl? Was that an issue?*

"Looked like there's more than a few years difference in your ages," he said, unsure if he wasn't walking into his own lion's den.

"She's six years younger than me," she said, adding a clipped, "It's your play."

He flipped a card on top of hers.

She nodded at the discard stack. "You put a seven on my six."

"Yeah, so?" he asked, studying her, more intent on

learning what about her sister bothered her than winning at the card game they were playing. He didn't buy for a minute it was *only* a blond vs brunette issue. There was more substance to Kelly than that.

"I could play an eight on your seven, which would give me a three point run."

"I see," he said, momentarily back-shelving his musings. "So, do you have an eight to play?"

"I do indeed." She laid her eight on the pile and moved her peg on the cribbage board three spaces. "Of course," she went on, "I could be setting you up for a nice play if you had a nine. You'd get two points for a go of thirty-one plus a four card run for a total of six points. But I'm gambling you don't have a nine or you'd have played it on my six which would have added up to fifteen and given you two points."

"Guess I missed that play," he said, giving her a sheepish grin as he placed a nine on her eight. "But hey, I'm just learning the game."

She gaped at the card, then at him.

He shrugged. "Beginner's luck."

The next hand, Dane made a play that netted him six more points. Kelly cursed.

He nudged her foot under the table. "I bet you thought I wasn't paying attention when you explained the game."

"Something tells me you pay attention to every game you play," she said, tucking her feet under her bench and out of his reach.

"I pay attention to everything that interests me," he said, holding her gaze until she blinked away. It'd been long enough for him to see she'd gotten his message…that *she* interested him.

They played one more round before running out of cards, counted the points in their hands, and moved their pegs along the cribbage board the appropriate number of spaces. She picked up the played cards and shuffled them into the deck.

"Where is she, your little sister?" he asked, well aware

his prodding might well be the equivalent to poking a sleeping bear with a stick.

Her shuffling faltered ever so slightly. "Student nursing in Marquette."

Much as he wanted to find out whether her terse responses to his questions about her sister came of jealousy or something deeper, he sensed he'd pushed as far as he dared go at the moment when she switched the attention to his family. "Yesterday, when you told me about your mother teaching you to cook, it sounded like you weren't the only boy."

"I have three brothers. There's Jake, Roman, and Renn, in addition to me and our little sister Dixie."

"Good size family," she said, dealing the cards. "Is Dixie the youngest?"

"No, Renn's the youngest. Dixie's the second youngest. But all us boys are protective of her."

"Because she's a girl," she stated, as she slapped the deck down on the table for him to cut.

"It's a brother thing," he said in an attempt to explain away whatever made her sensitive about him and his brothers looking out for their sister.

She snorted. "It's because she's a girl."

And another side to CO Kelly makes an appearance. But, was she touchy about protective men or men dominating women?

"We all look out for each other," he tested.

"How's that?" Kelly asked, an edge in her voice suggesting she and her sister didn't share the same kind of closeness he and his siblings did.

"When Dixie turned the first floor of Gran's farmhouse into a restaurant," he explained in answer to her question, "she needed a kitchen that met restaurant code. Roman's a contractor, so he drew up plans for her kitchen." He laughed, memories of his brother momentarily overriding his curiosity over Kelly's and her sister's relationship.

"Actually, Roman's a diehard planner. His latest five-year plan was to get married and start a family; and that's exactly what he did in spite of the fact he fell for a strong-willed woman who had plans of her own."

"As opposed to you, Mr. Impulsive?"

There was a sharpness to her question, almost a rebuke in it. He'd clearly pricked something touchy in her.

"Guilty," he quipped, determined to maintain the humorous tone to their conversation.

She picked up her cards and fanned them out, her tone deceptively neutral. "So Roman planned a restaurant grade kitchen for Dixie. What'd the rest of you do?"

"We bring brawn. We swing hammers."

She looked up from her cards, her pale brown eyes losing their shuttering. "Now I understand the calluses on your hands."

"You noticed those and still thought me as just a pretty face?"

There was a sheepishness in the way she lowered her chin and peeked at him through her eyelashes. "I didn't notice them right away."

"When did you notice them?" he asked, watching her, trying to figure out what she worked so hard to hide from him.

"When you held my chin to apply the sting stop," she said with such candor he forgot what it was he'd been trying to figure out she was hiding. His thoughts turned to the fact she hadn't noticed his calluses when they'd first shaken hands, but instead, when he'd touched her more intimately.

"So, where do you fit into the sibling line-up?" she asked, looking down at her cards.

"Smack dab in the middle," he said, gathering up his own.

Her eyebrow lifted a dubious angle.

"I know what you're thinking," he said. "Stereotypical middle child who always sees the glass half empty, who's always vying for attention. But let me remind you, Dixie is right there in the middle with me."

"But she's the only girl."
"Meaning?"
"It makes a difference."
"You think?"
"Uh, huh."

He shook his head. "I've never thought my brothers or sister got more attention than me."

"Of course you didn't notice," she said, picking at her cards. "You no doubt were very good at hogging the attention."

"I'm not an attention hog," he said, tossing two cards at her for her crib.

She smiled over her cards at him. "No. You just naturally flash your pearly white teeth every time I stop someone to check them out, making sure they recognize Mr. Action Movie Star."

"I can't help it if I have a great smile. It's in the genes. All of us St. Johns' got great smiles. Baby brother Renn is practically a mini-me."

She laughed. "Actually, I suspected you might be the youngest."

"The baby full of entitlement?"

"Yeah, something like that."

"Then Renn would surprise you, too," he said. "He's an old soul who'll readily give you the shirt off his back, if not his heart. Not that he isn't into having his share of self-serving fun," he added, fanning out his cards.

"Renn." She drew the name out. "Interesting name. And then there's yours, Dane. You two named after someone special?"

Dane chuckled. "Not exactly."

"Then what exactly?"

He shook his head. "I really shouldn't tell you how we were named."

She folded her cards and leaned across the table toward him. "Well, now, you're going to have to tell me. You've piqued my interest."

He smiled, not because he'd aroused her curiosity, but because she'd shortened the distance between them. And the closer she got to him, the better he liked it.

"Okay, but you have to promise not to tell anyone," he said.

"Promise," she said.

He chuckled again. "A few Christmases ago, us kids pooled our resources and had all the old family movies transferred to DVDs. So, here we are, the whole family watching one of those DVDs. It was endless images of Rennes, France. Us kids were bored silly.

But mom and dad sat there on the loveseat, their heads together, holding hands. Mom kept saying how beautiful the place was. Dad would point out something now and then and the two of them would giggle. *Giggle*. My parents were giggling and we're just watching scenery. Then Mom says, 'It was the perfect place to create our baby boy.'"

"Well, we all turned to Renn, whose full name is Rennes. He's sputtering away about our parents naming him after the place where he was conceived. The rest of us are teasing the hell out of him."

Kelly raised that dubious eyebrow at him, the one she raised way too often at him. He was going to have to do something about it. Unfortunately, what he had to confess wasn't going to help convince her he basically told truths.

"Okay, I was doing most of the teasing…which led to Mom turning to me and saying, 'What do you think is so funny about Renn being named after where he was conceived? You were conceived in Denmark.'"

Kelly slapped her hand over her mouth. "Dane, as in Denmark."

"You got it. Then Roman jumps up, sputtering about our parents' honeymooning in Rome."

"Hence Roman," Kelly said.

"Yup."

"And Dixie, what's with her name? Don't they know where in the south they conceived her?"

"Actually, the night they conceived Dixie, so the story goes, my parents stayed in a little town that straddled the Mason Dixon line."

"That's wild."

"If she'd been born a boy, they said they'd have named her Mason."

"So, where does Jake's name fit into this tradition?"

"Jake's actually our half-brother. Mom's first husband, Jake's dad, was military. He was killed while on a mission."

She eased back on the bench, a shadow darkening her clear eyes. "I'm sorry. It's tough for a kid to grow up not knowing his or her father."

"Dad has always considered Jake his son. Jake even took the St. John name."

"But there's always something about your real father that a kid can't let go of," she said, fanning out her cards and staring at them in a way that made him think she was seeing something beyond suits and numbers.

*Empathy*. That's what he was reading off her. But where did a girl who had a father find such empathy for a kid who'd lost his? Or was he reading too much into Kelly's simple compassion. Maybe her relating to Jake was for an entirely different reason.

He shrugged. "You might be right. Jake did follow his dad's path—joined the military. Guess you'd understand better than I would the allure of following in your dad's footsteps."

She grimaced, a strange tightness to her acknowledging, "Yeah."

CHAPTER FIVE

Dane didn't point out it was Saturday and they'd been working every day since Monday...at least *Kelly* had been. He'd spent Thursday lollygagging at camp, recuperating from his wasp attack. The rest of the time, he'd pretty much been along for the ride. And neither of them had brought up his returning to his motel room, other than the night they swung by the place in the wee hours so he could pack a few essentials. Fine by him. He wanted as much time with Kelly as he could get.

He didn't press further about her family, either, yesterday or today. But here they were, a full morning and half an afternoon of checking boaters behind them, turning onto the street where she lived.

"I'll just run in and get Max," she said. "You wait in the truck."

"Yes, ma'am," he said, wondering if she didn't want her family to meet him or if she didn't want him meeting her family.

When they pulled up in front of a two-story craftsman style house with a big front porch occupied by three people and Max, she cursed.

"Wait here," she reiterated as she unbuckled and hopped out of the truck.

He watched her sprint across the narrow front lawn and up the front steps, all the more curious why she didn't want him and her family to meet.

"Hey, Carrie," Dane heard her call as she crossed the porch.

A young blond woman sitting on the porch swing next to an older man gave Kelly a finger wave. Kelly gave the woman in the rocker on the far side of the door a quick peck on the cheek.

"Came to pick up Max," she said, reaching for the door. "I'll just run in and get his leash."

She disappeared into the house, the screen door banging shut behind her, the trio on the porch looking at each other and shrugging. Then Max spotted him and came bounding off the porch.

"No," the older woman in the rocker shouted.

"Max, no," the man commanded, struggling to stand with the aid of a cane.

"Max, come," the young blond called, standing and crossing the porch to the steps.

But Max was already leaping at Dane's open window. Dane stepped out of the truck and caught Max by the collar, not that the dog seemed intent on running any further. But the family on the porch seemed concerned about the dog running loose in the front yard.

Dane led Max back to the porch steps from the top of which the blond he'd guessed to be Kelly's sister smiled down at him. "Thanks. He's not supposed to leave the front porch. He knows that."

The man he'd pegged as her father, now standing between cane and porch railing, growled out, "The kids drive by here like the street's a racetrack."

Dane glanced back at the narrow residential street, not a moving car in sight at present.

"Max, here," the father commanded and Dane released the dog to go to his master.

But, when he looked up at the man, he found him studying him through narrowed eyes. "My dog seems to know you."

"Oh Frank," the older woman who had to be Kelly's mom said from her rocker, snapping the ends of fresh beans and dropping them into the bowl in her lap. "You know how Goldens are. Everybody's a friend."

She lifted a smile at Dane. "You must be the fellow who's job shadowing our Kelly."

He nodded. "Dane St. John."

"That's how I know you," the petite blond atop of the steps said. "You're the movie star."

"Guilty as charged, ma'am."

"Isn't he a polite one," the mother said.

"Come join us," Kelly's sister added, stepping aside from the top step and motioning him forward.

He thought of how adamant Kelly had been about him waiting in the truck as he strode up the steps to the porch…and her prickly reaction to his questions about the sister who now invited him closer. But it would be rude not to accept such a direct invitation.

The blond was the first to extend a hand and introduce herself. "I'm Carrie, Kelly's sister."

"Nice to meet you," he said, shaking her hand.

"And this is our mom, Alma," Carrie said, indicating Kelly's mother who was trying to disengage herself from her beans and bowls.

"Don't get up," he said, stepping toward her and taking her hand in his.

She lifted a soft, pleasant face at him that seemed accustomed to smiling, then nodded across the porch. "And that cussed old man is Kelly's father, Frank."

Dane turned and stuck out his hand. Frank wasn't as quick to offer his hand in friendship. But when he took Dane's hand, his grip was Alpha strong. Max took advantage of his master's distraction to jump on Dane, tail wagging and tongue lapping.

Frank frowned. "Max, down."

Dane turned his head to avoid a swipe of Max's big tongue and laughed. "I'm afraid it's my fault he's lost his manners. I'm not much of a disciplinarian."

"So," Frank said, drawing out his words. "My dog *does* know you."

"We've met."

"Not here," Frank said.

Max dropped back to all fours, no doubt feeling the tension in his master's voice. "No. I didn't meet him here. He was with Kelly."

"She took him to camp with her day before yesterday. Is that where you met him?"

The old man was interrogating him. For himself, he didn't mind so much. But what would Kelly want him to answer? Fortunately, he didn't have to wonder for long. The screen door creaked open and she stepped out onto the porch.

"Yes, Dad. I took Max *and* Dane to Camp." Her gaze met his. "Sorry it took so long. Someone didn't hang up Max's leash in its usual spot."

"That would be me," Carrie said. "Took him for a walk this morning. Sorry."

"Let's get going," Kelly said and started down the steps, but her father's words stopped her.

"Your sister is spending her day off visiting us."

Dane glanced from a dour Frank to a frozen in mid-step Kelly. It didn't take a rocket scientist to know Frank had all but ordered his oldest daughter to stay and visit with her younger sister. This was a different family dynamic than his, and all his curiosity about her avoiding to talk about her family came back to him double-fold.

Kelly peered over her shoulder at her dad. "Sure. I'll just drive Dane back to his place first."

"Dane's welcome to stay," her mother said. "I've got a pot roast in the oven and green beans fresh from the garden. You like green beans, Dane?"

"Yes, ma'am."

She looked at Kelly. "You and your young man should stay for supper."

"He's not *my* young man, Mom."

*Not my young man?* Funny how her emphasizing that fact bothered him, goading from him a "Thank you, Alma. I'd love to stay for supper."

Which netted him a glare from Kelly.

#

Dane quickly dispersed with the usual questions about his career. He wanted to know about Kelly's family. But he still had to wade through a barrage of questions about his family and upbringing, Kelly remaining silent through it all. When Carrie and Alma excused themselves to the kitchen to finish preparing supper, he noticed Kelly stayed on the porch with him and Frank.

Almost instantly, the topic of conversation turned to hunting, fishing, and being a CO. It was as if the ladies absence signaled it was time for guy talk…except Kelly wasn't a guy. Yet she seemed to loosen up, adding a comment here and there as her father related tales of a lifetime working and playing in the woods. No wonder Kelly had followed in his footsteps.

And Frank's understanding of the woods was such that it made Dane want to learn from the man. As had his daughter, no doubt.

The stories continued into supper, leaving Dane wondering if he'd been wrong to think anything amiss with her family dynamics until…

"How you liking the beans, Dane?" Frank asked from the head of the table.

"They're good," he answered, taken aback by the sudden subject change. "Excellent, actually."

Frank smiled broadly. "My Carrie cooked them. Said she had some new recipe that would make them healthier."

"Just made them with a butter alternative, Dad," Carrie said, glancing around the table. "Reducing the cholesterol."

Kelly shifted in her seat beside Dane.

"Carrie's a nurse," Frank said, beaming.

"Not quite yet, Dad," Carrie said, glancing across the table at Kelly, who intently cut into her beef roast. "Still doing my student nursing."

"Going to catch herself one of those rich doctors and marry him."

Carrie's cheeks reddened. "That's not why I want to be a nurse, Daddy."

Frank reached across the corner of the table and patted his younger daughter's hand. "I know you're a smart girl, Baby."

Was this Kelly's issue, that her father favored his

youngest daughter over his oldest? He wanted to shout that Kelly was smart, too. That she knew her way around the woods as well as any CO. Before he gave it further thought, he blurted out, "Kelly tracked a poacher yesterday morning. It was amazing, the way she read the trail the guy left."

Her head snapped in his direction, drawing his attention to the panic in her widening eyes. Damn. Maybe he wasn't doing her any favors by bringing up the events of the previous morning.

"Did she catch him?" Frank asked.

"She did," Dane answered cautiously, looking from daughter to father.

Frank looked past him to Kelly. "Did you bring him in, or just ticket him?"

She stirred her fork through her mashed potatoes, not looking up—not answering.

"Don't tell me you went soft on the guy," Frank said.

"Your daughter did what was right," Dane said. "You should be proud of her. I was."

#

Dane spent the bulk of their drive toward camp fending off Max's exuberant anticipation of a run in the woods until Kelly ordered Max into the cargo area behind the bench seat. The dog finally settled, and Dane turned his attention fully to Kelly.

"I'm sorry I brought up the poaching incident."

"You didn't know any better," she said, her gaze fixed on the road.

"It's just the way your dad kept going on about your sister while saying nothing about your accomplishments."

"It's okay."

"No, it's not. He should be as proud of you as he is of her."

"He is, in his own way," she said, a hint of longing in her voice.

"Dammit, Kelly! You followed the same career path he

did. For that alone any father would be proud of his child."

"And he is proud of my becoming a CO. It's just that it's a tough job, and he knows what I'm up against. He knows that me being a woman, I've got to be especially tough."

"And he thinks withholding praise will toughen you up?"

She expelled a heavy breath. "You don't understand."

"Then explain it to me."

"My father's black and white where the law is concerned."

He studied her. "You saying he'd have thrown the book at that destitute family over one dead rabbit?"

"He'd have given them a break. Just not as much of a break as I gave them."

"I don't think they had money enough to pay for gas. How the hell would they have paid a fine?"

Keeping her eyes straight ahead, she said, "Dad sees enforcing conservation laws as protecting the forest and everything in it. To do less makes being a CO just a job. And to him, it was never *just* a job. It was an avocation."

"And what is it to you, Kel?"

"I believe in protecting the forest, in conserving the wilderness."

"You can't do that and be compassionate at the same time?"

"Sure, but COs are law enforcement. I went through the police academy—had the same training as any Michigan State Police officer."

"I get it. I'm impressed. But your father should be, too."

She steered the truck off the highway and onto the county road toward camp. "It isn't about whether he's impressed or not. It's that he knows all the pitfalls—all the danger a CO faces. We confront more people with guns on them than just about any other police force." Her eyes glistened with unshed tears. "Toughening me up is just his way of protecting me."

He understood why she defended her dad. But Dane

understood something else as well, something equally fundamental that the woman in the driver's seat wanted.

"But you still want—need him—to be proud of you, don't you?"

She shot him a look so wounded, he knew he'd hit the bulls-eye.

They rode the rest of the way in silence. But, when she braked to a halt in front of the cabin, she stayed behind the wheel, staring straight ahead.

He had opened his door but closed it when he realized she wasn't moving. The silence stretched and he offered, "You want me to leave you alone?"

Her shoulders sagged. "Frank's not my biological father."

He recalled her reaction to learning Jake was his half-brother, and her questions about how he got along with their father, his adopted father. It put a new twist on why her interest in Jack and why Frank was hard on her.

"So he favors your half-sister because she's his biological daughter?"

"Not really." Kelly slumped back in her seat. "I was there first. His first little girl."

"But then she came along and you didn't have him to yourself anymore?"

She winced. "I really wanted a dad. It's not my sister's fault I felt threatened when she came along. But I needed a daddy, and if it took being his buddy, his hunting and fishing partner to hold his attention, that's what I did."

"So, what are you saying, he treated you tough like a son instead of a daughter?"

She shook her head. "No. It wasn't about me being the son he didn't have. He was tough on me because…"

"Because you were going to be a CO like him?" he ventured when she hesitated.

She gave him a small, sad smile. "Because my biological father is American Indian and Frank was afraid I'd get kicked around in a school full of blond-haired, blue-eyed Finish kids."

He eyed her dark brown hair and aquiline nose, drawing a glance from her pale brown eyes.

"I don't see it."

She shrugged. "Genetics. My biological father was only half Indian and my mother full Finn."

"Did the blond, blue-eyed kids in your school give you a hard time?"

She shook her head.

"So Frank thought he was toughening you up for reality, but reality wasn't what he thought it would be."

"I guess." She glanced away, not meeting his gaze.

"Yet you still want his approval."

"I'm a needy girl, Dane. Not that you'll be around long enough for it to become an issue for you. But, now you know."

He opened his door, stepped out of the truck and around to the driver's side where he opened her door, unsnapped her seatbelt and gathered her into his arms. "Bright Eyes, we all need something and right now I need to give you hug."

#

Kelly stretched, relishing the slip of the cotton sheets across her naked body and the warmth of morning sunlight. A contented moan escaped her, and slowly, she opened her eyes to find... Dane propped up on one elbow smiling down at her.

"What you doing?" she drawled sleepily.

"Watching you sleep."

She winced and swiped the back of her hand across her mouth.

"No, you weren't drooling," he said, answering her unspoken question, then grinned that soul-melting smile of his. "But you did moan a lot. I hope you were dreaming of me."

Oh yeah. She'd been dreaming about him alright. But he might be surprised to learn not all of them had been about him making love to her. Her dreams had been full of his defending her to her father—his caring enough to drag out all the harsh facts of her life—and his still wanting to comfort her. Such things were what love was made of.

*No, no, no.* Do not go there. This is a fantasy. An affair of epic proportion and short duration.

She smiled back at him, teasing, "In *your* dreams."

He lifted her hand to his mouth and pressed his lips to her palm. Damn, but he had a knack for finding her most sensitive parts.

"And if I *was* dreaming of you?" she all but purred.

He bowed his head and brushed his lips across the sheet tented over her naked breasts, the sensation making her nipples tighten almost painfully. "Then I'd say you were ready for an encore of last night."

Ah, but which time last night? The first time when he'd carried her from the truck into the cabin—from her confession to his tender ministrations? Or the second time, after they'd returned from scouting for night poachers and torn the clothes from each other as they stumbled to the bed?

"Are you always this responsive?" he asked, blowing his warm breath across her tender nipples.

He'd said everybody needed something; and his touch, the way he played her body made her come alive. And those goofy grins and wagging eyebrows he cast her way—his teasing manner made her feel desirable. Dane St. John made her feel like a woman, and no other man had ever done that.

But he was due back in Hollywood in a week. Who would make her feel this way when he was gone?

Her chest tightened, making her go still.

He pulled back. "Hey, where'd you go? I seemed to lose you for a minute."

She blinked at him. "Huh?"

"You left," he said, tapping her temple with a forefinger. "Up here."

What the hell could she say to him?

*You're too good to be true...and will be gone too soon?*

And there was something else. Something about how valued she felt by his simply listening—hearing her. It took her beyond the mindset of an affair.

But no way was she messing up the fantasy of a lifetime, not when she had only days left with a man who exceeded any fantasy she could have dreamed up.

She stroked his bare, broad shoulders, threaded her fingers through his shaggy, blond hair, and gazed into his mesmerizing blue eyes. "I've never spent a whole night with a man before you."

He gave her one of his impish grins. "I think I like that, being your first all-nighter."

"I've never jumped into bed with a guy three days after meeting him, either," she said, needing him to know this about her, too.

"I definitely like that," he said, his grin growing more serious.

Damn but the man gave her everything she needed, even when he didn't know he was doing it. Too bad her heart couldn't afford to buy into it, not with only days left to be together.

She smacked him in the shoulder, hiding her true feelings and spouting good-naturedly, "Sexist pig."

He laughed and scooped her close, the bed sheet slipping out from between them. "How would you like this *sexist pig* to serve you breakfast in bed?"

"Breakfast in bed sounds divine," she answered playfully.

He grinned, lowered his head, and pressed a kiss to the valley between her breasts.

A surprised, "Oh," escaped her.

Pressing her back against the mattress, he trailed kisses down her belly.

"When you said breakfast in bed," she said, "I didn't expect it to be meeee—"

He spread her legs and kissed her lower still.

"Oh. Yes. This is good," she said between tiny gasps.

And a glorious buffet he made of her before he flopped back on his pillow, panting. "Looks like we're going to get a late start on the morning marine duties."

"No morning duties today," she said on a contented sigh.

He groaned. "Tell me we aren't patrolling the woods this afternoon like the day I got stung?"

"Damn," she muttered, knowing she was about to lose her wonderful glow to another confession. "About that."

"What about it?" he asked.

She rose onto her elbow and side facing him. "We don't usually patrol the woods during afternoons in July. There's not much happening and it's too hot."

Confusion puckered his brow. "Then that day I got attacked by wasps, why were we—"

She pressed her fingertips against his lips, those artful lips that could tease both laughter and orgasmic delight from her. "You were enjoying the marine patrol way too much. I wanted to make things hard for you."

He blinked at her...then laughed. "No wonder you thought my getting stung was your fault."

"I *was* responsible for you *wherever* I took you."

He levered himself up on his side, facing her, mischief dancing across his lips. "That's right, and I wouldn't have run into that hornet's nest if you hadn't taken me into the woods."

"And you wouldn't have fallen into it if you had stayed on the trail like I told you to," she said, poking him in the chest.

He caught her by the wrist, stilling her finger, rolled her onto her back and straddled her.

"What do you think you're going to do with me now?" she asked.

"Maybe I'll cover you in honey and tie you down on an anthill in retaliation for you getting me wasp stung. No, wait. I think I'll lick the honey from your body, instead. Yeah, that's a torture I'd like to ply on you."

Though she itched in the most delicious of places at his idea of torture, she couldn't pass on the opportunity to tease him back...or teach him a lesson.

She raised an eyebrow at him. "And you think *you* with your meager stunt training can keep *me* pinned down?"

"I think I'm doing a pretty good job of it so far."

She had him face down on the mattress and his arms twisted behind his back in an instant. "Really?"

He spit out a corner of pillow and said, "No fair using your cop skills on me...unless you've got a special plan, sitting there naked on my bare butt."

"You're incorrigible," she said, even as she considered taking another spin in the proverbial hay. But Max chose that moment to whine at them from the bedside.

Dismounting Dane's delectable derrière, she scooted to the edge of the bed and patted Max on the head.

Dane belly-crawled after her, asking, "Don't you ever take a day off?"

She rose and opened a drawer on the dresser beside the bed, giving him what she hoped was a saucy look over her shoulder. "Actually, today is a pass day for me."

"Pass day?"

"What you'd call a day off," she said, plucking a fresh tee from the dresser rather than go for her camisole on the floor where she'd dropped it in their frenzied path to the bed last night.

"Then why are you even leaving this bed, Woman?"

She nodded at the dog dancing a path between the bed and door. "Max needs to go out."

"Max, old boy," he called, momentarily gaining the dog's attention. "Haven't you ever heard the saying, leave sleeping dogs lie. Well, we were lying...kind of."

She shimmied the t-shirt down over her torso, enjoying the way Dane's gaze followed the downward glide of the garment. Butterflies took flight in her stomach. Still she tsked and teased, "Middle child hogging the attention."

His eyes darkened on her. "Come here, I'll show you just how well I can *hog* the attention."

"I just bet you'd love that," she said, heading for the door instead.

A glance in his direction as she opened the door and let Max out confirmed his attention hadn't shifted off her. If only this moment could last forever. But it couldn't. It wasn't reality. This whole thing happening between them wasn't reality. He'd be back in Hollywood soon, and she'd be a notch on his bedpost.

But she could—would enjoy every moment she had left with him.

#

Max put out, he watched her stroll back to the dresser, thoroughly enjoying the womanly sway of her hips. She didn't walk like this when she was in uniform. But there was one thing he had noticed about her even when wearing fatigues.

"You have amazing, long legs," he said.

She huffed out a little, feminine snort and reached into the open dresser drawer as though his comment was of no interest to her. But he caught the upward tug at the corner of her lips.

He patted the mattress beside him. "Why don't you come over here and let me measure just how long they are?"

She faced him, the eagle emblazoned tee she'd donned before putting Max out stretched across her breasts. Were he a boob man, he'd have lingered on the wing span of that bird in flight instead of her long legs bared beneath the hem of that shirt...which only reminded him she hadn't put her panties back on.

And if she wasn't trying to tease him, she'd likely have already slipped on the shorts she'd retrieved from the dresser rather than stand there letting them dangle from her fingers while arching a playful eyebrow at him. "Don't you ever tire out?"

"Me," he said, thumping his chest, giving her his best Neanderthal imitation, "male in prime."

She groaned and flung the shorts *at* him. Then dove on him, pinning him with a knee to the solar plexus and a forearm to the throat, but not too forcefully. Clearly her intentions were not to incapacitate, but the exact opposite as she nipped at his lips and played tongue tag with him.

He reached for her. She slapped his hand away and rose over him, shaking a finger at him. "Na-ah. I had my breakfast. Time for yours."

She slid her knee off him and planted a trail of nips, licks, and kisses down his chest and over his abdomen. When she closed her lips over him, he groaned.

He hadn't asked for this. He hadn't expected it. But he shouldn't have been surprised. She'd already proven herself an ardent lover.

*Damn*, but he could spend a life-time losing himself in her enthusiasm. Too bad he had something to tell her that was going to dampen the mood, and there was no avoiding it.

But it could wait a little longer. No way was he interrupting what she'd started…or finishing without her.

About to come, he lifted her from him and slipped on a condom. Her bright eyes were all dreamy as she sank the length of him, riding him—the Eagle in full flight on her t-shirt riding her every stroke—the words printed below the image imprinting on him. Ottawa National Forest. When he heaved beneath her and she collapsed on top of him, he knew, if he lived another hundred years he'd always connect an eagle and the Ottawa National Forest with this moment.

They lay panting, chest to chest, until their breathing evened out. He stroked her head, her hair, the sweat-dampened back of her tee. His contentment waning as reality made its way back into his head. With utter tenderness, he kissed her temple, his lips lingering. Then he sighed.

"What's wrong?" she asked.

"What makes you think there's anything wrong?"

She folded her hands on his chest, rested her chin on

them, and peeked up at him. "You sighed and not in a satisfied way."

He stroked the hair back from her cheek. "You're one intuitive woman, Bright Eyes."

"Comes from being a—"

"CO, I know. But it also comes from being a woman. My mother has it. Dixie has it."

"So, what am I intuiting?"

"My sister's getting remarried."

"Nothing wrong with that," she said, tilting her head to one side, clearly unprepared for what he was about to tell her.

He drew a deep breath, feeling every inch of her sprawled atop him and hating he couldn't keep her there. "You know from what I've told you that our family is pretty spread out geographically. Roman's here in the U.P. and Dixie's just north of Green Bay in Wisconsin. But the rest are scattered. Renn works in Texas, Mom and Dad live in Japan, and Jake's usually in shadowland somewhere on another continent."

He purposely didn't bring up that he'd soon be heading to Eastern Europe to shoot his next movie. But she was picking up on the vibe coming off his words, trying to figure out what came next. He felt it in the tightening of her body—saw it in the darkening of her eyes.

"So," he continued, stroking her back, "since we were all here for the Fourth of July and none of us had anything major pulling us too far away at the moment, Dixie and Sam have decided to get married while we're all here in the States."

She slid off him to his side, putting her back to him as though anticipating his answer to her next question. "When is the wedding?"

He rolled onto his side behind her and cupped her hip. "Monday."

"Monday?" She sat up, breaking from his hold, her voice small, almost lost sounding. "Monday as in tomorrow?"

"Yes."

She swung her legs off the bed.

"Odd day of the week for a wedding," she said, pulling on her panties.

"It's the one day of the week Dixie's restaurant is closed."

"Sure. Makes sense," she said, snagging her shorts off the foot of the bed where they'd landed.

He watched her step into the shorts and pull them up those long legs that wrapped themselves around him every time he buried himself in her.

"Are you coming back afterwards?" she asked without looking at him.

He hadn't planned to. But that was before he'd discovered Kelly—before he'd gotten a taste of...

*A taste of what?* Love? Was that what this was? Or were they still exploring the possibility there was more between them than fantastic sex? Whatever the case, he wasn't yet ready to walk away from Kelly.

"I'm not needed on set for another week," he said, moving to the edge of the bed, closer to her

She tugged nervously at the hem of that tee he'd never forget her wearing as she made love to him.

"I'll be back," he said.

"Good," she replied in a small voice.

*No. Not good. They had so few days left together. He didn't want to squander a moment of that time by being away from her.*

"Come with me," he said.

She turned wide eyes at him. "To your sister's wedding?"

He stood and took her hand in his. "It'll just be a little family affair."

Something that looked like panic flashed across her eyes. "Wouldn't your family find my attending their *little family affair* presumptuous?"

He gave her hand an encouraging squeeze. "Not my

family."

She frowned. "I don't know."

Desperate, he added, "Besides, my brothers will all have dates. You wouldn't make me show up alone, would you?"

*Lie.*

"Don't make me go to my sister's wedding stag," he said, hating he'd resorted to a lie, even a small one, to persuade her.

"It's short notice to ask for a pass—a day off."

He lifted her hand to his mouth and kissed her white knuckles then said, "As little time as we have left together, Kelly, I don't want to spend a minute of it without you. Please, come with me?"

*No lie.*

## CHAPTER SIX

*He didn't want to spend a minute of the time they had left without her.* He'd actually said those words—voiced the same sentiments she felt. She'd have moved heaven and earth to get Monday off, if that's what it would have taken. Fortunately it hadn't taken that much effort.

But now, standing in Roman and Tess St. John's front parlor, watching Tess St. John descend the sweeping staircase of the grand Victorian mansion in a fine silk dress made Kelly want to sink behind the antique loveseat in her little cotton blend sundress.

*Casual*, Dane had told her when she'd fretted over what to wear. What other lies might he have told her?

Tess' smile seemed genuine as she approached, hands extended. "You must be Kelly."

"Yes," Kelly said, managing a smile of her own.

Then Tess gave her the onceover. "Cute dress."

Kelly's smile faltered. "Dane said to dress casual."

Dane stepped from his brother's side to Kelly's. "It is casual. Look at me. I'm wearing jeans and a blazer."

"He's right," Tess said. "The St. Johns are a casual bunch. Relax, Kelly, you'll fit in with that dress better than I will with mine."

Okay, so he hadn't lied to her. Kelly exhaled, but still couldn't let go of the fact Tess' dress looked designer-tailored.

Tess fidgeted with a seam. "I'm a little limited these days to what fits what with junior on board. Getting thick in the waist, you know."

Dane's brother, Roman slung an arm around his wife and patted her tummy. "I, for one, love every one of those extra inches."

Tess gave him a playful slap and added in Kelly's direction, "Besides, even a country transplant like me finds it hard to leave the city girl behind completely. We dress up even when we jog."

Kelly chuckled, momentarily distracted from her discomfort…which had begun to well up in her the minute Dane had steered his rental into the driveway of the biggest house she'd ever been in.

"You have a beautiful house," Kelly said.

"Which she would have flipped and sold," Roman said, hugging Tess to his side.

To which Tess shot back, "I had a business I was building."

"But he wanted to fill the house with babies," Dane said, slipping an arm around Kelly's waist.

"Guess who won out," Roman said, drawing his wife into his arms in a way that made Kelly long for the same.

"We both did," Tess and Roman said in unison and the longing tightened deep in Kelly's belly.

"We best get rolling," Roman said, glancing at his watch. "We've got a two-hour drive ahead of us."

At the car, Tess cut Dane off before he could join Kelly in the back seat. "I'm sure you boys have some catching up to do. Besides, I'd like to chat more with Kelly." And she slid into the backseat next to Kelly.

Kelly swallowed hard. Two hours chatting with a city-born girl who'd grown up on the moneyed side of the tracks. Whatever would they talk about?

They'd barely backed out of the drive when Tess asked, "Have you plans for a family, Kelly?"

Kelly blinked, catching a backward glance from Dane, and sputtered, "I-I haven't thought a lot about kids…yet. I've been concentrating on my career."

"That was my Tess, too," Roman said, glancing at them from the rearview mirror, "when I met her."

Between Tess having asked the question, Roman looking at her in the rearview mirror, and Dane with his ear cocked toward the break between the front bucket seats, panic swelled through Kelly. What did they want to hear from her—what did *he* want to hear—if he even cared about her response?

She looked at Tess. The woman patted her hand and gave her a knowing smile. "What Roman says is true. I was all about my career and proving men wrong when we met."

"What happened?" Kelly asked before she could edit herself, yet at the same time grateful for change in subject.

"Love happened," Tess said with a wink. "Damn that cupid."

Kelly's stomach gave a funny little twist. Was that what was happening to her? Was she falling into love, rather than lust?

Of course she was. She'd known it the minute Dane had offered her an out just before burying himself inside her that first night together. But what about him?

She eyed the back of his head. What did he want by asking her to be his date to an intimate family wedding? Was this the meet-the-family date? Did he feel more than lust as well for her?

*Ridiculous*. They'd known each other only a few days.

Want clogged Kelly's throat. She looked out the side window, hiding her emotions until she felt composed enough to face Tess again. "So, you're an architect. I'm a Conservation Officer. Looks like the two of us chose professions not too welcoming of the female sex."

#

Dane was glad Kelly and Tess had found something in common to talk about, even if it involved a little man-bashing. At least Kelly had finally relaxed, having found a kindred spirit in his sister-in-law.

But when he handed Kelly out of the car in the circular drive of The Farmhouse, the back half of which had been barricaded off with sawhorses, he saw the hesitation return to her eyes. Before he could say anything to reassure her, Tess snagged Kelly's hand and tugged her toward the house.

"Let's go freshen up before making our grand entrances. Besides, I've got a baby sitting on my bladder."

And off they went, into the house. Dane frowned at the closing front door.

"Come on," Roman said, slinging an arm around him and guiding him toward the back yard. "Tess'll look after her."

By the time the two women appeared on the back porch, Dane had hugged his way through his brothers, his cousins, his father who'd explained his mother was inside tending the bride, and one jittery soon-to-be brother-in-law.

At the top of the back porch steps, Tess and Kelly appeared. Tess was regal in her silk, but Kelly took his breath away. It was the second time today she'd had that effect on him. Maybe it was because all he'd seen her in up until today were her fatigues or jeans…and her underwear…and her altogether.

Those last two memories had him twitching in his pants. But there was something more going on with this girl—something that went beyond how good she looked naked or in that poppy-floral sundress with its wide t-straps hugging her beautiful, bare shoulders. There was a whole lot more to her than those lovely, long legs exposed by the tea length skirt of that dress and turned by the modest heel of her white pumps. He knew. She'd shared with him some of her darkest fears.

And he'd heard a lot more by listening to her talk to Tess about the trials of working in a man's world. Most of all, he'd sensed all Kelly could be in the passion she'd brought to their lovemaking. She was seeking more, whether she'd admit it or not.

And he too wanted more; the question being did he want more *now?*

He met her at the foot of the stairs with a smile, and steadying hands for both her and Tess as they took the last step. "Roman's saving seats for us. They're about to start the ceremony."

#

At least she'd been spared the immediate barrage of introductions she'd been dreading. Not that the reprieve could last forever, Kelly thought, as Dane guided her into a seat between him and Tess. But, before she could fret too much about the introductions yet to come, the bride's small entourage appeared on the freshly white-washed back porch.

That the procession should start from the side of where everyone was seated struck Kelly as odd. But, how nice it was to see the glow of utter happiness in Dane's mother's face as she was escorted to her seat by a thirty-something, dark-haired man who fit Dane's description of Jake, something few would have seen had she been escorted down the aisle from behind the congregation.

They were followed by a pair of junior bridesmaids, identical down to their giggles.

"Our Cousin Annie's girls," Dane whispered, his mouth so close his breath tickled her ear.

The grinning Maid-of-Honor in a matching tea length dress trailing the twins so resembled them Kelly knew, even before Dane whispered the woman's name, she had to be Cousin Annie.

Then it was just the bride and her father at the top of those steps, the bride in a white cotton peasant blouse, the neckline embroidered with blue morning glories. The matching full skirt ended just below her knees and well above a pair of ruby-red heels. She wanted to ask Dane about the dressy spikes with so casual a wedding-attire, but the bride was grinning in the direction of someone at the front of the gathering with such love, Kelly didn't want to break the spell of the moment.

Of course, the object of the bride's love was the groom, who was beaming back at her with the same intensity. This was the look of two people deeply in love, and Kelly envied them.

Then the music switched, but not to the conventional wedding march. Instead, Huey Lewis and the News belted out from the speakers *The Power of Love* and the bride and her father broke into a dance of a procession.

Kelly gaped from them to the laughing groom. Dane pulled her to her feet and she saw everyone stood swaying and gyrating and clapping in tune as Dixie and her father danced their way to Sam. The father of the bride swung her into the groom's arms, took a turn in the aisle with the mother of the bride, the music faded out, and everyone but the wedding party and minister sat down.

Dane leaned close and, in a low voice, stated more than asked, "Wasn't that fun?"

"It was...unconventional," she replied, not sure what she thought of what had just transpired.

"That's my family," he said, beaming.

#

By the end of the service, Kelly ruled the orientation of the seating well thought out and not just so the guests could have easily watched the father of the bride dance her into the arms of her groom. Granted it was the most unusual *giving away of the bride* she'd ever witnessed, not that much beyond the conventional ever happened in Copper Falls. In any case, she was certain her father would never have danced her down any aisle, even if he hadn't taken a bullet to his hip.

She'd decided the seating arrangement was perfect because of the natural slope of the yard that set the flower-trimmed trellis and the bride and groom in easy view of all who witnessed their loving exchange of personal vows. Even little Ben, the bride's preschool son whom Sam had chosen to be his Best Man, wasn't lost behind a sea of heads.

"Sam would have no other," Dane had told her when she asked about Sam's having chosen a five-year-old as his Best Man. "He said it was the next best thing to having his cousin Michael at his side."

The cousin whom Sam had been raised alongside like a brother, Ben's father and the husband from whom Dixie had been widowed.

"Marrying like that within the family must have taken some time to work through," she'd said.

"Not nearly as much as you might think," Dane said, then switched gears, hauling her off to meet the first round of relatives.

Brothers Jake and Renn, like Roman, were tall like Dane. But, while Renn was practically a twin to Dane with his Viking blond hair and blue eyes, Jake was dark, his musculature lean, and his eyes watchful.

She shook hands with the oldest of the St. John siblings, the one who was a St. John by adoption and found him sizing her up with the same intensity with which she sized him up. "Dane tells me you're military. Special Ops?"

"Formerly," he said. "I've moved on."

*But not too far,* she surmised given his guarded demeanor.

Renn accepted her extended hand, but instead of shaking it, lifted it to his lips for a light kiss. "A pleasure, my lady."

"Don't let the act fool you," Dane said, extricating her hand from his brother's. "And it is an act. He plays a Renaissance knight at one of those theme restaurants where they joust while the patrons dine."

"The Joust," Renn said, giving her a courtly bow. Then, to Dane, he added, "At least I do my own stunts."

"I do my own stunts," Dane snapped back.

"Not all of them," Renn said with a wink.

"Most of them," Dane grumbled.

Jake just watched his two brothers with something just short of amusement. Then he caught her watching him.

"Join me at the punchbowl while these two verbally duke it out?" he offered.

"Oh no," Dane said, tucking her arm into his. "She has more people to meet."

As he steered her off, she nodded back at Renn and Jake. "Where are their dates?"

A triumphant grin split Dane's face. "They don't have

any."

"But, one of the arguments you gave me for my accepting your invitation to your sister's wedding was that you didn't want to be the only one here stag."

"So I wanted to show them up. We can sometimes be a bit competitive."

"You lied to me," she said.

He frowned. "Hang up the damn CO cap for one day, Kel."

"Hey, I left my phone back at the camp." Then, unable to keep the smile completely off her face, she said, "I've never seen you annoyed like this."

He pulled her into a shaded alcove behind a lilac bush, pressed her against the porch with his body, and kissed her.

"What's that for?" she asked when he let her up for air.

"To shut you up," he said and tugged her back out into the yard.

Before she could give her muddy heels or potentially smeared lipstick a second thought, he towed her to the edge of the lawn to a couple she recognized from the wedding ceremony.

"Mom, Dad," he said, hugging her close to his side with a hand around her waist. "This is Kelly Jackson. Kelly, this is my mom, Sarah, and dad, James."

Kelly extended her hand, but she'd barely gotten a "Nice to meet you" out before his mother enveloped her in a warm hug.

"How very nice to meet you," his mother said, stepping back without fully releasing her. "We so seldom meet any of Dane's lady friends."

His dad stepped in and gave her a light hug, "Hell, the boy never brings any girls home. You must be someone special."

She stood there, her head spinning as she tried to digest what his parents, his father especially, had said. Had he brought her here to meet the family after all?

"Looks like they need help setting up the tables," his father said, clapping Dane on the shoulder.

The next thing she knew, Dane and his dad had joined the other men in rearranging the chairs from the wedding ceremony to accommodate rows of long tables and she was left standing alone with his mother. Afraid his mother might ask her something as straight forward as Tess had, Kelly fell back on her CO habit of chatting up a person.

"So, Dane tells me you and your husband live in Japan."

His mother's smile was gentle. "Yes. We felt we'd seen all we wanted to see of Europe during our years living there. Time to explore the Orient."

Kelly nodded, knowing there was a plethora of questions she could be asking but lost to think of one. She was saved from the awkward silence by Cousin Annie propelling Dixie into their mix.

"I've told her she's the bride," Annie said in rush, "that she has to leave all this rearranging stuff to the rest of us."

"But someone needs to make sure the tables are set right," Dixie said. "You know the boys. We'll have wobbly, undecorated tables if it's left to them."

"Which is what your Maid-of-Honor is for," Annie returned. "You stay here and visit and I'll make sure the tables are set and decorated perfectly."

And just as quickly as she'd appeared, Annie was gone.

Dixie laughed, her blond curls dancing in the late afternoon sunlight. "Isn't this the most perfect day?"

Then she made eye contact with Kelly, and brightened even more. "You must be Dane's Kelly."

"H-he's told you about me?"

Dixie pulled her into a hug even warmer than the one Dane's mother had given her. "Of course he's told me about you. We tell each other everything."

"But we only met a few days ago," she said, extricating herself from the hug as gracefully as she could.

Dixie grinned at her, a grin so much like Dane's know-it-all grin. "Yeah, we St. Johns are pretty quick about knowing what we want."

*Knowing what we want?* Just what the hell was Dixie telling her? For that matter, what did his telling his family about her imply? Even if Dixie and her mother weren't now deep in conversation about setting up the buffet, she didn't feel comfortable enough with any of the St. Johns to ask bluntly whether or not she might mean more to Dane than *a love the one you're with* moment. Maybe if she got Tess alone she could *interview* some information out of her.

#

Dane made sure she and Tess were seated together. Though thankful to be sitting with someone she knew well enough to talk comfortably with, at a table full of St. John family and close friends was no place to ask the kind of questions she wanted answers to. Then there was the fact the St. John in question was seated beside her, his arm slung across the back of her chair.

And damn, but she liked his nearness. But, was it for her or for the sake of one-upping his brothers?

*We can sometimes be a bit competitive.*

And his attentiveness, always seeing to it her punch cup was filled, offering her his last hot wing, asking if she wanted him to fetch her more potato salad…leaning close enough to brush her ear with his lips with each offer. She hadn't once caught him looking at Jake and Renn as though to make sure they saw he had what they didn't, a date.

"There's one more family member you need to meet," Dane said when they'd finished eating.

He hauled her off toward the back of the yard where the children in attendance played on a swing set. The smallest boy broke away from the group and came running toward them. Dane released her hand, caught Ben, and swung him around.

"Uncle Dane," the giggling Ben hooted.

They faced her and Dane did the introductions. "This is

Ben."

She bent to accept the kid's extended hand, saying, "I know. I recognize you as Sam's Best Man."

"Sam said I was standing in for my dad," the child said, chest puffed up with pride.

"That's really great," she said around the lump in her throat, knowing that someday this little boy was going to look back on this day and understand how very profound his standing in for his father was.

"Ben," Dane said, "this is my friend, Kelly."

"You're very pretty," Ben said in that candid way little boys had about them.

"Thank you, Ben."

Dane ruffled the kid's head. "Where's Bear?"

"Mama said he had to stay in the house until everybody was done eating."

Dane gave the mostly vacated tables a glance. "They look done enough to me."

Ben whooped and took off toward the house.

Kelly smacked Dane in the arm. "I don't know what or who Bear is, but I don't think everybody is done with their meal."

"Bear'll help them finish," he said, just as Ben emerged from the back door, a full grown, black and white Great Dane bounding past him down the steps straight for the dining tables.

"You're a bad influence on that boy, Dane St. John."

"I've got to do something to stand out among the uncles."

What was she, a law and order girl, doing being attracted to a guy who played fast and loose with the rules? What was she doing laughing alongside him as they watched Bear vacuum his way about the tables for any dropped food?

She was falling hard for him. That's what she was doing.

#

The first dance for the bride and groom took place in

the small barn on the far side of the circular drive, its floor swept clean and its open space lit by strings of white Christmas lights. Dixie swayed in Sam's arms on her impossibly high, ruby-red heels.

But it was the way Sam and Dixie gazed into each other's eyes as if they were the only people in the room as they danced that made Kelly want to sink back against Dane—made her wish he would be as moved by the scene and the music to want to hold her the way Sam held Dixie.

It almost took her breath away when Dane slipped his arms around her and pulled her back against him. Once the parents of the bride, uncle of the groom, and the rest of the wedding party had joined the newlyweds on the dance floor…when the rest of the guests were invited to join in, Dane swept her onto the dance floor and into the fairytale.

He held her close and they moved as one. How far around the dance floor they moved, she hadn't a clue. She knew only the feel of his arms around her, the ardor of his eyes locked on hers, and the singular movement of their bodies. When the music stopped, they were in a dimly lit corner in front of an unlit stall. He didn't release her and she didn't let go of him. Something unspoken passed between them and he lowered his mouth to hers.

The kiss was gentle, sweet yet deep, the sweep of his tongue across hers full of promise. She answered with a promise of her own.

"Get a room you two," a voice that sounded much like Dane's said.

She jerked back from Dane, tearing her mouth from his. Dane's hold on her loosened but he didn't let her go as he addressed Renn.

"Get lost, little brother."

Renn's grin slanted a mischievous angle. "Without at least one dance with this delightful gal you brought here to tease us with?"

Renn's words jolted her from the comparison of the brothers' grins. That Dane was using her to show off to his brothers had been among her fears of why he'd brought her to the wedding and it stung to hear that fear put into words.

"She doesn't want to dance with you," Dane said, his hand tightening on her hip.

She'd observed the possessive tendencies of men all her life—possessive over land, space, objects...women. Not that she'd ever been the focus of any man's possessiveness—not that she'd ever thought she'd like being possessed. But if Dane's possessiveness was for the sake of some competition with his brothers, she was having none of it.

Peeling away Dane's hand, she said, "I can answer for myself and my answer is—" She lifted her face to his brother and held out a hand. "—I'd love to dance with you, Renn."

Renn swept her onto the dance floor, the music Latin-inspired and far too sensual for her comfort. Too late, she realized she'd rather be in Dane's arms...even if he was using her.

"You're really stuck on him, aren't you?" Renn asked.

She looked up at him. "We've only known each other a few days."

"Yet you'd rather be over in the shadows with him than dancing in the light with me?"

"I— It doesn't matter."

Renn laughed, the sound so familiar it pinched at her stomach. "The hell it doesn't. You can't stop looking over there at him, you blush when I call you on it, and, even though we dance a dance that cries for two bodies to press themselves together, you haven't once given into the allure of my hard, hot body."

She stumbled. He held her upright.

"Easy there," he said, his teasing toned down. "I'm just kidding about the hard, hot body. Don't mean to unsettle you."

"Fine. I get it. I'm the game-piece you boys are using to show each other up. When does Jake take me on?"

Renn sobered. "I'm the only one playing here and my

game is about riling Dane. Didn't mean to make you feel used."

She shrugged. "I suspect Dane didn't bring me to your sister's wedding just so I could meet the family. He probably had a game or two in mind as well."

"I wouldn't be so sure about that," Renn said. "Take a good look at him."

She followed the direction Renn nodded, and found Dane pacing the edge of the dance floor, watching them with eagle-eye focus, and scowling. "You sure he's not just pissed that you won me out of his arms?"

"I know my big brother. That look he's giving us has nothing to do with any game."

Renn pulled her close and Dane's hands balled into fists.

*For her?* She wished.

But she couldn't be sure. She just didn't know him that well yet.

When the dance ended and Renn released her, she thanked him and turned to where she'd last seen Dane. He wasn't there. She scanned the barn and still didn't see him. Even Renn had disappeared. Someone announced they were putting on some line-dancing music. Dixie appeared mid-floor wearing red cowboy boots rather than the ruby stilettos. With a final glance around the room, Kelly still didn't see Dane but she spotted Tess filling punch cups.

As Kelly approached, Tess nodded between the punch bowl and beer keg. "Which will it be?"

"Make it a beer. I need something stronger right now."

Tess filled a tall plastic cup and handed it to her, filled a shorter one with punch for herself, and nodded toward one of the hay bales scattered around the perimeter of the room.

"Let's sit," Tess said. "That last dance just about did me in."

They found a bale that had been draped in oil cloth for comfortable seating and sat.

"Where's Roman?" Kelly asked.

Tess nodded toward a stall where a laptop-run music station had been set up. "He's setting up the file of country music for the line-dancing. Myself," Tess went on, "I prefer salsa. But baby plus heels—" she chuckled. "—I'll happily concede to the country music fans tonight."

Kelly sipped at her beer, her gaze snagging on the bride's red cowboy boots. "What's with Dixie's red footgear? Is it her favorite color?"

"Ah, you noticed that," Tess said. "There's quite a story behind the red footgear. Last Christmas, the boys conspired to add some humor to Dixie's Christmas."

"Of course. A joke."

"It was more than just another St. John brother prank," Tess said, the look in her eyes consoling. "They wanted to add a little humor to the holiday because the second anniversary of Michael's death was looming."

"Ben's father," Kelly murmured.

"Yes," Tess said. "So, the boys each picked out a different kind of red footgear for Dixie."

Kelly grunted. "Dane gave her the high heels, didn't he?"

"No, Jake did."

"Jake?" Kelly looked across the room at Jake who stood a little apart from everyone else, stoic Jake who watched the partiers with a hawk's eye.

"They came with a note," Tess went on. "It read, *for when you're ready to dance again.*"

The reason Dixie had worn the precarious high heels for her wedding ceremony and danced hers and Sam's first dance in those uncomfortable shoes punched Kelly in the gut. She swiped a tear from her eye.

Tess patted her on the knee. "That story chokes us all up."

Kelly took a deep breath. Much as she was touched by Jake's story, there was another St. John brother who interested her more. "So, what kind of footwear did Dane give her?"

Tess smiled. "Dane gave her a pair of fuzzy, red slippers. Pretty enough to make her feel girly, but warm enough to be practical."

"I have no problem seeing the pretty girly part," Kelly said. "But I didn't see the practical part coming."

"There's a lot more to Dane than what you see on the surface," Tess said.

"That's something I've been discovering every day since meeting him."

"You're just jealous," a familiar voice carried heated words from the far end of the barn.

Kelly stood, honing on Dane's voice. There, in the loft, near the edge, Dane and Renn squared off.

"At least I do all my own stunts," Renn shouted, a repeat of the earlier banter the two had tossed back and forth.

"You may be a big fish in your little arena, brother," Dane returned, "but my face graces the big screen and it's about to grace it big time."

Renn took a swing at Dane. Dane ducked, his shifting weight bringing his foot dangerously close to the edge of the loft.

Kelly gasped. "Someone needs to stop them before one of them falls."

When no one moved and Dane shoved Renn, Kelly kicked off her heels and headed for the loft ladder. She hadn't gotten more than two rungs up when Dane fell from the loft. Thank goodness he landed on a stack of hay bales. Still, he wasn't moving.

She vaulted from the ladder and ran to his side, shouting, "someone to call 9-1-1."

But, when she put her ear close to his mouth checking for breath, she was met with a whispered, "Hey, Bright Eyes." Then he nipped her ear.

She straightened. "Don't move. You might have hurt your back or your neck."

He reached up and stroked her cheek.

"Don't move," she repeated, placing her hands on his shoulders.

He frowned. "You're really worried about me."

"Dammit, Dane. Stop trying to move."

He sat up and hooked a hand around her neck. "Didn't mean to scare you, Kel. I was just showing off for you."

Action star Dane St. John a.k.a. The Hawke...who did *some* of his own stunts. Of course he was okay. She glanced around and realized she wasn't hearing gasps of horror but laughter.

"Move your fat head," Renn called from the loft, "so I can show you how a real stuntman takes a fall."

Dane climbed off the hay bales, taking Kelly with him.

"I'm so embarrassed," she said. "Everyone's laughing at me."

"They aren't laughing at you, Kel. They're laughing at Renn and me."

She punched him in the arm. "You scared the hell out of me."

"Ow," Dane said, grabbing his arm.

An arm slipped around her shoulders, Tess'. "These St. John boys have a wicked sense of humor. If you're going to be part of this family, you better get used to it."

*Part of this family?* Is that how they were all seeing her? Is that how she wanted them to see her—how she *wanted* Dane to see her?

#

"Reading people is life and death to you, Jake," Dane said, having joined Jake outside the barn where he was having a smoke. "What do you think? Have I thrown her into the deep end too soon?"

"You always were impulsive," Jake said on a stream of exhaled smoke.

"Yeah. But have I scared her off?"

"That stunt you and Renn pulled put a powerful fear into her."

Dane frowned. "That was my fault. I was showing off for her."

"I know," Jake said, taking a long draw on his thin cheroot.

"I should have known it was a mistake. The last time I showed off for her dumped me into a nest of ground hornets."

Jake choked out a laugh. "I'd liked to have seen that."

"It wasn't pretty."

Jake grunted. "I bet."

Dane brightened. "But it did get her to see beyond my pretty face."

Jake shook his head. "You and Dixie, the two of you can't help but make lemonade out of lemons."

"That's not so bad. Look where it's gotten Dixie."

Jake gave him a sidelong look. "But Dixie has always known what she wants. She had herself a direction. Do you, little brother?"

Dane stuffed his hands in his pants' pockets and stared off into the night sky. "I have strong feelings for her."

"I can see that."

"You think she's a keeper?" Dane asked, eyeing his big brother.

Jake gave him a long, hard look. "Are *you* ready for a keeper?"

Dane stared at the ground, kicked at the dirt. "I think that's what I'm trying to figure out."

Jake stubbed out his cheroot. "Just don't keep her if you're not ready to give her everything she'll give you."

Dane stared at his brother for a long moment. Was he ready to give Kelly everything she deserved?

#

Midway through the evening, Dane, Kelly, Tess, and Roman had congregated together near the front exit where the music wasn't so loud.

"Was yours and Roman's wedding so…interesting?" Kelly asked.

"We opted for a justice of the peace," Tess said, her chin sweeping the air in the kind of arc perps used when they were about to play the distract-the-CO with indignance card, not that she thought Tess was being anything more than indignant.

"What with my family so spread out," Roman interjected, "the logistics of bringing everyone together at that time was impossible."

"I couldn't afford the trip," Dane said with such a sad note to his voice, Kelly slipped her fingers into his and gave his hand a squeeze. That he smiled back at her told her he'd read the support in her gesture.

"But you were there via Skype," Tess said, patting him on the arm. "Renn Skyped in, too."

"Jake, unfortunately," Roman said, "was off doing some of his *in the shadows* stuff."

"But Mom and Dad St. John were there in person to witness their son's wedding," Tess said a little too vehemently. "And Dixie and Ben, of course."

But not a word about Tess' family, Kelly noted, sensing there was more to the story. Then Tess dipped a bittersweet smile in her direction and said as though reading her thoughts, "My family, however, did not attend. I was somewhat *persona not grata* at the time."

Recalling their conversation on the drive to the wedding about their personal experiences as women in male dominated professions, Kelly commiserated. "Just because you started your own architectural firm separate from your father's?"

"Daddy's nose got bent out of shape because, as he saw it, I abandoned him when he could have most *used* me."

"Breathe," Roman said, rubbing his wife's back. "Raising your blood pressure isn't good for you or the baby."

Tess pulled in a long breath and slowly let it out. Then she smiled and patted her tummy. "Seems Daddy's not so unhappy with me anymore, not with me carrying a potential grand*son* to take over the family firm." At which point, Tess lowered her face toward her stomach and said, "You do *not* want to be an architect. You do *not* want to join your grandfather's firm."

She straightened, a sly smile on her lips. "I repeat those words to the unborn every chance I get. I'm hoping all that research about sounds filtering into the womb influencing the fetus works."

Kelly couldn't help but laugh, and she wasn't alone. Roman lifted his beer cup in toast. "To a well-informed fetus."

To which Dane and Kelly likewise raised their beer cups and drank as Tess drank from her punch cup.

"Looks like you four are toasting something," Dixie said as she and Sam joined the quartet, hand in hand, and grinning like a couple teenagers.

"We are," said Tess. "And here's another," she continued, holding up her punch cup. "To the newlyweds. May they be forever as happy as they are today."

"Here, here," said Roman, hoisting his cup.

"To happiness all around," said Dane, giving Kelly's hand a squeeze as they all drank.

As she lowered her cup, Kelly caught Dixie glance up from hers and Dane's entwined fingers. Dixie's smile widened. "Thank you for sharing this day with us, Kelly."

And she leaned in and hugged Kelly, whispering in her ear, "You seem to make my brother very happy."

When she stepped back beside Sam, he slipped his arm around her waist and drew her close. "Yeah. It was great of you all to come. Stay and enjoy the festivities as long as you guys want, but we've got an early breakfast service in the morning, so we're calling it a night."

Dixie's eyelashes dipped flirtatiously. "We're heading off for an early start on the honeymoon."

"You be good to my little sister," Dane said, "or you'll be hearing from me and remember, I'm an action star who does his own stunts."

"Dane," Dixie scolded.

Sam laughed. "Your baby brother says you do *some* of your own stunts while he does *all* his own."

One corner of Dane's mouth betrayed the combative edge to his words. "Watch it. I'm now in the financial position to move around the country at will. I can easily come after you."

To which Sam countered, "Jake said he could take me out before I even knew he was in the same room as me."

They all laughed at that, hugged, and said their goodbyes. As the newlyweds finally strolled off toward the house, Roman looked at his watch. "It's only ten o'clock but we've got a two hour drive and Dane and Kelly have two more hours to go after that. We should head out."

It took another half hour to make the rounds of goodbyes with the rest of the family and friends. On the way to the car, Dane draped his blazer over Kelly's shoulders and Tess held out a hand to Roman. "Give me the keys. You've been drinking."

"Always the voice of reason, Princess," Roman said, digging in his pocket.

Dane chuckled as he guided Kelly past the couple toward the car, his hand feeling so right against the small of her back.

"Don't be a smart ass with me," Tess countered.

"Doesn't she like being called Princess?" Kelly asked.

"*That*, she's gotten used to," Dane said. "What's funny is—"

"Is that an admission you aren't always the voice of reason?" Roman teased amidst the jingle of a passing key fob.

"That's what's funny," Dane said as he all but shoved Kelly into the backseat and followed her, barring Roman admittance with, "Backseat's full, Brother."

"Come sit in front with me," Tess called from the driver's side. "Leave the back to the lovebirds."

Kelly blushed. The whole family already seemed to think she meant more to Dane than he'd ever expressed to her.

Dane leaned through the fading interior light and kissed her. It was a sweet, but lingering kiss that, when ended, made her glance self-consciously at Roman and Tess. They seemed not to have noticed, though, both staring straight ahead as Tess steered the car toward the highway. Still, she muttered to Dane, "Buckle up."

"Sure," he said, scooting close and buckling himself into the middle position.

"You're riding on the manifold," she said, "your feet on either side of the hump in the floor. That can't be comfortable."

"I'd suffer any discomfort to be close to you, Bright Eyes," he said, then draped his arm across the backrest behind her and laid his head on her shoulder.

Her heart kicked up a notch at his words and she pressed a kiss to his brow. If only this could be forever. That's the thought that tapped at the inside of her skull as the miles rocked them to sleep.

#

They woke to a tapping on the side window and Roman's, "Wake-up sleepyheads. We're home, at least our home."

Dane stretched.

Unsnapping her seatbelt, Kelly opened the door and climbed out and likewise stretched.

"Tess made a mad dash for the bathroom," Roman said. "You two are welcome to stay the night here. Tess said to tell you she just changed the linens in the guestroom."

Dane was instantly at Kelly's side. "I've slept off whatever beer I drank."

"But if you two are too tired to drive the rest of the way—" Roman continued.

"I'm good to go," Dane said, shaking his arms. "Just give me a minute to get the circulation flowing again."

Kelly folded her arms across her chest and cocked a knowing pose. "Told you the middle seat was going to be uncomfortable."

He wagged his eyebrows at her. "But I had the best pillow."

Her cheeks grew warm at the reminder of exactly where his head had been nestled when they woke up to Roman's rapping. And had Roman said guest *room*, as in singular?

Granted, they were all grown-ups. But, the idea of sleeping with Dane outside the privacy of the camp...and *sleeping* was definitely a euphemism for making love where Dane was concerned...took her back to all her father's lectures about being a *good girl.* Her throat tightened and panic sweat broke out along her spine.

"Besides," Dane said to Roman, "I promised Kelly I'd have her home for work tomorrow."

Her breathing evened out; and, even as she silently thanked Dane for removing her dilemma, she questioned why she should still be so controlled by the dictates of her father. She was an adult, dammit.

"Thanks for the ride and everything," she said, hugging Roman good-bye. "Tell Tess it was great meeting her. I really enjoyed her company."

"I know she enjoyed yours as well," Roman said.

He and Dane slapped each other on the shoulders, then she and Dane headed for the all-wheel rental Dane had traded his sedan rental in for.

"Don't be a stranger," Roman called after them, no doubt meaning Dane. Surely he couldn't mean her, a virtual stranger, a girl his brother had just met a few days ago.

Not girl, she reminded herself as they climbed into the SUV. Woman. Funny, she'd never really thought of herself as a woman before. That's what Dane did for her, made her feel like a woman.

She eyed him as they backed out of the driveway, but, for all she had to say to him, what came out of her mouth was, "Are you sure you're okay to drive? If not, I can."

The dashboard lights detailed his grin and glinted off his eyes as he looked her way. "The only driving problem I'm going to have in the next two hours is that these damn bucket seats are going to keep you way over there while

I'm way over here. But as soon as I get you back to camp, there's going to be nothing but skin between us, Bright Eyes."

What he said made her itch in all the right places. Still, she shook her head, and teased, "You're incorrigible."

"I try to be," he chirped, pulling out into the quiet residential street.

She sank back in her seat, figuring she had two hours ahead of her to talk to him about *things.*

But the last thing she remembered before they pulled up to the camp was a string of streetlights as they left Pine Mountain.

"You should have woke me," she said, climbing down from the SUV and heading into the camp. "I could have helped keep you awake."

"We made it," he said through a yawn, "so I clearly didn't fall asleep at the wheel."

Lighting a gas lamp, she gasped. "It's nearly three in the morning."

He didn't answer and she turned around to find him face down on the bed. "Dane?"

He didn't stir. She sat on the edge of the bed beside him, thinking how he'd half promised, half threatened to strip her bare once they got back to camp. She studied what profile his squashed-against-the-mattress face presented her. Open-mouthed. Shaggy-haired. Half-man, half-boy.

She stroked a blond lock back from his brow. She wanted him and she didn't mean in terms of sex. She wanted this man with his boyish ways to be hers forever. And, given the events of the night maybe, just maybe he could be.

She rose, folded his blazer on the bench at the foot of the bed then added her own clothes to the pile. One by one, she tugged off his shoes and socks. Rolling him onto his back, she undid the buttons on his shirt and the zipper on his pants. Other than a few moans and a snore or two, he didn't stir as she peeled away his clothes. When he was naked, she crawled onto the bed beside him, pulled a quilt over them and lay next to him, nothing between them but skin. Helping a man keep a promise, even an implied one, was what a woman did for her partner, right?

## CHAPTER SEVEN

A ringing woke Dane. *An alarm clock?*

He blinked into the darkness, Kelly rolling away from him.

"Hell," he muttered. "It's still night."

She was talking, but not to him.

Her satellite phone. That's what woke him. He dropped his head back on the pillow.

"He's been out there all night?" she stated more than asked.

Dane elbowed himself into a half-sit. "Who?"

"Where do you need me?" she asked. Then, "I'll be there in ten."

He was in a full sit now. "What's going on?"

"Lost four-year-old," she said, scrambling into her uniform. "Family was camping. The dad woke up about midnight and realized the boy was gone. Kid's been in the woods at least five hours."

Dane jumped out of bed and pulled on his jeans.

"You don't have to come with me," she said. "Stay and get some sleep."

"The hell I will," he said, pulling on a t-shirt and following her to the door, boots and socks in hand.

She gave him a head to toe glance. "Bring a jacket. This early in the day, it'll be cold and wet."

#

"Dad, just give me a quadrant to search," Kelly said.

"If you'd had your phone with you when you were first called, you'd already be in the field searching."

Dane stepped up to the awning-covered table where Frank sat with maps spread out. "Frank, even if she'd gotten the call when it first came in, we were still on the road a couple hours away."

"She *shouldn't* have left the area."

Dane gaped at Frank. "It was her day off. She wasn't on call."

"This is more than a job. She knows that," Frank said, jabbing a finger at Dane. "I'm retired and I'm here."

As they headed for Kelly's truck with their assignment, Dane couldn't let go of how she'd let her father treat her. "Just because this gig was everything to him doesn't mean it has to consume your life, too."

"He has high standards," she said, climbing into the driver's seat.

"You have high standards, too, Kel," Dane said, taking his seat. "But I don't see you letting any job take over your life."

She pulled away from the command center at the campsite, frowning. "This is more than *just* a job."

"As opposed to acting?" he shot back, his anger getting the best of him.

She frowned at him, a hurt look in her eyes. "I didn't mean to imply other jobs were less important."

He grimaced. "What you do *is* more important than acting. I just meant, even brain surgeons have days off."

"And you're trying your damnedest to be my hero," she said, turning onto a service road into the woods past the campsite.

"You once said heroes are just ordinary people who do extraordinary things," he muttered. "I haven't done anything extraordinary."

She blinked at him with what he could only call confused wonder. "You stood up to my dad for me, Dane. You make me feel…worthy."

"And that's extraordinary to you?" he asked, mystified

She shrugged and focused on the narrow road they traveled.

He likewise turned his gaze to the road. But his thoughts strayed back to the conversation they'd had about Dixie and Sam—strayed to what she'd said about Sam walking into the lion's den on Dixie's behalf—how that made him a hero. Had he just done something heroic for

Kelly?

*You make me feel worthy.*

He glanced over at her, caught the concentration in her profile—all CO focused on finding a lost boy. *She* was the hero.

Yet she needed someone to remind her she was *worthy.*

It made him want to be the man who did that every day for her—to be her hero.

#

By noon, the sun was hot and high in the sky. Teams trickled in and out of the command center, restocking their drinking water, grabbing sandwiches, looking for new quadrants to search. Nobody looked happy. Even the tracking dogs from the state police and a local tracker, lay in the shade looking beat down.

Dane leaned against the trunk of a hardwood, chewing at his ham and pickle spread sandwich, watching Kelly as she squatted at the campsite with the lost kid's parents. She was deep in conversation with them, had been for some time. When she rose, she shook the dad's hand and patted the mother's shoulder, then headed for the command tent.

"I think we're searching too far afield," he heard her say to her post commander as he approached the table where her father still sat with the area maps.

"We started closest to the campsite," her father said.

"In the dark," she responded to her father, barely taking her attention from her commander to whom she added, "He'd have been easy to miss in the dark. You know little kids. They'll sack out wherever they are and there're plenty of spruce with their branches touching the ground bordering the campground. Just yesterday, when he and his family played hide and seek, Jimmy and his dad hid from the rest of the kids under a tree like that."

"And kids that age can sleep like the dead," her father provided.

Dane hung back, smiling inwardly at Frank supporting his daughter's theory.

"He could have slept through everyone calling for him," Kelly said.

The commander studied the maps on the table. "We've already searched well beyond the radius a four-year-old theoretically could have traveled on foot." The commander peered through the park toward the lake it bordered. "Bringing the search in closer beats dragging that lake."

"Sir," Kelly said, "given the heat and his state of mind, Jimmy might have gone back to sleep under one of those trees. The pros know to sweep under low slung branches. Some of the volunteers are experienced, too. But we've got a lot of rookies helping us."

"Reminder well taken, Ranger," the commander said, then sent her and Dane to start searching outward from the area where the family was camped, his radioed commands to outlying searchers crackling from the mobile unit mounted on her shoulder.

"He called you *Ranger*. I haven't heard him call anyone else Ranger," Dane said as they headed into the woods fringing the park.

A smile twitched at the corner of her mouth. "It's what they used to call us before someone higher on the food chain decided *Conservation Officer* was a more modern title."

"Judging by how your eyes lit up when he called you Ranger and that smile now tugging at your lips, I'm guessing there's something special in him giving you that title."

She straightened from having swept aside some ground-hugging evergreen branches and moved on. "CO is a title the old-timers see as fitting the new-comers, especially those of us college educated rather than *woods trained.*" She paused at the next tree and grinned at him. "Ranger is a term they save for an officer they consider the real deal."

He grinned back at her. "A term of respect."

She nodded and turned her attention to the tree. "Lesson over. Get sweeping under these trees. We've got a little kid to find."

#

They found Jimmy about half an hour later under the ground-sweeping branches of a spruce barely a quarter mile from the campsite, hungry, thirsty, and wanting his mother. But safe. Family reunited and, with the commander's blessing that Kelly could write up her report after she'd gotten some rest, she and Dane climbed into her truck and headed out.

"Damn, I'm happy we found that kid," Dane said, letting his head fall back against the truck headrest. "But I'm so tired I think I could sleep for a month."

"I'm wired," Kelly said, turning onto the county road leading to camp, her smile as wide as the lane.

He smiled in return. "You done good, *Ranger* Jackson," he said, reinforcing the old term of respect she'd earned. "Well deserving of a long nap."

She drove past the camp road.

Dane sat up and twisted in his seat, pointing. "Wasn't that our turnoff?"

She smiled. "I've got a better idea."

"Better than sleeping?" he asked.

"I think so," she said.

He crossed his arms over his chest. "So, where you taking us?"

"There's a pond in the valley below Angel Point."

"You're taking me swimming?" he all but whined.

"I'm hot and sticky. Aren't you?" she asked, following two grassy ruts off the main road.

"More tired," he muttered, took the cap from her head, settled its brim low over his eyes, and hunkered down in his seat.

A moment later the truck rocked to a halt. Dane knuckled the cap back from his eyes and squinted over the dashboard at a pool of water more pond than lake in size. "It looks murky."

"It's not," she said, opening her door and jumping out

of the truck. "It's spring fed," she added, shucking her shirt and tossing it on the bench seat of the truck.

"Cold then."

Her boots hit the floor of the truck. "You don't shy away from those cold-water cistern showers at the camp."

Next came her fatigues and she peered across the bench seat at him, mischief in her eyes. "Come cool off with me and I'll give you a far better reason to get all hot and bothered."

"I don't have a bathing suit," he said through a grin, beginning to catch her drift.

"Neither do I," she responded, tossing her camisole at him and taking off for the pond.

"I do believe I could use some cooling off," he said, opening his door and yanking off his tee in one motion.

#

She was sans panties and floating on her back by the time Dane came running bare ass naked toward the lake. She couldn't help but laugh. Muscled hunk that he was, there was just something too funny about how man-parts jiggled and bounced about when men ran.

Dane dove in and came up beside her, shook the water from his hair, and, treading water, asked her what was so funny.

"You," she said, shoving his head back under water.

He came back up spitting, caught her in his arms, and pulled her against him. She swatted him and wriggled against his hold, but not too hard. And when his mouth fit over hers in a long, deep kiss, she slipped her arms around his neck and let her body settle against his.

When their lips parted, he said, "I didn't see anything funny about you naked."

"That's because I don't have any little dangling parts bouncing around when I run to make me look funny."

"There you go calling me little again. Then again, the water is really cold."

"Excuses, excuses," she chirped.

"On the other hand," he said, slipping a hand between

them and rolling his palm over one turgid nipple, "there is one or two—" He caught her nipple between his finger and thumb. "—advantages to cold water."

"You're a bad boy, Dane St. John," she said in a breathy voice.

"I can be worse," he said, clamping his hands around her waist and lifting her high enough her nipple lined up with his lips.

She felt the pull of his mouth all the way to the core of her womanhood, and she wrapped her legs around him, opening herself to him even though they weren't lined up well enough for her to accept him. Then again, they were in over their heads…at least she was, and she wasn't thinking only about footing.

She closed her eyes against the reality of their situation—that he would be gone in mere days, choosing instead to lose herself in the moment and the sensations of his teasing lips.

He licked and nipped and suckled her until she begged for more.

Later on shore, where the late afternoon sun warmed the soft, green grass, he entered her, moving inside her until she shuddered with her orgasm. But he pulled out without finishing himself.

"Dane," she cried out, reaching for him, wanting to feel him finish inside her.

"No protection," he murmured, letting the touch of her hand finish him instead.

They lay a long time in silence side-by-side in the soft grass, their fingers entwined. Clouds scudded across the blue sky above. Birds sang and twittered from the woods surrounding the clearing. The scent of clover and wild mint engulfed them. If they could stay like this forever—that's what she was thinking.

But, as ever, with thought came reality. He'd pulled out because they weren't wearing protection.

But protection against what? Disease? That damage

had already been done their first night together...if there was any such damage to be done. But, she didn't think that was what he was talking about when he'd brought up the subject of protection. The notion of what else they protected each other against churned through her belly.

Her fingers tightened among his, and she asked the question that hammered at her heart. The one she hadn't been able to get out of her head since Dixie's wedding. "Do you want children, Dane?"

His fingers moved among hers. "Sure. Someday I'll want a bunch of them. It's great growing up in a big family."

"*Someday*, but not now."

His fingers stilled within hers. "I love my nephew and I look forward to Tess and Roman adding to my uncleness. Hopefully, Dixie and Sam will add to the family tree soon, too. Kids are fun little people and I love watching them explore and discover new things. Good huggers, too. Makes a guy really feel what it is to be part of a family."

"But they're not for you just yet," she pressed.

He rolled onto his side without releasing her hand and looked down into her eyes, his dead serious. "There's a lot changing in my life right now, Bright Eyes. Kids aren't something I could commit to just yet."

She turned her head away, feeling foolish for asking him such an intimate question when she knew there was no future for them. Or, had she been hoping for an answer that would tell her he was ready for something more?

He lifted her hand to his lips and pressed a kiss to her knuckles before speaking again. "What's up, Kel? You saying you're ready for babies now?"

She waved him off with her free hand and forced a laugh. "I hadn't really thought about it. It's just, you seemed to have such a good time with Ben and you were so good with that little homeless girl..." She shrugged, giving herself time to regroup. "I was just wondering."

He tugged on her hand. "Someday."

She forced a smile. "I get it. Right now, you're having

too good a time with this movie stuff."

His nod was slow and his eyes too serious. *Damn.* If he hadn't already seen right through her questions, he was on the brink of doing so. And if he did, he'd see how truly pathetic she was.

She grunted. "Really, I get it. You're still working out your life, planning it."

He gave her a gentle smile. "Roman's the planner in the family. I tend to just go with the flow. Whatever falls into my lap, I check it out. Heck, I never even gave acting a thought until a year ago when I was skiing moguls in Italy and some producer asked me if I wanted to be in a movie."

She couldn't bear the tenderness of his smile—the sympathy in his eyes—and she huffed to cover how much his sentiments hurt. "No wonder you relate so well with kids. You're still one yourself."

"That I am, and I'm not afraid to own up to it," he said, tucking her hand against his chest just above where his heart beat. "But I'm also adult enough to know my being gone months at a time shooting films doesn't make for good parenting."

A kid with the good sense to know he wasn't ready for parenthood. Give the man credit for knowing his mind and being honest about it.

#

They'd slept through the evening and the night, but were up before dawn the next morning, this time scouting the creeks for violators. Their conversation in the clearing by the lake was never far from Dane's thoughts. What she'd asked him had been important to her and he'd badly wanted to tell her whatever she wanted to hear.

But he couldn't; and, even if it was in his nature to be dishonest, *she* was too important to him to lie to. He'd told her the truth about how things were for him right now. Yet, he felt there was more he should have said, more he wanted to say. He just wasn't sure it was fair to tell her how he felt for her just yet.

"Here," she said, pointing out a couple brook trout in the brush above the creek bank. "It's a favorite tactic of violators. Toss them in the grass rather than put them in their creels and retrieve them later."

"So they don't get caught with too many if a CO checks on them," he said.

She nodded and they moved on, finding two more caches of trout in the brush before she stopped him and pressed the side of her finger to her lips. She cocked an ear at the woods upstream. Dane tried to hear what she was listening for, but all he heard was the babbling of the brook and the chatter of a squirrel.

She motioned him to turn around and herded him along the path they'd just come. She didn't speak again until they passed the first cache of fish she'd shown him.

"Our violator is on the move," she said in a low voice. "Coming this way, no doubt retrieving his catches."

Keeping his voice low as she steered him around a stony outcrop, he said, "You're going to nab him when he's got all the fish, huh?"

"I'll nab him when he's got all the evidence," she said and motioned him to follow her up the backside of the glacially carved rock slab cutting into the creek. Belly down at the top, they watched for their violator to appear.

It didn't take long before a lanky guy in well-worn jeans and a holy tee broke through the brush with a lidded bucket and headed for the hidden trout.

She shimmied back from the peak. Dane did likewise.

"It's Simo Tuome," she whispered. "Repeat offender. I'm going to have to take him in."

The small hairs at the back of Dane's neck prickled. "Is he going to be a problem?"

She shook her head. "He's okay, but you better watch from up here."

He nodded, though something about her suggesting he stay back niggled at the back of his mind. When she adjusted her sidearm, alarm bells went off.

He caught her by the arm, whispering when he wanted

to shout at her, "If he's *okay,* what're you checking your sidearm for and why do I have to stay behind the rocks?"

"Wherever Simo is, his big brother Raimo's not far behind and he's done hard time."

He tightened his grip on her. "If Raimo's so dangerous he's got you checking out your gun, shouldn't you call for back-up?"

The hinge of her jaw popped, and she clenched her teeth hard. "He's nothing I can't handle on my own."

He eyed her narrowly. "You're not showing off for me, are you, Kel?"

"Showing off is your shtick, not mine."

The look she gave him as she peeled his fingers from her arm warned him against debating the issue further and, as if for good measure, she ordered, "Whatever happens down there, you stay put."

"Whatever happens?" he squeaked out.

She jabbed a finger in his face. "Stay or I'll handcuff you to that tree over there and you won't even get to see anything."

He caught her by the shoulders, leaned in, and gave her a quick kiss and a long look that pleaded for her to be careful. Her features softened a degree and she whispered, "On the off chance something does go wrong, haul your ass back to the truck and call for help. Do not, I repeat, do *not* come charging in thinking you're going to rescue me. This isn't the movies. The guns used here contain real bullets and if we both get put down, then neither of us gets help. Got it?"

Numbly, he nodded. Then she was gone and he was left there on the slab of rock trying to process the reality of what she'd just said. His every instinct screamed for him to go after her—protect her.

But she was right. He couldn't help her down there. She knew her job. Then there was that look she'd given him… Commanding. It said she was in charge—that she knew what she was doing and he reminded himself she was the real deal.

Still, he couldn't help thinking her father had been shot doing this job.

Dane shimmied back up to the crest of the rock from where he watched her approach Simo, his gut churning. Kelly must have said something or made some sound as Simo dropped his bucket. The din of the brook cutting around rocks drowned out most other sound. He heard nothing of what she was saying and only an occasional plaintive word from Simo.

Simo's shoulders drooped, he turned his back to her and she cuffed him. She'd apprehended the guy just by talking to him. Impressive.

He let out a pent-up breath. Below, she glanced around herself then bent for the bucket Simo had dropped. That's when he caught the movement out of the corner of his eye.

The guy charging from the woods hit her before Dane's warning shout had even left his mouth. Kelly and her attacker went tumbling toward the creek; and, for several anxious seconds as Dane scrambled down from the rocks, he was blind to what was happening to her. He bolted around the outcrop in time to see Kelly flip her attacker over her head into the creek. Instantly, she was in the water with the guy, one knee dug into his back between his shoulder blades as she tie-wrapped his hands together behind his back.

Hauling the guy onto his feet, she turned, and catching sight of Dane, growled, "I told you to stay put."

"I know. But he hit you so hard."

She pushed her apprehension onto the creek bank and climbed up after him, talking to Dane through clenched teeth. "I knew he was in the woods. I saw him coming."

"Sorry, but all I could think was there were two of them and only one of you and one of them had hit you, hard."

She paused in front of Dane, her face close to his. "He didn't hit me. I took him down with me."

"But what if the other guy…"

"Raimo," the first cuffed guy said, "you shoulda stayed

in the woods. All they got me for is over the limit."

"Habitual offender," Raimo snarled out. "That's jail time."

Kelly pushed Raimo to his knees. "That's *only* jail time for him. Attacking an officer puts you back in prison."

She dug a key from a pocket and handed it to Dane. "Here. You want to be helpful? Unlock Simo's cuffs."

"Unlock them?"

If the look she gave him had been a knife, he'd have been skewered. "You still questioning me?"

"No, ma'am," he said, turning to Simo and unlocking his cuffs.

She held out her hand for the cuffs. Dane handed them to her. She slapped them on Raimo and lifted a tight smile at Dane. "Raimo's an expert at getting out of plastic wraps and we don't want to lose him."

She hauled Raimo to his feet and looked at Simo. "Do I need to put tie wraps on you or are you going to cooperate?"

"I'm coming along, ma'am."

#

She had her eight hours in and then some by the time she processed Raimo and Simo. Back in her truck and alone with Dane, she shook her head.

"Every time I think about you running into the middle of—"

"I know," he cut in. "I was stupid to come running."

"Dammit, Dane. You grew up playing alongside old minefields. You know better."

"But it was you, Kel."

"What does that mean?"

"It means I care a lot about you. When that guy hit you—"

She opened her mouth and he held up a silencing hand.

"You knew he was there, coming for you. But *I* didn't know that. I acted on instinct same as…"

"Same as what?" she asked.

He looked out the side window of the truck and sighed. "Luka was my best friend in Lithuania. I'd gotten a soccer ball for my birthday and took it out in the streets to play with my friends." He shook his head as though he were remembering. "I was so damn proud to be able to bring a real ball to our games."

His shoulders sagged. "But my friends weren't as familiar with the action of a proper soccer ball, let alone one properly inflated."

She caught the sadness in the look he cast her way. "The ball went into one of the fields my friends had warned me against entering."

She blurted, "You went after it?"

He shook his head. "No. Luka did." Dane closed his eyes. "And he stepped on a mine."

She reached over and placed her hand on his forearm. "Oh, Dane, was he killed?"

He shook his head. "But if someone hadn't gone after him and tied off the stump that was left of his leg, he'd have bled out before the adult emergency crew got to him."

"You went into that field after him, didn't you?"

He stared out the front window of the truck, his gaze unfocussed. "I used my belt as a tourniquet."

"I'm sorry, Dane," she said, squeezing his arm, reminded yet again how much more there was to the man than met the eye.

"I cared about him and I care about you," he said, turning his gaze on her. "And I do stupid, impulsive things when the people I care about are in danger."

"I got it."

"That's just the way I am. Stupid and impulsive."

She patted his arm. "You're not stupid, Dane. Impulsive, yes. But not stupid."

"Jury's still out on that one."

"Your friend, Luka, he survived?"

"Yeah." He gave her a wobbly smile. "Talk about stupid. He went after that damn ball because it was my ball and I was his friend; and, as he put it, he couldn't bare the sadness it would cause me to lose such a beautiful soccer ball.'"

They rode in silence, Kelly pondering what he'd just revealed of himself. And not just that he cared for her. This was a man who would risk his life for the people he cared about. What more could a woman want in the man she loved?

## CHAPTER EIGHT

Loved? Yes, loved. There. She'd admitted it…at least to herself. She loved Dane. If she weren't such a coward, she'd have told him, too—talked to him about some kind of future. But, like he said, he wasn't into making plans.

Besides, she didn't want to waste a minute of their remaining affair on pleas or arguments, which any serious talk would no doubt lead to. Or not. He'd been gentle in his candidness about not being ready for kids.

In any case, she'd come off as pathetic and that wasn't how she wanted him to remember her. Then there was the very real possibility *pathetic* would poison the proverbial well of what they did have. The last thing she wanted was Dane making love to her out of pity.

The breakout of a forest fire the next day didn't help her dilemma, either.

For two days, they helped fight the blaze, taking breaks only allowing for a few hours' sleep at a time. Dane could have bailed—ended his *research* and taken an earlier flight back to his world. But he stayed.

"Never know when some crazy writer will throw the Hawke into a forest fire," he'd said during one of their breaks, grinning at her, his pearly whites bright against his soot-stained face.

"Then don't let them see how handsome you look in a hardhat and soot," she'd said back to him, then kissed him long and hard in the shadows behind her truck.

Friday night's moon rose full and bright. The best part of that, it could be seen. The fire had been contained, the hotspots covered, and smoke no longer filled the sky.

At camp, she and Dane stumbled out of the truck toward the cabin. They stopped outside the door, shedding their smoky clothing. And looked into each other's eyes, the message the same.

*Two nights left together. Day after tomorrow, he'd*

*board a plane and fly away.*

He pulled her into his arms, his kiss hard and hungry. She answered in like. And, when he lifted her in his arms and carried her around the cabin to the cistern shower, she knew only that she wanted to spend every moment of whatever time they had left wrapped around him.

They doused themselves with tepid water and soaped each other's bodies with a thoroughness and tenderness that was meant to create a forever memory. Then, in the soft glow of moonlight, they peered into each other's eyes—explored each other's bodies. When she slid her leg up the outside of his thigh, he cupped her backside with his hands and lifted her onto him.

After two days of denial, their lovemaking should have been hard and hot. Instead they moved together like slow dancers—moved and touched and tasted, memorizing every nuance of the other's body.

The water was cold against their heated bodies when they rinsed themselves off, but neither cared. They had their shared warmth as they held each other beneath a lover's moon on a point so high it had been named for angels.

#

Dane and Kelly slept in on Saturday morning, a perk of having worked the fire almost nonstop for forty-eight plus hours. They took a swim in the pond in the afternoon and loved and dozed in the warm, green grass.

When they woke, they ate their way through a wild blueberry patch and she took him fishing. One pole of course. He didn't have a license. But she caught enough fish for supper.

Thus they shared their last day together, exchanging stories, laughing, talking about everything but the future—about what was coming the next morning.

Stomachs full of brook trout and supper dishes cleaned and stowed, they sat on the picnic table, their feet on the bench, she between his legs, watching the sun set over the valley beyond Angel Point. Their last together. Somehow, she'd found a way to accept it.

His arms tightened around her and she laid her head back against his shoulder.

"So beautiful," he murmured.

"I like the purples best," she said of the sky.

"I'm not talking about the sunset," he whispered in her ear. "I'm talking about you."

His words were the most intimate either of them had spoken all day and she swallowed against the lump it brought to her throat. "You make me feel desirable, Dane."

He brushed his lips across her ear. "Good, because you are desired."

*Just not enough to stay—to tell me you love me.*

She closed her eyes against the thought, blocking the tears she was determined not to shed in front of him.

"I don't want to leave you," he said.

*Then don't.*

"You believe me, don't you?" he asked, nudging the outside of her leg with the inside of his.

She nodded, not trusting her voice.

He pressed his lips to her temple, murmuring, "Talk to me, Bright Eyes."

She swallowed back her feelings best she could, venturing, "I don't want you to leave, either, but some things can't be avoided."

"Like me leaving."

"Uh huh."

"If the star of the movie doesn't show up, it'll cost the production company big bucks, not to mention a lot of people will lose their jobs."

"Can't shoot an action film without the hunky hero," she said, forcing a lightness into her voice.

She felt his smile stretch against her temple. "So you think I'm hunky?"

"Aarg, but you're such a middle child," she said, clutching at whatever humor she could find in the moment.

He pulled her closer, his chest tight against her back,

his lips brushing her cheek. "I don't need that kind of reassurance."

"Of course not," she managed to quip. "You know you're a hunk."

She felt his smile slip. "If my next two movies bring in the kind of bucks the first one did, I'll be getting a whole lot more attention than that one paparazzi camping out in the motel room next to mine. Could you handle that?"

She shrugged. "What difference will it make? You'll be gone tomorrow. Out of my life."

"Kel, I don't want to be out of your life."

Her chest tightened but she kept her voice steady. "I work and live here. You work and live all over the world."

"Doesn't mean we can't keep in touch."

"Like a letter now and then? Maybe a phone call on special occasions…until the novelty wears off?"

"I don't think you're a novelty," he said, brushing his cheek against her. "And I'm thinking more along the lines of emails and texts."

"Sure. Type your fingertips off."

"You'll text and email me back, won't you?"

"Sure," she managed on a tight breath.

He nudged her. "Never know when I might need a little technical advice about checking a fishing license."

"Don't make fun of me," she said, stiffening, sounding more churlish than she intended.

"I'm not. I'm just trying to make light of a moment neither of us want to face," he said with a sincerity that nearly undid her.

She sank into his arms, wishing she could be as optimistic about their keeping in touch as he was. Everyone knew long distance relationships didn't work. Like what they'd been doing the past ten days could even be called a relationship.

No. She might as well get used to the idea right now that she'd had an affair of a lifetime—that maybe he'd text her for a week—or maybe not at all. In any case, any correspondence was sure to fade away with time.

#

The next morning, she stood with him beside his rental, her bare feet soaked with dew and her heart aching.

"I'll call when I can," he said, his voice quiet. "And email you."

She managed a small smile. "That would be nice."

"I'll text you every day."

"Sure," she said, the smile still fixed on her lips.

An unusual uncertainty flickered in his eyes, "You'll write back, won't you?"

"Of course."

He slipped a hand around her neck, palming the back of her head. They'd already kissed inside the cabin...and made love and kissed some more. She wasn't sure she could handle another good-bye kiss.

Pulling against his hold, she said, "You've got a long drive to the airport. You better get going."

But he didn't let her pull away. He leaned in and kissed her long, hard, and deep.

Then he was gone.

And she was left alone with her fear she would never hear from him again.

## CHAPTER NINE

She'd been wrong...at least so far. Eight weeks had passed since Dane had headed back to Hollywood to prepare for his next movie, and he still sent her daily texts and emails, this latest an email from his on-location shoot from Eastern Europe.

*Good morning, Bright Eyes. Wish I was waking up to those beautiful eyes of yours instead of a mug of coffee being waved in my face by a producer. Did a night shoot that ended just before dawn and now they want to get an early start on today's filming. Got to keep moving, they say. Production costs, they say. I understand low-budget production costs from the first movie with a no-name lead like me. But you'd think, after that movie went blockbuster at the box office, they'd have loosened up a bit on the production budget.*

*Oh, wait. They did. They're spending a lot more on blowing things up. Okay. I'm also getting more money this time around. Still, I wish they'd chosen the U.P. rather than Eastern Europe to shoot this film supposedly set in the Upper Peninsula of Michigan. But they tell me production costs are lower in Europe.*

*Not that I'd have had much time to spend with you even if we'd filmed in the U.P. Being in almost every scene, my shooting schedule doesn't give me much more than a few hours of downtime each day. But, if we were shooting there, an hour with you would be better than no time at all. Miss you.*
*Dane*

Kelly sat at her dressing table-turned desk staring at her laptop screen—at Dane's final words. Normally, she'd have already hit reply and begun to type her response. But, given what she'd learned just before opening her laptop and downloading her emails—before searching out that morning message she always hoped would be waiting for her, she wasn't sure what she would email back to him.

So she moved the email into the file labeled "Dane." She needed time to think and a day's work should be enough to clear her head.

She closed her laptop, picked up her cell phone, and tapped out a quick text to him.

**Sorry about ur schedule. Work calls. Gotta go.**

But she didn't *go*, not quite yet. She picked up the slim, white plastic tester from beside the laptop. The results hadn't changed. Still two pink lines. Still pregnant.

#

But Kelly wasn't any closer to knowing what to write to Dane after a day's work than she'd been that morning. Probably because every attempt at composing something in her mind was interrupted with what Dane had said about *someday* wanting what his brother Roman and sister Dixie had—what his parents had—a monogamous relationship defined by a marriage license and kids.

*Someday.*

*Not now.*

Oh, he loved his nephew and soon-to-be-born niece. No doubt about it, judging by the way he lit up when he talked about them and how eagerly he shared with her new pictures of Ben and the sonogram of Roman's and Tess' baby-in-utero. But nieces and nephews didn't come with the responsibility of a child of your own. And the last thing she wanted to do was *trap* Dane, especially now that they seemed to be building such a good friendship.

Besides, trapping a man—getting pregnant by him hadn't worked out well for her mother. The last thing she would ever want for her child was for him or her to grow up knowing their father hadn't wanted them. But, would it be any better for her child to grow up knowing her mother hid his or her existence from their father?

In the end, Kelly simply wrote a short note about her day at work and that she missed him, too. There was still time to figure out what, if anything to tell Dane. After all, if she spared him the responsibility now, by the time their child figured out what she'd done, Dane should be all grown up and ready for the responsibility of fatherhood.

Now all she had to do was tell her parents. But, in some ways, facing her dad—facing his disappointment—was going to be a more daunting obstacle than telling Dane. That too could wait...for a while.

#

The morning sickness hit with a vengeance. Kelly thought she'd hid it well through the first week until... She opened the bathroom door and found her mother standing there, a pile of laundered towels in her arms.

"Time we had a talk, girl," she said, ushering Kelly back into the bathroom, butt-shutting the door behind them.

Alma sat her on the edge of the tub, put away the towels, lowered the commode seat, and sat facing her. "It's not the flu, is it?"

Kelly shook her head.

"Don't imagine I have to guess who the father is."

Again Kelly shook her head.

"I'd ask how this sort of thing happened, but I know."

"We used protection." Kelly bowed her head. "After the first time."

"I understand, baby." Her mother stroked a lock of wayward hair back from Kelly's brow. "Does Dane know?"

Kelly shook her head.

"But you are going to tell him."

"I-I don't know."

"I never saw you so happy as when that boy was around...and since. You two are always emailing and texting."

"I know, Mom. But…"

"He strikes me as a real nice fellow. He's got strong family values."

"He's all that, and more. But he's not ready to settle down with a family."

"Kelly, look at me." Kelly met her mother's eyes. "Isn't that *his* choice to make?"

Kelly lowered her gaze. "I don't want Dane to ever feel like I trapped him."

"Is this about your biological father—about how he cut and run when I told him I was pregnant with you?"

"No. Maybe. Yes. I don't know."

Alma took Kelly's hands in hers, making her meet her gaze. "Whatever choice he makes, Dane has a right to know. You need to tell him."

"And if he runs?"

Her mother drew a deep breath before answering. "You'll survive. I did."

A memory twisted through Kelly's gut. *Whatever falls into my lap, I check it out.* He'd said that and there was something entirely too temporary-sounding in that statement.

"Besides," her mother said, "Dane might surprise you. He might be more ready for a family than you think."

"Sure," Kelly said. "Just give me some time to figure out how to tell him."

*And time to figure out whether I'm willing to settle for being* checked out.

#

Kelly let work occupy her for the next few days, hoping an answer would come to her as to whether or not to tell Dane. It didn't. Of course such a decision wouldn't come so easily.

At shift's end on the fourth day, sequestered in her bedroom, she searched for the answers she needed. With cell in hand, she scrolled back through the string of texts she'd saved on her phone to the first four Dane had sent her after leaving her at the cabin their last day together.

**At highway. Miss u already.**

**In town. Still missing u. Do u miss me?**

**At Marquette airport and missing u like hell. Y AREN'T U TEXTING ME?**

Followed by: **Figured out y u haven't texted me. Ur still at camp out of cell phone range. U likely haven't even gotten any of my texts yet.**

Then: **Flight about 2 take off. Must shut off electronics. Miss u bad.**

When she'd finally checked her phone that day and found all those "Miss yous," she'd been giddy as a school girl. Of course the infatuation was still fresh. That's what she'd thought at the time. She'd still been willing to live the fantasy rather than the reality.

She scrolled forward to the first text after she'd responded to his first four.

**Luv that u miss me, 2.**

He'd used the word *love*. But he'd never said he loved her. But that would have been a stretch even for a fantasy. They'd been *together* ten days.

She opened her laptop, scanned past his initial emails from Hollywood that told of boring meetings, and brought up his first email from abroad.

> *First day of shooting. Guess who's on the production crew? Luka, my friend from Lithuania. Remember me telling you about him?*

She remembered all right. She remembered him telling her how Luka had stepped on a mine running into a field for Dane's soccer ball...how Dane had gone after him and applied a tourniquet. That Dane could have been lost that day still made her gut twist. But, that Luka survived—that he seemed to have flourished, judging by Dane's excited description of reuniting with him, made her smile.

She read on, feeling his excitement as he wrote about the special effects planned for the project and how good it felt to be back in action again.

> *Didn't realize how much I missed rolling around in dirt until I was back doing it. Of course, it's nowhere near as much fun as rolling around in bed with you.*

Her stomach pinched at the reminder of what it was like to have him inside her...and holding her and kissing her.

> *Tomorrow we're shooting a scene where I have to dive into a lake to avoid getting shot. Remember our swim? Remember what the cold water did to your body? I can still taste you between my lips.*

Without thought, she touched herself and found her breasts had responded to his mere reminder of that day.

> *Remember how fast I ran after your bare ass into that cold lake? I'm using that memory tomorrow as motivation. Don't want to suffer through too many takes where a cold lake is concerned.*

She remembered frowning the first time she'd read that passage, unsure how to take his reference to using that incident as motivation to *minimize* the number of takes he'd have to *suffer through*. But his next line had chased away her doubts.

> *Though, for you, Kel, there's no limit to how many times I'd run into a freezing lake.*

This was the kind of talk that made her want to call Dane and share the happy news of their pregnancy. But she was a woman of reason, trained to not make assumptions without all the evidence. Besides, if she looked beyond his words, there *was* all that excitement for being back on a shoot.

She closed that first email and scrolled down the list to one from the middle of the second week.

> *The director took my cell away from me today like I was a school kid. I'd shut off the ringer. I wasn't even keeping it on me. I even kept it off camera. But he said the*

> *way I kept checking it between takes was distracting to everybody. 'Suppose I could pull the demanding star act and walk off. But it's not in me to make the whole crew suffer. So, no more mid-take tweets from me. Sorry.*

She chuckled, same as she had the first time she'd read the message. He really was such a boy.

Kelly sobered. That was the question, wasn't it? Was the boy man enough to deal with fatherhood in the midst of a rising career that excited him?

She caught the last line before she shut down the email.

> *I wish I'd stolen one of those little cotton camisoles of yours so I could smell you right now.*

Her cheeks warmed. How could he still have this effect on her eight weeks later with thousands of miles between them?

Pregnant. Hormone overload. Of course.

Which is why she wasn't looking at more of the saved text messages from him. They were full of "miss yous" and veiled innuendoes that would only make her miss him more. And missing him would get in the way of reason. And reason relied on facts—facts she'd glean from his emails.

She scrolled down to an email four weeks into their separation. More talk about his day on the set and the progress of the onsite shoots. Not that that meant much. She wrote him about her workdays as well. And he was still playing the *remember when we...* game. Though, in this email, he'd begun the question game.

> *What's your favorite color? I thought mine was blue. But I've grown partial to hazel with hints of green, as in a certain pair of bright, hazel eyes.*

He wrote such beautiful things to her. He'd said such amazing things to her. The kinds of things that made a woman feel cherished, desired…loved. Yet, he'd never said he loved her.

But, neither had she.

She'd fallen for him almost from the first time he'd taken her to the moon and stars. It'd happened so fast, she saw now how she'd tried to dismiss it as lust.

But, in mere days, she'd learned enough about the man to know what she felt wasn't lust, but love. Maybe it was the same for him. Maybe what made him hesitate was the same thing holding her back, the lightning quickness with which it all happened.

Then there was his latest entry.

*Great news! Little sis Dixie is pregnant!*

She closed the lid on her laptop. She knew what she had to do. She'd call him tonight. Might as well face her father with the news today as well.

#

Kelly found her father in his recliner in the living room, some game show on the television.

"Where's mom?" she asked.

"Grocery shopping."

She thought for a moment about waiting for her mother to return before telling her father about the pregnancy. Mom had a way of calming Dad when he got riled, and her news wasn't going to make him happy.

She took a step toward the kitchen, but stopped. Whether she told him now or later, it wasn't going to change the situation or make it any easier.

She faced her father. "Dad, I have something to tell you."

He glanced up from the TV screen. "Yeah?"

"Something important. Something you're not going to like."

This time when he looked up his gaze stayed on her.

She drew a deep breath. "Dad, I'm pregnant."

There was a beat before he responded. *"You're what?"*

"Pregnant. I'm having a baby."

"What about the DNR?" he demanded, sitting forward

in his chair. "How're you going to work if you're pregnant?"

She blanched, confused and hurt.

"It's the busiest time of the year. Bow hunting opens in a few days. Rifle season is just a couple months away," he went on, his voice rising, his face reddening. "You'll be leaving them short-handed."

"I tell you I'm having a baby and all you're worried about is hunting season?" she returned, her hurt turning into an anger of her own.

The veins in his neck pulsed. "Fall is the busy season!"

"I guess I'll have to transfer to forestry or some other job," she said, not backing down.

"You didn't even think through how this was going to affect your career before you got yourself pregnant, did you?"

"I didn't plan to get pregnant, Dad."

He was on his feet now, leaning over his cane at her, shouting at her about all of her mistakes. She shouted back.

"I'm a grown woman, Dad. I'll deal with my own mistakes."

"But what about your career as a CO?"

"Maybe I don't want to be a CO *like you*."

He opened his mouth, but nothing came out. He just stood there, propped up on his cane, his face red, the veins standing out in his neck. He went down like a sack of potatoes.

"Dad!" she screamed, dropping to her knees beside him.

#

That evening, her father lay in a hospital bed, her mother and sister each holding a hand, as Kelly slipped out of the Intensive Care Unit, seeking a place to be alone. The nearest waiting room being occupied by family of others in the Unit, she continued past and ducked into an alcove where she pulled her cell from its case on her belt.

Why, she didn't know. She had no one to call...except Dane, and now was not the time to talk to him. But she couldn't stop thinking about how badly she wanted to hear his voice.

She stared at the phone for a long time before turning it on. She'd had to shut it down upon entering ICU. A tone announced missed messages. She tapped the text icon and several popped up from Dane. She almost smiled. She could always count on him to be there for her...even when he didn't know she needed him. She flicked open the first message.

**Morning, Bright Eyes. Wish u were here.**

She'd seen that one this morning at home and had sent him back a similar greeting. Of course, with the time difference, her greeting had been more of a *good afternoon.* His second text came when she was driving her mom to the Marquette hospital where her dad had been taken because they had a special stroke unit. She remembered hearing the ping but hadn't checked the cell, her entire focus on the road and willing her father to live.

**Rain. Midnight break. Soggy subs and water-logged coffee. Be glad ur not here,** she read.

Third message.

**Drying off 4 next take. Missing u.**

The time stamp told her he'd messaged about the time they were being told Dad was in a coma and it was a matter of time before they knew if he would survive and what damage had been done.

For the first time in her life, Kelly deferred to her little sister, as the nurse in Carrie took over. The three had sat in the small waiting room, Kelly and her mother holding each other while Carrie elaborated on what the doctor had told them, comforting them, giving them hope. She was good. Dad would have been proud.

Kelly pressed the phone to her chest and closed her eyes. What she wouldn't give for one of Dane's hugs right now. Her fingers stroked the back of the cell as though she could feel his warmth through its plastic case. Even just to hear his voice.

She looked at her watch. It was late evening here. What was it where he was? Early morning? Middle of the night? Damn, she couldn't think. He might be back in his trailer. She tapped his image on her screen, seeking a connection.

She didn't even think through what she would say if she got his voice mail. It rang once, twice, three times. Maybe she should disconnect.

The thought had barely lumbered through her brain when an enthusiastic, albeit sleepy, "Hey, Bright Eyes," filled her ear.

Emotion clogged her throat, preventing anything more than a weak, "Hi," to escape.

"What's wrong?" he said, his enthusiasm turning to concern.

She swallowed hard. She could do this. "My dad. He had a stroke."

"Aah, Kel. I'm sorry. Is he…"

"He's alive."

"That's good."

"He's in a coma," she said, her voice cracking.

"Do you need me there?"

She slumped into the alcove where the adjoining walls met, sobs taking over.

"I'm going to check flights," he said. "I'll call you right back."

"No," she managed between sobs.

"I want to be there for you, Kel."

She spread a hand across her abdomen, remembering how she'd planned to call him tonight but with entirely different news, knowing she couldn't handle facing him right now.

"My mom and sister are here," she said, her throat tight.

"They're there for your dad. Who's there for you?" Dane asked.

"J-just hearing your voice, knowing you'd have come, that helps."

"It doesn't feel like I'm helping much," he said on a thick voice that only made her cry harder.

"Kelly, it's killing me to hear you like this and know I'm not there for you."

She rolled her forehead against the cold wall and bit back her tears. "This is just the first opportunity I've had to let go since it happened. Sorry to be such an emotional mess."

"Let it out, Babe. That's what I'm here for."

She wanted to. Oh, how badly she wanted to. But she was afraid he'd get on that plane if she kept sobbing. Or maybe she should let him come.

Her sister appeared at her elbow. "He's awake."

"He's awake," she repeated into the cell.

"That's real good news," Dane said.

"I-I need to go."

"Call me later," he said. "I'll keep my phone with me…even on set, director's dictates be damned."

"Yeah. If I can."

She disconnected but didn't move.

Her sister touched her arm gently. "Kelly?"

Kelly shook her head. "I don't think Dad wants to see me."

"Of course he does."

"We were fighting, Carrie. That's why he had the stroke." She broke down in sobs again.

Carrie's arms encircled her. "You didn't cause his stroke. He's a stubborn old man with high blood pressure, high cholesterol, who smokes and has a short fuse."

"We were fighting," Kelly sobbed as if she needed to make someone understand she was to blame here.

Her sister rubbed her back and stuffed a tissue into her hand. "You need to calm down. This isn't good for the baby."

Kelly all but strangled on a sob, and glanced up at Carrie. "How do you know about that?"

"Mom."

"Of course," Kelly said, swallowing back her tears.

"Come on. Come see Dad."

"I can't," she said. "I just can't."

"You're emotionally drained. At least come back to the waiting room and sit down."

She shook her head. "I don't want to be around other people right now."

Carrie patted her shoulder. "Okay. I've got a place for you." She guided Kelly down the hall far from the ICU to a dimly lit waiting room barely big enough to hold a loveseat and padded chair. "No one's likely to bother you here."

Numb, Kelly sank onto the small couch. Carrie placed a box of tissues within easy reach.

"Rest," her sister commanded then stepped out of the room.

Kelly thought of calling Dane back. But just the sound of his voice was bound to start the waterworks all over again. She blew her nose in a wad of tissues, fragments of thoughts poking through her numb brain, like why had she told Dane not to come?

*I want to be there for you, Kel.*

She didn't doubt he did. He was that kind of guy. But he was working and he was the star. The star leaves and nobody works. She understood about people depending on you. Look at the lost boy they'd found and the fire they'd fought side-by-side, keeping it from spreading through the nearest town.

She braced her elbows to her knees and propped her chin in her hands. And, right now, *she* needed *him*. Was that enough to take work away from dozens maybe hundreds of people?

Her mother appeared in the alcove opening, hands on hips. "What's this I hear about you not wanting to see your dad?"

Kelly dropped her arms and hung her head. "It's not

that I don't want to see him, Mom. I don't think he…should see me right now."

Alma sat on the couch beside her and hugged her to her side. "I'm sure he wants to know you're here with him."

Kelly shook her head. "I'm afraid I'll just make him angry all over again and that can only hurt him."

Her mother stroked Kelly's cheek and tucked her head against her shoulder. "Sometimes you can be as stubborn as he is, almost like his blood flows through your veins."

A single shuddering breath escaped Kelly. Her mother's arm tightened around her.

"Carrie said you were on the phone when she found you. Dane?"

She nodded against her mother's shoulder.

"Did you tell him about the baby?"

Tears rolled down Kelly's face. "I already gave one man a stroke with that news. I'm not chancing killing another."

"Oh Sweetie, you've got to stop taking the blame for everything."

"I just can't handle any more tonight," Kelly said.

"I understand."

She eased back from her mother. "You should be with Dad. Not here with me."

Wiping the tears from Kelly's cheeks, her mother said, "I think you need me now just as much as your father does."

Kelly shook her head. "You should go."

Alma sighed. "I'll go, but only if you promise me you'll lie down here and rest. All this stress isn't good for you."

Kelly grimaced. "Not in my condition, huh, Mom?"

"Not for you under any condition," her mother said, rising and pressing a kiss to her forehead as she had when she was a child being tucked into bed. "Try and rest," she said. "We'll let you know if there're any changes with your dad."

Kelly nodded and her mother left. She stared at the empty chair facing the couch. She was too weary to think about what an empty chair represented to her right now.

She tucked her legs up onto the short couch, her cell phone digging into her hip. She pulled it from its holder and looked at it. She should call Dane before he decided to jump on an airplane and fly to her. Part of her so wanted that. But another part, the part of her that was too fragile to even talk to Dane right now wanted him to stay away.

She glanced at her watch. Midnight here. Eight hours later where he was. With luck he might already be on a shoot.

She texted him. **Dad's holding his own. Exhausted. Going 2 sleep.**

Then she shut off her phone.

#

As gently as the hand shook her shoulder, Kelly started. Seeing her mother she jerked upright. "Is it Daddy?"

"Your father is fine. He survived the night. That's an excellent sign."

Kelly glanced about her surroundings, her disorientation slow to dissipate. She was in the little waiting room where her sister had put her last night. She must have fallen asleep. But it was much brighter than it had been then, and she realized the source of the brightness was sunlight. She'd slept for hours.

Stretching, she asked her mother, "Why'd you wake me?"

"You need to call work and let them know where you are. And I need you to drive me home so I can get a change of clothes."

"What about Daddy?"

"He's stable and resting. Carrie will stay with him until I get back."

Kelly nodded, conceding, the drive back to Copper Falls long and silent.

Once home, her mother dashed into the house. Kelly sat a moment in the car, readying herself to face the scene of hers and her father's fight—preparing herself for the evidence left behind by the paramedics who'd taken him off in their ambulance.

Her cell buzzed. She knew even before she saw the ID image it would be Dane. Still too fragile to talk to him, she chastised herself for not having shut it off after she'd called the DNR office.

She exited the car and climbed the steps to the house, letting Dane's call go to voice mail.

#

Kelly didn't visit her father in the ICU, though she tried to visit him when he'd been moved into a regular room. Standing outside his doorway listening to him struggle to speak all but brought her to her knees.

Once, after he started physical therapy, she slipped just far enough into the therapy room to see the therapists manipulating the damaged side of his body. He looked so small and frail. This was not the father she knew.

At her mother's and sister's urgings she attempted a visit just after he was moved to the nursing home for extended therapy. His speech was still garbled. But the minute he saw her, he started banging on his bed tray with his good hand.

She left, refusing to return no matter how much her mother and sister insisted he hadn't been hitting his tray out of anger. Kelly knew better.

And through it all there'd been Dane's texts, emails, and the calls she didn't take until he threatened to show up on her doorstep.

"I'm sorry about answering your calls with texts," she said when she finally called him back.

"I don't want you to be sorry," he said. "I want you to be okay, or at least to know you're okay."

Cell pressed to her ear, she sat in the middle of her bed rubbing her forehead. If he thought she wasn't okay, he'd likely show up and she couldn't handle him and her father's medical condition at the same time. But, she wasn't a good enough liar to keep Dane from seeing through one so she stayed as close to the truth as possible.

"We're all focused on Dad's rehab."

"He's still in the nursing home, isn't he?"

"Yes. He'll be there about four weeks. But the more family and friends he has around him, the better it is for him. There's even exercises family can help him do." She grimaced at her attempt to imply she was among those helping her dad exercise and the half-truth she was about to tell him. "We're all pretty busy."

"Didn't mean to intrude on your time. It's just… Your texts, they've been…short."

"I haven't had much to say."

"I would have thought you'd have had a lot to say between your dad's situation and hunting seasons starting."

Was that a hint of irritation she heard amidst his concern? She pulled in a breath. "I've kept you updated on everything going on with Dad. Work is…just work."

"But you haven't told me anything that's going on with you," he said.

She closed her eyes as if that was enough to shut away *all* of what she hadn't told him, knowing she had to tell him something. And soon.

"I'm tired. Really tired." She wasn't completely successful at keeping all the emotion from her voice and her final words wobbled a bit. But she'd told him all she could handle sharing for the moment.

"We're wrapping up the exterior shoots. We'll be moving onto a soundstage for interior shots and green screen stuff. Maybe I can beg a couple days off—"

"No." She cut him off. The dead silence coming from his end told her she'd come off too strident, too desperate. She forced a laugh and went for teasing. "You, Mr. Big Movie Star *begging* for time off? How does that work?"

There was another beat of silence before he responded. "Like I've told you before, Bright Eyes, I'm not the *big* star you think I am. I'm in no position to demand anything…yet."

Schooling a lightness into her voice, she joked, "Yet?"

"If movie two goes blockbuster like number one did, then I rise to demanding status. But about you…"

Damn the man's intuitiveness. She sighed. "Dane, things are just too complicated here for me to have to deal with you, too."

There was a slight hesitation before he responded. "I didn't realize I was something you had *deal with.*"

She winced. "I didn't mean for it to sound like you're a bother or anything. I—" She splayed her hand across her abdomen, remembering what it was like to be with him, feeling what *being with him* had left inside her. "I know what happens when you and I get within arm's length of each other and I just can't handle *that* right now along with everything else that's going on."

"Flattered as I am you still got those kinds of feeling for me, Bright Eyes, I really want to help you out any way I can."

Biting back the tears scratching at the backs of her eyes and silently damning her hormones, she said, "Stay where you are. Keep working. That's how you can help me."

"By keeping out of your way," he said, a flatness to his tone that didn't reassure her. "And by not calling, either, I take it. How about the texts and emails? You want me to stop bothering you with those, too?"

"No," she said in a small voice, knowing she should say yes—knowing that answering yes would end their connection. But she wasn't sure she was ready to let him go yet—wasn't sure she was ready to risk losing him.

"Don't do this to us, Kel."

*Us?*

"We've been getting to know each other beyond the sex, haven't we?"

Is that what all this texting and emailing had been about? She rubbed at her temple, her head beginning to hurt.

"Kel?"

"Yeah, I guess."

"You don't sound convinced."

This was exactly why she didn't want to talk to him on the phone. He heard way more than she was ready to reveal. "My head's in a bad place right now. Between my dad and—"

She caught herself before she said baby. Another reason she shouldn't be *talking* with him. She was too weary to watch her every word.

"And what?" he asked when she didn't continue.

"Work," she said, covering. "We're into the busy season—hunting season. Lots of meetings and strategizing. You know how it goes. You have job obligations."

"I guess," he said slowly.

"I better let you go," she said. "Middle of the day, you must have a shoot to get to."

"Yeah, sure."

He sounded like he wanted to say more—wanted her to say more.

"Take care," she said, disconnecting before the conversation went any further.

#

Sitting in the tall make-up chair, electric heater blasting his legs, Dane stared at the blank screen on his cell.

"Long distance relationships are the pits," said the make-up girl who'd been waiting for him to finish talking so she could freshen up the fake blood dripping from the corner of his mouth.

"Yeah," he said absently as he pondered Kelly's *you must have a shoot to get to.* Is that why she'd chosen to call him in the middle of the day, because she thought he'd be working and she could have left a voice mail rather than talked to him?

Or was she really just overwrought about her father?

"Yep. This business is hard on relationships," the make-up girl went on as she applied the last touches to her artistry.

He hoped not.

## CHAPTER TEN

*Hey Dane,*
*Dad comes home from the nursing home*
*tomorrow. He still needs therapy, but it'll be*
*in-home. Mom and I rearranged the living*
*room so they could put a hospital bed in*
*there, and Carrie moved home to add her*
*nursing skills to his care.*

Kelly's fingers stilled over the laptop keyboard. Yeah, right. Like her mother would let her move furniture. She slid a hand over the little bump rising from her abdomen. She was growing into a first rate liar...at least as long as she could avoid phone calls with Dane.

She sighed and continued typing.

*First floor, in front of the TV, and close to*
*where Mom can watch over him. Should be*
*a boost to his morale.*

Like she knew anything about her father's morale other than what her mother and Carrie reported to her. Like it mattered how he was in the nursing home. The real test would come tomorrow when he and she faced each other for the first time since...

*We're all looking forward to being together*
*again.*

And the lies keep rolling. Now, what lies could she tell him about herself besides that big one by omission?

"Got any whites that need washing?" her mother asked from her bedroom doorway.

"I'm a big girl, Mom. I can do my own laundry."

"Just figured, since I'm throwing in a load of whites..."

"Got no whites, Mom."

But instead of leaving, her mother sat on the bed beside where Kelly typed at her desk on her laptop. "You still haven't told the boy he's going to be father, have you?"

"Dad's my priority right now."

"You've been using that excuse for weeks."

"It's not an excuse. I can't deal with anything else at the present besides Dad."

"I don't see you dealing with your dad, either. All I see is you avoiding him."

"Won't be able to do that any longer come tomorrow," Kelly muttered, "unless one look at me puts him right back in the hospital."

"Still beating that old horse of an excuse too, huh?"

She gave her mother a sharp look. "What does that mean?"

"You and Frank face down angry bears, forest fires, and men with guns. But you're both afraid to face up to your feelings."

"I think I've been dealing with a helluva a lot of feelings lately."

Her mom patted her shoulder. "Sweetie, I don't think you've dealt with your feelings ever, at least not the ones at the core of why you haven't told Dane about the baby."

Kelly scowled. "You don't know what it feels like to grow up knowing you were rejected by your own father. I don't want that for my child."

"And you're afraid Dane will reject his child." Her mother rose from the bed and headed for the doorway. "I think *you* don't want to risk being rejected again."

Kelly jerked around so fast she nearly fell out of her chair. But her mother's footsteps were already fading off down the stairs, leaving her alone with her absurd theory.

It was absurd, wasn't it?

#

"I don't know what to do," Dane said into the mouthpiece of the headset he'd attached to his cell in anticipation of a long talk with his sister.

But the one and only time Dixie had met Kelly, Dixie's attention had pretty much all been on Sam. He couldn't blame her. It had been her wedding day. Though Dixie had consoled Dane and promised him her support whatever his decision, she'd had no real advice for him.

Tess, on the other hand, had spent hours chatting with Kelly.

"Long distance relationships are hard, Dane," Tess said.

"I already got that message," he said, impatience thick in his voice. "I just can't figure out if I should call it quits or not."

"Do you want to end the relationship?"

He shifted forward on the couch in his trailer outside the sound stage where they'd begun shooting action shots against green screen and interior shots, his answer an emphatic. "No."

Tess didn't say anything and he continued through a tight throat, "But, I need to know if it's over for her."

"Then you need to talk to her face-to-face," Tess said.

"Every time I suggest visiting, she puts me off."

"From what you've told me, she's got a full plate what with her father's stroke and a busy work schedule. You can at least understand the heavy work schedule, can't you?"

He groaned. "Yes, Tess. I get it. Career women are work-focused."

Tess' voice softened. "Maybe she's trying to spare you because she thinks you'll expect too much of her attention."

"You going to give me that middle child crap, too?"

"I don't know if it's about being a middle child or not, Dane. But you do like the spotlight. You've got to concede that."

He had to admit, he did like the attention the first movie had brought him. Hell, he'd always enjoyed the way women were attracted to him and the admiration his athleticism gained him. Still, he frowned at the cell in his hand.

"I thought I did a good job making her the center of attention, at least the center of mine. Hell, she was—is my center."

"Judging by the way you treated Kelly on the day of the wedding, Dane, you did an outstanding job focusing on her. There were times you two seemed to be in your own world."

He closed his eyes, recalling their first dance—recalling how, when the music stopped, they hadn't.

"Roman said he's never seen you like that before."

Dane rose from the couch and paced from the living area into the narrow kitchen galley. "I've never felt for any other woman what I feel for Kelly."

"Then listen to me, Dane. Don't call, email, or text her that you're coming," Tess said. "Don't give her a chance to dissuade you. Just go there and see her."

He stopped on the far end of the galley just short of the bedroom. "And if she still refuses to see me?"

A sigh filled his ear and he didn't like the finality it seemed to convey. "Then you have your answer."

#

Inside the back entrance, Kelly shucked her boots and hung up her jacket, mumbled a greeting to her mother as she passed through the kitchen, and entered the living room where the hospital bed was. Her father hadn't stroked out when he'd seen her the first time after coming home a month ago. He didn't even bang on anything with his good hand at the sight of her, lending credence to her sister's claim that the event in the nursing home wasn't done in anger, but frustration, or maybe even excitement at seeing her. Or maybe the old man had mellowed…or given up on her…or was depressed as her mother and sister kept insisting.

But he had stared at her that first time he saw her after coming home and she'd sworn she'd seen fear in his eyes. *Impossible*. Dad feared nothing. But it was enough to give her the courage to face him, say a few words to him…tell him she was sorry.

After that, she convinced herself what she'd seen in his eyes was expectancy because that's what she saw every time she came home from work and he lifted his face in her direction. So they'd fallen into the routine of her sitting with him at the end of each day, telling him every detail of her workday while feeding him cookies and cocoa and wiping his chin. Like she was now.

*It was her fault he was like this, silent and helpless.*

Her mother strode into the living room, hands on hips. "Make him ask you questions about your day."

Kelly blinked at her mother. "What?"

"The speech therapist says he isn't making the progress he should be, that we should make him ask for things."

"He's progressed to sitting up in his recliner," Kelly said.

"Physical therapy…and that could be going better, too."

Kelly looked from her mother to her father. Her father stared straight ahead, his way of avoiding things he didn't want to face these days—refusing to look at them.

*Like he never looked at her expanding belly.*

This was the sort of stuff she would have talked to Dane about, if she weren't pregnant and afraid he'd make good on his threats to visit her. Maybe it was time to stop lying to him about how well Dad was doing—how well she was doing. Maybe it was time to confess all to Dane. Goodness knew she could use the comfort of his arms.

And if his response to the news of impending fatherhood was to reject the baby—reject her?

*What the hell.* Between her father's snail's-paced improvement, deer hunting season in full force, and a pregnancy that was exhausting her, she couldn't feel much worse.

Up in her room, Kelly flipped open her laptop and turned it on. A lightness floated through her stomach as it always did in anticipation of an email from Dane. Though he didn't email and text every day anymore, he still did one or the other each day. And since she hadn't gotten a text today…

The computer screen populated. She clicked on her email icon, bringing up a handful of messages. She scanned the list, reading it. Having not seen Dane's name, she read it again. There was no email from Dane today, either.

She slumped back in her chair, staring at a screen that held nothing for her. It was bound to happen eventually, that he'd stop corresponding with her. It's what she'd expected from the very beginning. What she knew all along would be the outcome. To be stunned by it was…pitiful…and painful.

Or the result of pregnancy hormones, she'd convinced herself by bedtime. She'd also convinced herself this is what she wanted, for him to stop contacting her—show his true colors so she could move on. Yet, when her cell pinged and woke her up at pre-dawn, the possibility that she'd received a text from him sent her heart into her throat.

She grabbed her phone and opened the message without even taking the time to note who it was from.

**Pre-dawn shots reported from the flats just outside town. Ur closest. Check on them. Respond 2 verify. Didn't want to wake household.**

Meaning they hadn't wanted to wake her dad who slept closest to the hardwired DNR phone downstairs. She jumped out of bed and pulled on her clothes when she'd rather have pulled the cover over her head and cried herself back to sleep.

But time was of the essence regarding an illegal shoot. Wait too long and there'd be no proving when the deer had been shot and no catching the bad guy who disregarded the rules of good sportsmanship.

She slipped out of the house, and out to her truck without notice.

By sundown, Kelly'd apprehended her illegal shooter, checked out a half dozen camps for tagged deer, followed up on a complaint about a stolen kill, and eaten only power bars to keep her going. She pulled into a local gathering hole, Big Lil's, for a late supper and whatever gossip the hunters brought in from camp.

She'd barely stepped onto the porch of the bar-café when a text ping alerted her.

With a weary sigh, she pulled out her cell and glanced at the ID. Dane.

Her stomach bottomed out and she stutter-stepped to a halt.

**Hi,** the message began. **Flew to New York yesterday 2 promote movie. Big push 2 release it 4 the holidays.**

Then: **Good 4 movie. Bad 4 any of us thinking we were going 2 get some time off.**

Ending with: **Not happening with whirlwind promotion tour. Catch u when I can.**

She stood there on Big Lil's porch, tapping out a reply with numb thumbs.

**Understand about work. Gotta do what u gotta do. Beyond busy here, 2.**

And she did understand. His career was just taking off. There were sacrifices to be made. She'd made her share to become a woods cop. She was still fighting for the respect of the old-time COs. At least she had been until she found out she was pregnant.

That's when it struck her how little she cared any longer what the old COs, Pykkonen and Grieg, thought of her. Had she been that distracted by her father's stroke and recovery, her guilt? Could she be *that* broken up about losing Dane?

Except she hadn't so much lost Dane as pushed him away before he could reject her. Yeah, her mother had nailed that one. She *was* afraid of being rejected.

So, was that what distracted her to the point she no longer cared who she impressed or didn't?

Something moved in her belly. A distinct fluttering as though something or *someone* was announcing their presence. She opened her jacket and splayed her hand across her abdomen.

Life. A baby. Her baby. This was what mattered.

Family. And it was time to find out how much of a family her baby had, especially now that Dane was back in the States.

But, of course, this news merited a phone call, not a text.

She tapped out Dane's cell number before she lost her nerve. But her call went directly to voice mail. He must really be on a tight schedule since he'd just texted her. And her news wasn't the kind to be left on a voice mail, either.

#

The next day proved as busy as the previous. Kelly pulled into a gas station-convenience store to replenish her supply of power bars. At the checkout, she came face-to-face with a rack of tabloids. A glossy magazine caught her eye. It wasn't the big image on its cover that stopped her dead, though, but the trio of smaller pictures next to the one labeled Sexiest Man of The Year. The top shot of the three, to be specific. Dane's picture. If his picture was on the cover of *Hollywood Magazine's* Sexiest Man issue, it could mean only one thing.

She snatched the magazine from the rack and flashed it at the clerk. "Add this to my bill."

"Never known you to buy those kinds of magazines," Shirley Sempe said as she made change.

"Thought I'd bring Mom a treat. She likes this stuff," she lied.

Kelly pulled out and turned onto a service road about a quarter of a mile from the store. If she'd opened that magazine while parked in the one-stop, Shirley Sempe would have fed the fact into the rumor mill before she'd even found the page that went with that headshot at the top of the trio on the front page. Everybody within twenty miles of Copper Falls had speculated about her and the handsome movie star who'd visited the area last summer. Only the fact that the town kept its gossip to itself saved her from becoming infamous. But, once they figured out she was pregnant... Then what?

She found a two-rutter off the service road and parked. She flipped the pages of the glossy until she found the one she was looking for. *Sexiest Action Star*.

There he was with that damn grin that made her melt. Dane St. John. Would he still smile at her if she threw a monkey-wrench of an unwanted pregnancy into his sky-rocketing career? What would the tabloid headlines read then? Would she be labeled a gold-digger, or a publicity-hound?

She stared at the picture of Dane all ripped and tan and smiling. Everything was going his way. Could—would he find a place for family in his life right now? This was something she needed to know before she subjected her child and herself to public exposure.

She took out her cell and tapped out a text to him, something cute, inviting…testing.

**Hey there Mr. Sexiest Man! Congratulations. 2 think I can say I knew him back when he was just the sexiest man in Michigan's U. P.**

She couldn't help but add: **Don't get 2 swelled a head.**

His reply came late that evening.

**Only Sexiest \*Action\* Star. Still room 4 more head-swelling.**

Finishing with: **Write more when I can keep my eyes open. It's no exaggeration when they call it a whirlwind tour, this promotional stuff. Sweet dreams.**

*Whirlwind tour.*

Meaning he's busy.

**Write more when I can keep my eyes open.**

Meaning he's dead tired busy.

**Still room 4 more head-swelling.**

But having the time of his life. Not the time to spring family responsibilities on a man.

#

Dane had intended to take Tess' advice and visit Kelly

unannounced when he got back to the States. But the very reason he'd been shipped back to the U.S. proved to be the very reason he couldn't get away to see Kelly. The closest this publicity tour took him to her, or any of his state bound family had been Chicago, which had been little more than a touch-down stop for a major talk show.

Then there was the fact it was the busiest time of the year for her workwise. Even if he had showed up in Copper Falls, she might be off keeping the woods clear of poachers and gun-toting deer hunters safe from each other. But he saw a chance for a break in both their schedules after rifle season ended at the end of November. She'd said there was a week break before black powder season began in December.

Then that damn Sexiest Man list came out. He'd learned real fast that kind of exposure notched up one's demand tenfold. The producers must have had some inkling he would be on that list given how fast they'd increased his interview schedule with the east and west coast talk shows. Maybe it even had something to do with their rushing the movie through post-production for a coveted holiday release.

Great stuff for a new actor's career. Not great for a floundering relationship.

Still, Kelly's congratulations had been the best part of making that list. Her text had sounded like the old Kelly. She'd even signed off with a smiley face.

Then she emailed him only twice in the following weeks and her texts came pretty much only in responses to his. Even his were growing more sporadic.

Still, when his movie premiered Christmas Day he texted, **Wish it had been you on my arm for the premiere.**

She texted back a short congratulations with a seasons greeting message.

Maybe he didn't have to face her to get his answer about where their relationship stood. Maybe he already had his answer.

#

Curled up on her bed, Kelly stared at the magazine picture of Dane attending his movie's premiere, the beautiful actress who'd played his love interest in the film on his arm. They made a striking couple, him with his boyishly, charming smile, shaggy hair slicked back befitting the tuxedo event and she with her blond curls, big, blue eyes, and perfect petite size two body.

He'd written that he'd wanted her on his arm for the premiere. Kelly stroked her swollen belly.

"Not like this you wouldn't, Mr. Sexiest Action Star."

The baby kicked. For the briefest of moments, Kelly let herself imagine the hand on her stomach was Dane's. But it wasn't. He wasn't here. He'd moved on.

He had, hadn't he?

The baby kicked again, harder this time. Kelly smiled in spite of her indecision about Dane, and spoke to the daughter the sonogram had revealed she was carrying.

"Fight for all your worth, Little Girl. It doesn't get any easier out here."

#

> *Earliest box office receipts indicate number two is another blockbuster,* he emailed on the first day of the New Year. *So the powers-that-be are hotter than ever to get number three in the can. Shipped me off to the next shoot location day after the premiere. They think an African desert looks like the Tex-Mex border. Production costs are priority of course. So here I am, half a world away and wishing I'd gotten to see you before I left the states.*

Kelly wanted to believe what he wrote about wishing he'd gotten to see her before he'd left again. She should believe what he wrote. He wasn't the liar. She was.

She texted back.

**It's work. U gotta do what u gotta do.**

**Heading into bush. Am told cell service is sketchy there. If u don't hear from me 4 a while, u know y,** he'd replied.

And that was the last she heard from him for the month of January.

Kelly sat at the desk in her bedroom and arranged the pillow at the small of her back. She hadn't gained a lot of weight and she was carrying high. Still, her back ached, and every time she went to the bathroom, she remembered what Tess had said about having a baby sitting on her bladder.

She'd connected with Tess even though they'd spent barely a day together. Wished she could talk to her. Tess who must have had her baby by now. She'd been due in January. But, to talk babies with Tess was tantamount to telling Dane he was about to become a father, and she couldn't have that. She knew firsthand *biology* could mean nothing to a man.

But Dane was a man who found baby announcements something to celebrate, as evidenced by his October email about Dixie and Sam being pregnant. He was a man who valued family.

Kelly pulled up her emails, one jumping out at her making her stomach flutter, and it wasn't the baby this time, either.

She opened the email from Dane.

> *Long time no write. Too long. So much to tell you. Tess and Roman had a girl born on January $10^{th}$. See attached pictures.*

She opened the attached file. The first picture was of the newborn with closed eyes and a round, red face. In the next, her eyes were open with the third appearing about two weeks after the birth. The infant's coloring had softened to a healthy pink and a pink ribbon adorned her wispy, blond hair.

How'd that happen when Tess had dark hair like her?

Didn't the dark gene dominate the lighter one? Until this moment, Kelly had envisioned her daughter with dark hair—looking just like her. What if her daughter looked like Dane?

Heaven help her, her daughter would be a daily reminder of the one and only man she would ever love. And every time she hugged her daughter it would be like holding a piece of him.

Blessing or curse? Only time would tell.

> *Little Madeline is a heartbreaker already. Mouthful for such a little girl. I've already decided to call her Maddie.*

And his own child, what would he call her... if he knew about her?

> *They're flying me back to the states next week to present some award. Gotta keep the face in the public eye, they tell me.*

And if the Sexiest Action Star of the Year should drop in for a visit, how would she explain her expansive waistline? Before she could debate whether or not she wanted him to see her in her present condition, she read on.

> *It'll be a one day hop in and out of New York.*

Disappointment niggled at her in spite of her fears about what his reaction might be at seeing her.

> *Then it'll be back on-site for final exterior shots. I'll be glad when we move indoors for interior and green screen shots. Hot and dry here. But I'm working with some great stunt guys. Wait 'til you see the amazing stuff they have me doing.*

He sounded happy—like he was enjoying what he was doing. She sighed, recalling what he'd told her that day at the pond, that he didn't have time for kids right now. He had been right.

#

Kelly's water broke a week earlier than expected. Nothing unusual for a first time baby, so her doctor, her nurse sister, and mother assured her. So there she was, in the birthing suite of the Marquette hospital, her sister rubbing her back as she rode out a labor pain, her mother off getting ice chips for her. She was surrounded by family and caregivers. But the one person she wanted here wasn't. Dane.

She'd been wrong not to tell him about the baby. He did have a right to know—to choose. And, at this moment, she was certain his choice would be everything she needed it to be. As soon as her mother returned, she'd send her out with her cell to call Dane.

A nurse bustled into the room with a handful of magazines. "Thought you guys could use some reading material. This labor business can take a while."

The nurse dropped the magazines on the tray table beside the bed, the top one featuring a photo of Dane arm in arm with a blond starlet, a blow up of her ring finger sporting a hefty rock, and the headline:

### *The Hawke engaged?*

At the same moment what she was seeing in front of her sunk in, another labor pain hit Kelly. She cried out louder, deeper, longer than that pain created.

Carrie clutched her hand and whispered in her ear, "Don't look at it."

"That's a big one," declared the nurse.

"Heard that one all the way out in the hall," her mother said, entering the suite, cup of ice chips in hand.

"Move those magazines out of the way," Carrie said, "and set the ice chips there."

"Certainly there's room for both—" Her mother's words stopped abruptly as she reached the tray. She flipped the magazines over, set down the cup, and cradled Kelly's head, murmuring, "Ride the pain, Sweetie. Ride it out. You can do this."

Tears streamed down her cheeks. She could only hope

the nurses thought it was the labor pains.

Baby girl Jackson entered the world with the soft cry of a lamb. When they put her in Kelly's arms, Kelly's tears streamed for an entirely different reason than those she'd shed an hour earlier upon seeing Dane's engagement picture. These were the tears of a mother's love.

"You have a name for her yet?" Carrie asked.

"What a little angel," her mother sniffed out.

Her mother's comment reminded Kelly how Dane's parents had named their children after the places where they were conceived. And she thought about where she and Dane had conceived this child, the place where she'd fallen in love with the only man she'd ever want—Angel Point.

"She is an angel," Kelly said. "My angel. My Angela."

## CHAPTER ELEVEN

Sitting on the living room floor at the foot of the Christmas tree, Kelly pasted another picture of her daughter's first Christmas into the scrapbook she was creating for her daughter. In his recliner beside her, her father played peek-a-boo with the eight and a half month old Angela, making her giggle.

Kelly smiled at the pair. After all the months of his avoiding her advancing pregnancy, the moment Angela had been placed in Frank's lap, he'd wept, she'd wept, and they'd talked.

In his broken speech, he'd told her she'd never been a disappointment to him, said that he was sorry he'd been so hard on her. She understood deep down. She probably always had. But hearing it from him had lifted the burden of doubt from her soul.

The next day, Frank had worked his rehab with a renewed vigor so he could hold his granddaughter on his own. Angela, whom everyone called Angel, seemed to have brought harmony into their home.

The house phone lying on the floor at her hip chirped. Kelly picked up the handheld, out of habit checking the caller ID. A blocked number. Probably a sales or survey call. But, it could be work-related even if it didn't come in over the hardwired work phone or her cell. In a small community where everybody knew everybody, sometimes tipsters didn't bother with the usual channels.

She answered the phone. The hesitation on the other end was almost enough for her to hang up. Then...

"Kelly?"

She knew that voice. Stunned, she turned away from the chair where her father and daughter played.

"It's Dane," the voice on the other end of the line said. "Dane St. John."

"I know," she said, working her best to sound normal. "What's up?"

"Nothing good," he said through a weak chuckle. "But anybody who reads the rags would know that."

How well she knew. Her mother had religiously pointed out every headline, every picture, every story that showed up in the rags and movie magazines in the months since Angel had been born, since she'd stopped answering Dane's texts.

"Sorry about the breakup of your engagement," she said, her voice sharp even in her own ears.

"Kel, I wrote you about that being a fabrication of the rags," he said, frustration rolling through his words. "I told you I was never engaged."

"So you did," she said, her tone softening with the memory of that long ago email. At the time, she'd wanted to believe he was lying to her. But he wasn't the liar. She was. Which had been the reason she'd stopped responding to his emails and texts. She couldn't keep lying to him.

"Sorry," he said. "Didn't mean to snap at you, Kel. It's just… You sound like that crap is still bothering you when it shouldn't. How are you doing?"

*Fine until you called.*

"If you wanted to chitchat about how I've been, you'd have called my cell," she said, all business sounding, "not my parents' number. Why're you calling, and from a phone with a blocked number?"

"Ever the CO, huh?"

"That's me."

He sighed. "The blocked number has nothing to do with you. It's a burner so no one can trace my calling you."

"Except you didn't call *me,*" she said. "You called our house."

"Semantics."

"Reality. I see the facts like any good CO," she said, not entirely sure she didn't mean what she said as a warning to him, a man whose personal life of excess was spiraling into the toilet…according to the gossip rags.

"What do you want?"

She heard him swallow. "I have a favor to ask. A big favor."

She hugged her knees up against her chest. She could tell him he'd get no favors from her. End it all right now. But then she'd have to explain why she wouldn't grant him any favors.

"What is it?" she asked.

"I need a place to hideout, someplace where the paparazzi won't think to look for me."

Her heart thudded in her chest, afraid she knew just which *someplace* he was going to ask about before he even put it into words.

"I was thinking of your family camp," he said. "Any chance I could rent the place?"

She closed her eyes. The last thing she wanted was Dane St. John that close to Angel...or her.

"I know I'm asking a lot, Kel. But I'm desperate to find a place where I can hideout for a while. The paparazzi are turning my sister's restaurant business upside down with me here."

That he was within four hours of Copper Falls made her heart stutter-step.

"Roman and Tess will take me in. But the press will only follow me there and make their lives miserable. They know about Renn, too, so I can't go to him. There's Jake, but even I don't know where he is right now."

"What about your parents?" she asked.

"Action films are huge in Japan. The fans will tear me to pieces. I know. I've done promotions there."

Behind her, Angel giggled at some antic of her grandfather's. At her hip, Angel's bright blue eyes peered up at her from the photo album, Dane's eyes. One look and he was sure to figure out she was his.

"We just closed the place up for the winter," she said, hedging.

"I'll pay anything it'll take to reopen it, Kel. Please. I'm really desperate to find someplace where I can be alone."

*Desperate to be alone.*

She understood desperate. She understood wanting to be left alone.

"Not that I'm agreeing to this, but," she found herself asking, "when?"

"As soon as possible."

"The big snows start in January," she said. "You could get snowed-in up there."

"Sounds like just what the doctor ordered."

*Doctor? Did he mean that figuratively or literally?*

She thought of the headlines and pictures in the latest papers her mother had left for her on the kitchen table. *Action Star Parties Hard* and *Dane St. John's Drinking Binge,* were two that read above pictures of a disheveled Dane. *Action Star Stumbles,* captioned a shot of him in a restaurant apparently falling over a table.

She'd dismissed most of them as fodder for the tabloids. Anyone could be caught on a bad day. But, given his comment and headlines like *Action Star Dane St. John Causes Set Shut-down* and *Dane St. John Headed for Rehab,* the possibility he was out of control didn't sound so far-fetched.

"Kel? You still there?"

"Yeah."

"Can I stay at the cabin?"

Every nerve in her body screamed for her to keep him away. But he sounded so pitiful, so broken, so in need. Besides, he'd said he wanted to be alone. She could meet him away from the house, have him follow her up to the camp, and…leave him there. Heaven knows the family could use the rental money given the expenses of her father's extended rehab.

"I'll need a couple days to get someone to plow the place out and another to heat the place up."

"Thank you, Kel."

He sounded so relieved, it was almost enough to make up for her lingering doubts. "Make sure you rent yourself a four-wheel drive this time," she added. "Nothing less will get you in or out of that place."

"I remember."

She remembered, too, every detail of their ten magical days together. She drew a calming breath. "Especially this time of year, you'll need something heavy-duty to drive in there."

"I'll take care of it."

*Like you did me by leaving me pregnant?*

Wrong. She'd been as willing a participant that first night when they'd made love without protection.

She swallowed back any condemnation she might have let slip into her tone and asked, "You want me to stock the place or will you pick up your own supplies?"

There was a pause at the other end as though he were recalling, just as she was, the first time she'd bought him groceries.

"I'd appreciate you stocking the pantry and fridge," he said. "You know what I like."

Indeed she did. Her stomach pinched at the thought. He shouldn't still be able to have this effect on her.

But he did…

#

Kelly sat in her truck in front of the Buck Inn watching the entrance to the parking lot through frosty windows. She'd made her family and friends swear, should they happen to run into Dane, no one would tell him about Angel. Why she was still so adamant to hide her from him, she wasn't sure. And those she'd sworn to secrecy were quick to press her for a reason.

Especially her mother and sister, her mother insisting his coming back to Copper Falls was a sign she should tell him, her sister flat out urging her to take the opportunity to come clean about the baby. To what end, she'd argued back. So he could reject them both face-to-face? Their responses had been a unified, "You don't know that's how he'll respond."

And that was the truth. She didn't know what his reaction would be. She knew he was big on family, close with his, and wanted a family of his own…*someday*.

Yeah. There it was. *Someday*…whatever that meant for a guy who loved everything about his skyrocketing stardom.

Okay, he didn't love the publicity or he wouldn't be looking to hide out.

But Dane was an adventurer. Always game to try something new. She'd be damned if she let her daughter become just another adventure for him.

So she'd countered her mother's and sister's arguments with, "And if he does welcome his daughter with open arms, if he wants custody of her? He's got the money now to buy whatever he wants."

That had shut them up. Not that either looked any more convinced Kelly shouldn't tell him. Then there was her father's reaction. He didn't like the deception at all. He was the wildcard among those who knew the whole truth of Angel's parentage. But he and Dane weren't likely to run into each other, unless Dane came to the house…which she wasn't giving him any reason to do. She'd even arranged to keep him out of Copper Falls by meeting him in the next town south, giving him the excuse that it didn't make sense for him to come all the way to Copper Falls when the camp was south of town.

A navy-blue SUV rental pulled into the lot and parked. Even with a knit cap pulled low over his ears covering his blond hair, there was no hiding the broad shoulders or the height of the man exiting the vehicle. No hiding the profile of Dane St. John backlit by the late afternoon sun. If she'd been standing, she'd have dropped to her knees.

*No, no, no.* She couldn't react to him like this. Maybe if she just let him walk into the Inn, she could drive away and avoid ever seeing him in the flesh again. Except, if she didn't show-up for their meeting, he'd come looking for her at the Ranger Station or, worse, the house.

She gave her horn a tap, drawing his attention. Hands

shoved in his pockets and shoulders hunched against the cold, he headed toward her truck. She powered down her window. He ducked his head, his "hi" a white cloud reaching for her. She wanted to open her door, step out, and follow that vapor cloud right back to his smiling lips, a smile, she reminded herself, that melted all women.

"Follow me," she said and rolled the window up between them instead.

#

He hadn't been wrong about the tone of their phone conversation. She was angry and that anger was definitely aimed at him.

He cursed, slapped his steering wheel, and pulled out of the parking lot after Kelly. Where did she get off being mad at him? He hadn't been the one to stop emailing and texting. She'd been the one who let his calls go to voice mail. She'd been the one to let *them* go.

And if that's the way she wanted it, then it was her problem if she was angry. He just needed a place to hideaway for a while and her family's camp was the perfect place.

*But it did matter to him because he hated seeing her unhappy.*

Because he'd never stopped thinking or caring about her.

Her directional light signaled the turn onto the highway. He followed, rehashing the one question he'd never quite been able to let go of. What had gone wrong between them?

*Long-distance relationships are the pits.*

The make-up girl from his second Hawke movie wasn't the only who'd warned him that maintaining a relationship long-distance was a long shot and building one under those circumstances was next to impossible. He'd made a mistake going for the taking-the-time-to-get-to-know-you-better route. He should have told her how he felt about her before he'd left Copper Falls. At least she'd have known how he felt and maybe then they might have had a chance for something lasting. Maybe she'd have thrown herself into his arms back at the Buck Inn parking lot instead of rolling up a window between them.

This is what he got for letting his head take the lead instead of his heart—for going against what came natural to him.

But, what was natural for Dane was to be impulsive. All his life, his siblings had teased him about his impetuous ways. How many times had his laidback parents shaken their heads, warning him someday he'd make a rash choice that didn't pan out? Is that what had happened here with Kelly?

No. Because he hadn't been impulsive about his choices where she was concerned. If anything, he'd been too cautious. He should have moved heaven and earth to come to her at the first sign of trouble rather than letting her talk him out of returning to Copper Falls. If he'd acted on impulse, he might have been riding beside her in her DNR truck, sharing the heat blasting off its heater—sharing dreams, plans for a future.

But she'd been so persuasive in her arguments that he stay away—continue shooting his movie. And moving heaven and earth to be with her would have involved breaking his film contract. He frowned. Might he have let her persuade him a little too easily because breaking that contract would have killed his acting career?

The tires of the SUV droned along the blacktop.

Who was he kidding? He had no *acting* career. He played at being an action movie star, a big boy rolling around in the dirt and thrilling at the stunts. A man couldn't live forever on adrenalin rushes. But love…

Had he failed to see beyond her words that he not visit when her father had his stroke that she really *wanted* him with her?

By the time they turned off the highway onto the county road winding through the woods toward the camp, he'd replayed every phone conversation they'd had and every email and text she'd written him in their earliest days apart.

By the time they'd turned onto the single lane camp driveway, he'd come to two conclusions. One, she hadn't just been persuasive in telling him to stay away. She'd been adamant.

And two...

That she was angry with him meant she still had feelings for him. And, if she had feelings for him, he yet had a chance with her. He just had to figure out what the problem was.

He parked beside her in front of the cabin where it'd been plowed out wide enough to allow for a turn around. She climbed out of her truck and headed for the cabin without waiting for him. He stepped into the building behind her, noting she had removed her mittens but not her jacket.

"Almost toasty," he said, his tone light, testing.

"I came up this morning and started a fire to get the chill out," she said, all business as she lifted a tin box from the fireplace mantel. "We keep the matches in the tin in case any mice get in. Mice chewing on matches have caused more fires than you might think."

She glanced at him. "Then again, maybe you already know that. As I recall from your last stay here, you knew a lot more than I expected."

He pulled off his cap and stuffed it into his jacket pocket with his gloves as he watched her bustle about the cabin.

"Andi Johanson will keep the road plowed when it snows," she said. "Pumps been primed and the fridge is stocked."

She opened the appliance as though she needed him to see the contents. All he saw was her nervous energy. The way she kept moving—avoiding looking at him.

"I'm leaving our old bag phone with you in case you have any problems. It's clunky but it's has greater signal power in places where heavy woods, copper rich hills, and sparse towers reduce cell service."

"Worried about me, Bright Eyes?" he asked.

Calling her by the nickname he'd given her got her attention. For the briefest of moments, she looked at him with hurt eyes before she glanced away.

"I feel responsible for your safety," she said. "That's all."

"Ever the responsible CO."

"You're renting my family's cabin," she said, facing him but avoiding his gaze. "You're going to be up here alone. You get hurt or snowed-in, you'll need a way to connect with the outside world. It *is* the responsible thing to do. So, keep that phone charged."

He gave her a salute, keeping to himself the fact he had bought a satellite phone for his stay. "Yes, ma'am."

She pivoted away from him, picked up a couple logs from the wood bin, and opened the stove door. "The wood stove will heat the camp more efficiently than the fireplace."

She tossed the logs into the fire box, their striking the glowing embers within making them explode into flames, their light dancing in and out of the weave of her braid as it slid over her shoulder. It was more than he could resist and he reached out and touched her hair.

#

The moment he'd stepped into the building behind her, the cabin had shrunk around Kelly making her feel there was no place she could go within its walls to escape his nearness. Even with his blond hair untrimmed and his face thinner and more angular than when she last saw him, the impulse was to throw herself into his arms. Fortunately, he'd stayed in place just inside the door…until he touched her hair.

She wheeled around, facing him. "What are you doing?"

"I'd forgotten how shiny firelight makes your hair."

Instantly, a memory of toasting marshmallows over the

fire pit on the point surged through her. He'd unbraided her hair and threaded his fingers through it for the first time there.

Shaking off the memory, she closed the stove door and stepped out from between it and him. "There's plenty of dry wood in the shed out back."

"I've missed you," he said so quietly had she not been hyper-sensitive to his presence she might not have heard him.

She turned halfway back toward him, finding he'd pivoted after her, and said, "I doubt you've missed much of anything in your life."

"Kelly, I missed you," he said with such earnestness, she couldn't help but look him in the eye...where she found a matching intensity. "I missed you more than you know."

*So much that you didn't come back until you needed some place to escape to.*

That's what she wanted to say to him out of hurt feelings. But she was more to blame for his staying away than he was. Because she was afraid he'd have run at the news of her pregnancy just as her own father had at the news of her impending birth.

He knuckled her chin up a notch and leaned in, his lips parting, lowering toward hers. Those beautiful, artful lips that knew how to make her body sing. Without thought, she tilted her face to accept them—*him*.

A knot popped in the wood stove snapping her back to her senses. She pushed away from him. "Don't."

"Sorry, I wasn't thinking. I was—"

"You think you can waltz back into my life and pick up where you left off?"

He settled back on his heels. "Why are you so angry with me, Kel? Did I fail some test by not coming back when your father was sick? Was it something I wrote or something written in the rags?"

She could have rebutted the last part of his last

question. She'd had a year and a half of practice at debating the tabloid headlines. But *fail her? Something he wrote?*

She had no rehearsed answers to those questions and she sputtered, "W-we had a nice fling, Dane. That's all."

"Is that all it was to you?" he asked.

She squared her shoulders and put on her best CO mask. "I knew what it was when it was happening. I knew when you left, it was over."

"I wrote to you. I called you," he said. "You responded, at least in the beginning. You didn't see a relationship growing there?"

She had, she admitted to herself. Even through all her insecurities, she'd clung to the fantasy...until reality intruded in the form of pregnancy, bringing back all her fears about rejection amidst an avalanche of guilt over her father's stroke. Maybe she'd made a mistake not telling Dane about the pregnancy—about Angel? He looked so confused—so in need of answers.

But she was confused, too, every instinct screaming for her to protect her daughter. Now was not the time for hasty decisions. She needed a clear head to think things through and she couldn't clear her head as long as she was in the same room with Dane.

She pushed past him, heading for the door. "I'm sorry if you thought that's what was happening. I need to get back to town."

## CHAPTER TWELVE

He didn't believe for a minute she saw their affair as nothing more than a fling. She'd been caught up in the moment as much as he had been...before she'd pushed him away just shy of their lips meeting. He'd also glimpsed fear in her wide, bright eyes before she'd gone all CO on him.

He lifted the hood off the snowmobile he'd found in the shed behind the cabin, glad to have found something new to tinker with. Three days puttering about the cabin had left him with too much time to think. Not conducive to decompressing from the load of negative press he'd come here to escape, especially since all he'd been able to think about was Kelly and her reaction to their meeting again.

He poked at the wiring inside the engine. Didn't appear the rodents had chewed anything up. He glanced about the windowless shack lit only by what sunlight the open door let in and the narrow space where the corrugated metal roof didn't quite match up to the top of the walls.

Spotting a metal tool box on a back shelf, he retrieved it, set it on the sled's seat, and opened it. Taped to the inside of the lid was a faded picture of the big sled with two little girls on the seat. The bigger girl with the dark hair knelt on the seat reaching around the smaller, blond girl, clearly in charge of the throttle. Kelly, in control even then.

But, she'd almost lost control when he'd tried to kiss her.

And he knew she was capable of letting go. She'd made love with him with utter abandonment through their ten incredible days together. It'd been one of the reasons he'd fallen for her, that openness—that honesty.

But where'd that open honesty gone to? He'd already figured out the anger was a cover for some big hurt.

What was it he had done that had hurt her so much? His leaving? His not returning sooner?

Their correspondence had been steady—their relationship growing…right up until her father's stroke.

Could it really be about his not returning to her when her father was in the hospital—when she needed him? But, he'd never read anger in her voice or in the tone of her texts and emails back then, or in the months following. Besides, she was the one who'd insisted he not jeopardize his career by leaving his shoot…adamant even, that he stay where he was.

Adamant. There was that word again.

For a long time, Dane had believed the engagement story had been the death knell. He'd *heard* it in the tone of her text when she'd *congratulated* him. *Heard* it the politeness with which she responded to his explanation that the story wasn't true. But it wasn't until he'd looked back over their months of ever-growing sparser correspondence leading up to that damn story, he'd realized the relationship he'd hoped to build with Kelly had been dying a slow death for months.

He snatched a sparkplug wrench from the tool box in an attempt to break the loop that had played through his mind for the past couple days. But he couldn't let it go.

*Why* had she let go so much earlier than he had? Not that he had ever really let go of her. And, given her emotional reaction to him upon his return, he couldn't believe she had stop caring about him, either.

He positioned the wrench around the exposed end of the sparkplug and twisted it free.

Now all he had to do was ferret out the reason she'd pulled back. And to do that, he had to get her to come back to the cabin or…

He looked at the sparkplug clamped in the wrench. He could go to her, and he had just the excuse to do just that in the gummed up sparkplug in his hand.

#

Her truck wasn't in the driveway. Did he keep driving,

checking the house until her truck was there? Or did he go in now and hope she'd show up sooner rather than later? If he went in now, he might learn something from her parents. But, if she saw his rental in the drive, maybe she wouldn't stop.

He opted for parking on the opposite side of the street half a block up from the house. Her mother and Max answered his knock on the back door, her mother's eyes going wide when she saw him.

"Kelly's not here," she said, standing in the doorway almost like she was blocking his entrance while Max wiggled his way between them. This was not the same woman who'd welcomed him to her dinner table two summers ago.

"I'm not here to see Kelly," he said, using Alma's odd behavior to rationalize the half-lie. "Can I come in?"

"Um. Sure. Of course," Alma said, stepping out of his way, leaving the exuberant Max his only obstacle.

"Hey there, Big Fella," Dane said, scratching the dog's ears as he shuffled himself and the dog far enough into the mudroom so he could close the door behind him. "You remember me."

Dodging Max's wet tongue, he said, "I came to ask permission to use the snowmobile up at the camp. It looks like it hasn't been used in a while and needs some work."

"Who's th-there?" her father shouted from deeper in the house.

"Dane St. John," Alma called back. "He wants to use the snowmobile up at the camp."

Frank appeared in the archway between the front rooms of the house and kitchen, leaning on a cane. "Needs sparkplugs."

"Hey, Frank," Dane said, smiling over Max's head at Kelly's dad. "Yeah. I already picked some up. Figured you wouldn't mind me fixing up the sled."

Frank ordered Max to his side and tottered over to the nearest kitchen chair from where he motioned Dane into the kitchen.

"I'm sure Dane wants to get fresh gas and get back to that snowmobile," Alma said, still standing between him and the kitchen.

"I'm in no rush," Dane said, sitting on the mudroom bench and removing his boots. "It's not like I'm on any schedule these days."

His boots on the boot tray, he side-stepped Alma and headed for Frank at the kitchen table. Dane stretched out his hand for a shake, too late remembering Frank had had a stroke that affected his right side. Without missing a beat, Dane grasped the trembling hand Frank had lifted halfway to him in both his hands and shook it.

"Good to see you, Frank."

"Good," Frank said, his speech clearly limited. Motioning Dane into a chair, he added, "Down."

Dane sat across from Frank, Max settling under the table between their feet, tail thumping. "Sorry about your stroke, Frank. I'd have visited if I hadn't been tied up with work."

"Got you—your—" He made a scribbling motion in the air with his good hand, then scowled and flipped his hand as though giving up on the word that escaped him.

"He's saying he got your letters," Alma said, standing behind Frank's chair.

"They were more like cards with a few lines I added to them," Dane said.

Frank nodded.

"He appreciated your remembering him," Alma said, still at Frank's shoulder worrying the dish towel in her hands.

What was the woman all nerved up about? Probably had to do with how Kelly now felt about him. She'd have likely confided her feelings to her mother. Much as he'd have liked to ask Alma what those feelings were, he feared a direct question might get him thrown out. He turned his attention back to Frank.

"I'm glad my cards made you feel better, Frank."

Half of Frank's mouth lifted into a smile. At least her father seemed happy to see him.

"Is it okay with you if I use the snowmobile up at camp?"

"Sure. Need—need—" Frank scowled again and shook his head.

"It needs an overall tune-up and some greasing up," Dane said, trying not to step on Frank's words while clarifying what the older man was trying to say. "I'm pretty handy with machines. I've already taken a close look at it."

The half-smile pulled at the good side of Frank's face and Dane was pretty sure he read approval in the old man's eyes.

"Gas," Frank said.

"I'll drain the old gas," Dane said. "No sense taking a chance gumming up new plugs with bad gas."

Frank leaned over the corner of the table and slapped Dane's arm, managing to get out, "G-good man."

"Think you could take a ride with me once I get the sled running?"

Frank gave him an enthusiastic thumbs-up with his good hand. Alma placed a hand on Frank's shoulder.

"Great," Dane said, noticing how Alma's fingers twitched on Frank's shoulder. "Maybe Kelly could drive you up to the camp for that ride."

Alma's fingers tightened noticeably on Frank's shoulder. Frank frowned and waved her off with a harsh, "Beer. Two."

Alma went white, her eyes widening at Dane. "W-we're out of beer."

"Go," Frank said, flipping his hand toward the door. "Buy."

Dane shook his head. "It's Sunday."

Frank and Alma looked at him with such confusion, he explained, "When I stopped for supplies, they wouldn't sell me any because it was Sunday."

Alma blinked owlishly at him. Frank frowned at him

like he was loony.

"You know, the county ordinance about not selling liquor on Sundays?"

"W-who tell you that?" Frank asked, both sides of his mouth frowning.

"The store clerk," Dane answered, sensing he was missing something.

He looked to Alma for further explanation. But she just glanced around the room as though avoiding his gaze.

"It doesn't matter anyway," Dane said, giving up trying to figure out what was off. "I'd rather a cup of your coffee, Alma."

Alma hesitated, worrying that towel through her fingers again. She glanced over her shoulder toward the adjoining room before moving to the cupboards, filling two mugs, and setting them down in front of him and Frank, quick to return to her position behind Frank.

Frank tapped the table by his cup. "Milk?"

Alma sucked in her bottom lip and turned to the refrigerator positioned to one side of the archway between kitchen and dining end of the front rooms. Strange how she seemed to open the fridge only wide enough to squeeze out the gallon jug of milk. Stranger still was the six pack of beer he spotted on a shelf inside it before she shut the door.

He hadn't spent much time with Alma, but she didn't strike him as a woman who lied. Yet, she had lied about having beer. Strange. Then again, maybe she didn't want Frank drinking this early in the day.

He sipped at the coffee. "As good as I remember," he said, gaining a nervous smile from Alma as she repositioned herself behind Frank.

Frank tipped the gallon-size milk jug over his mug, lost his grip, and dropped the jug, spilling milk across the table. Dane jumped up, righting the jug, while Alma mopped at the spill with her towel as Max lapped at the milk dribbling off the table. Frank cursed. The commotion seemed to spark interest from a sunny spot in the dining room behind Alma and Frank.

The gurgling of a baby. Over Frank's shoulder, he saw the tow-headed child in the playpen, up on her knees, peering through the mesh at him. He smiled at her and she smiled back.

"Hey, I didn't know you two had become grandparents," he said, drawn to the playpen like a bee to honey.

The child, a girl judging by the pink bow in her wispy, blond hair, looked up at him with huge blue eyes. He squatted to her level and she giggled.

"What's your name, sweet thing?"

"Angel," Alma said in a tight voice, instantly at his side.

"Babysitting?" he asked, glancing up at her.

"Yes," she said.

"Kelly never told me her sister had had a baby." He straightened and sighed. "But, judging by this little lady's size, Kelly and I weren't communicating much by the time she was born."

Something flickered in Alma's eyes, like there was something she wanted to say to him. Braced against his cane in the archway, Frank was spitting out words that made no sense to Dane.

Then it dawned on Dane, the fact that Kelly had never mentioned her sister's pregnancy—her *unmarried* sister. People in small towns could be pretty conservative. Maybe all there was to the discomfort he was reading from Alma and agitation in Frank's voice was about a baby born out of wedlock.

"May I?" he asked, reaching for Angel.

Alma gave Frank a nervous glance, but nodded. Dane picked up the child who immediately reached for his eyes.

"They're so curious at this age," he said, smiling.

"I didn't realize you knew babies so well," Alma said.

"My sister Dixie's baby is about the same age as this one and I just spent a week with them. And my brother

Roman and his wife, who've got a little one who'll turn one this month, send me videos all the time. My co-star in my last movie brought her kid to the set every day, also." He shrugged. "I get a kick out of babies and they seem to like me, too."

Angel curled her fingers over his lower lip. He popped his lips together. She giggled.

"That Angel likes you is apparent," Alma said in an oddly speculative tone.

#

"He was here? With Angel?"

Her mom nodded.

Kelly darted into the front room where her daughter played.

"Hey there, Sweetie," she said, picking Angel up and brushing kisses across her forehead, cheeks, and nose. Angel giggled and Kelly hugged her close. Over the baby's head, she gave her mother an accusing look, and, keeping her voice quiet so as not to upset Angel, asked, "How could you let him see her?"

"It's not like I could have snuck her out of the room without him seeing her," her mother answered in a low voice.

"But you let him in, Mom," she went on, cooing a smile out of her daughter while she examined her fingers and toes as if some monster might have taken pieces of her daughter.

"He showed up unexpected," her mother said. "Your father invited him in."

*Dad, who had* not *promised to keep her secret from Dane.*

She glanced at her father's empty chair. "Where is Dad?"

"Napping." Alma nodded toward the little room in back of the kitchen where they'd converted Frank's office into a bedroom so he wouldn't have to deal with the stairs.

"They had a nice chat, Dane and your father. Really cheered your father up."

"And just what did they talk about?" Kelly asked, struggling to keep the panic from her tone.

"Dane wants to use the snowmobile up at camp. Him and Dad talked about what needs to be done to get it back into running shape. Dane even promised to take dad for a ride when he has Big Blue up and running."

"He thinks Dad is up to riding a snowmobile?" Her voice rose in spite of her attempts to contain it for Angel's sake. "There's no way he's in any shape for snowmobiling."

Angel patted Kelly's lips, reminding her how easily little ones picked up on tension while Alma defended Dane's invitation. "It's the only thing other than Angel I've seen your dad get excited about since his stroke."

Kelly winced. Dane's visit might have been a good thing for her dad, but it was dangerous for Angel and her for more than one reason.

Even though panic screamed through her, she tempered her voice. "Dad didn't say anything about Angel, did he?"

"Nothing Dane could understand. You know how jumbled your dad's speech gets when he's excited."

Some of the panic eased from her, but she still had to face the possibility Dane had recognized himself in Angel's eyes. Over the lump forming in her throat, she probed, "Did Dane ask any questions about Angel? Did he seem suspicious?"

"He thinks she's Carrie's baby."

Hope surged through Kelly. "Is that what you told him?"

"It's what he assumed," Alma said.

Kelly stroked Angel's silky, blond hair, frowning. "So, he just looked at her?"

Her mother sighed. "And held her a while."

"And you let him?" The question came out strident and Angel lifted her head, her little brow puckered. "Shhhh," Kelly soothed.

"He asked if he could," Alma said.

Kelly frowned, suspicious and confused. "Why?"

"He said he liked babies and they like him."

"Had a lot of experience with babies lately, has he?" she asked, barely containing her sarcasm.

Angel's fingers covered Kelly's lips as though reminding her she had no right judging Dane.

Alma sighed. "He talked about spending a week with his newest niece."

Kelly kissed Angel's fingertips, murmuring, "So, Dixie and Sam had a daughter, too."

"He said her and Angel couldn't be more than a month apart in age."

"Roman's and Tess' daughter must be about a year old," Kelly said, wishing they could have stayed friends given how well they'd hit it off the day of Dixie's and Sam's wedding. But circumstances had gotten in the way of that. "He no doubt stopped and visited them on the way up here."

"He also said his leading lady brought her baby on set," Alma said.

"Got himself a baby fix right on set, even. How nice for him." *But not with his own daughter.*

There she went, automatically blaming him, even feeling jealous when she had no right to. He didn't *know* he had a daughter. She'd seen to that.

"So, how'd Angel take to him?" Kelly asked, more curious than she wanted to admit.

"She's a sweet-natured baby."

"So she took to him," Kelly said, dying a little inside, knowing what it was to long for a father who wanted nothing to do with you, wondering if Dane could be a different kind of father.

#

Kelly tossed and turned that night, sleep eluding her. Had he seen his eyes in Angel? Could he even now be adding up Angel's age and coming up with one particular night of unprotected sex? Even though Mom had assured her he couldn't know exactly how old Angel was, guessing her age wouldn't be a stretch.

Then there was her name. How long before he figured out the connection to Angel Point where she was conceived?

Maybe Dane had figured it out and was playing dumb to avoid taking ownership. Could a man who doted on kids the way he did turn his back on one of his own? Could the man she'd fallen in love with two summers ago really be that shallow?

She kicked off her blankets and padded barefoot across the nightlight-lit bedroom to the crib occupying the far wall. She stroked the wispy blond hair of the child in question, a halo for an angel. Her Angel sleeping like an angel, not a worry in the world. She'd give anything to insure every night of her daughter's life would be so peaceful, that she'd never have to live with the pain of knowing her father had rejected her.

That's why it was better that Kelly not tell him—that no one told him and forced Dane into making a choice. Better for Angel to grow up with the hope her father would have chosen her had he known about her.

*If only he hadn't come back and risked her daughter's happiness?*

Then there was the argument she used to keep everyone quiet about Angel's parentage, that fear that had wormed its way under her skin ever since he'd returned. If he knew he was her father, he might take her away.

She wanted to pick up Angel and hug her to her chest—hug her so close nothing and nobody could ever separate them. Was that the real issue she faced—that Dane would try to take Angel away from her?

That wouldn't—couldn't—happen, could it? No court would take a child from her mother...even a mother who'd denied the father knowledge of his child, right?

Arms folded against the crib rail—folded against taking up her daughter and running off into the night with her, Kelly looked out the dormer window between the crib and her desk. Huge snowflakes fell outside the window, gilded by the streetlights. It was the kind of snowfall that turned streets slick and dangerous for fleeing vehicles.

It was also the kind of snowfall that turned a landscape into a wonderland. The kind of snow that invited an adventuresome man to play.

This last thought made her think of Dane alone at the cabin. Had he taken out the snowmobile to play tonight? What if he hadn't fixed the sled as well as he'd thought he had and he'd broken down somewhere out there in the beautiful but deadly woods? Or maybe Mr. 'I-Do-Most-of-My-Own-Stunts' hadn't been able to resist pushing the machine to full throttle and he'd hit a tree and…

Her stomach bottomed out. She didn't even want to think how an accident could end the dilemma of Angel being rejected. The idea that Dane could be injured and freezing to death sent a shiver through her. She couldn't leave him to such a fate.

Then there was the CO part of her. That protector-of-all-things-in-her-woods couldn't simply watch the snow accumulate outside her dormer window while there was a chance a man's life hung in the balance.

Dressed in her winter gear, she tapped on her mother's bedroom door, opened it and stuck her head inside. "I have to make a run. Keep an ear open for Angel."

"Be careful," her mother said as she always did.

Even though it had stopped snowing, the drive from town to the camp on slick roads took Kelly nearly twice as long as normal. Palms sweaty, she pulled up to the cabin in her DNR truck, trailered DNR sled in tow. She'd come prepared.

Turning off the ignition, she stepped out into the frosty air.

Silence.

She squinted through the dim pre-dawn light at the footprints outside the cabin half-filled with fresh snow and decided they were no more than an hour or two old. Heart pounding, she rapped on the cabin door and walked in.

The place was empty, nothing moving but the occasional flicker of a flame from the embers in the wood stove. She cursed and headed back outside to the storage shed. The tracks—the packed snow still visible through the new fall, pretty much told the story. But she looked inside the shed to make sure.

Just as she suspected, the snowmobile was missing.

"Cowboy," she muttered under her breath and returned to her work truck where she retrieved her night-vision gear. Solo night rides on a decades old snowmobile that hadn't been run in way too long were an iffy bet, worse with a fast sled driven by an adrenalin junky like Dane.

She followed the packed footpath out onto the bluff where she stood in the silence, listening.

Nothing.

She flipped her night-vision gear over her eyes and scanned the terrain below. Nothing out in the open. She thought about the direction the tracks leading away from the shed had taken and scoured the wooded hills to the east for the heat signature of a body. Again nothing.

There was a trail through the fresh snow, though. But, with the trees laden with new snow, she quickly lost it.

She removed the night-vision gear and listened once more, hoping to hear the distant whine of a snowmobile engine. Still nothing but silence.

*Where are you, Dane?*

With the gray of false dawn creeping in, she stowed the night-vision gear, unloaded her sled from its trailer, and set out on Dane's trail.

She found him a couple miles away on the neighboring camp road beneath a canopy of snow-covered trees end-lit by the promise of a rising sun. He was sprawled out on his silent sled, hands folded behind his head like he didn't have a care in the world. She pulled up beside him and turned off her sled.

"Breakdown or run out of gas?" she asked.

Instead of answering her question, he asked one of his

own. "Isn't this just about the prettiest sight you've ever seen?"

She looked down the narrow roadway all but turned into a white tube by the snowy limbs bowing over it. She nodded. "Our winters have their moments."

"And listen," he said.

"To what?"

"The silence. Do you have any idea how much a treasure silence like this is?"

"It's the snow. It muffles sound."

He nodded. "Beautiful."

It was beautiful. She'd always found a fresh snow magical. And she loved the utter silence a layer of the white stuff could create. That Dane St. John did, too, stirred through her. It was almost enough to make her want to snuggle up with him on the seat of that sled and lose herself in the silence…and his arms.

*Almost.*

"Pretty but potentially deadly," she said. "You're lucky Mom told me you were fixing up the old machine—that I came checking on you."

He looked at her and grinned. "Were you worried about me, Bright Eyes?"

She wanted to tell him to stop calling her that. But, she didn't want him to know the nickname meant anything to her, and she gave him a CO answer. "I'm responsible for everything in these woods. It wouldn't look good if the guy renting my cabin wound up frozen to death in them."

He studied her as though searching for something. Or maybe he'd already figured out what she was afraid he knew after seeing Angel. Maybe he was contemplating…

*What?* How to call her out on not telling him he had a daughter? How to go on pretending he didn't know Angel was his? Which did she want it to be…providing he'd figured it out?

As much to distract him as to distract herself, she nodded at his sled. "Think it's something we can fix or do you need a lift back to camp?"

"I never said there was anything wrong with the snowmobile," he said, mischief glinting in his eyes.

"You've been sitting here since predawn on a stilled sled, and don't deny it. I haven't heard a sound since arriving at the camp."

"Can't enjoy the peace with a motor roaring in your ears," he said. "And peace is what I came here for."

She frowned at him, not quite sure he was talking entirely about escaping the scrutiny of the paparazzi. He righted himself, and with a twist of the ignition key, the sled roared to life.

"Ah," she yelled over the noisy puttering, more than ready to put some distance between them. "As long as you're all right, I'll go see to people who really need my help."

"Race you back to camp," he shouted, revving the engine, the whine all but deafening her.

She rolled her eyes at his boyish challenge but found herself unable to resist. That free-spiritedness had been part of what had attracted her to him and made their affair so muchfun.

Besides, the competitor in her had turned on her own ignition and was spinning her machine around on the trail before he'd likely even realized he was facing the wrong direction. As an added bonus, her machine was a newer model and in topnotch condition. There was no way he was going to catch her.

She glanced back at the fishtail of snow pluming off her track. She couldn't even see him. Teach him to challenge her.

Lost in the moment, she laughed....but not for long.

An earsplitting whine filled her ears. The next instant he was alongside her. He gave her a grin and a wink, then throttled past her.

Kelly hunkered down, well below the profile of her windshield and gave her machine full throttle. She pulled up almost even with him. The turn off the road into the woods would be coming up soon. Whoever got there first would have the advantage on the single track trail. But, no matter how much she urged her machine onward, he inched ahead.

She almost caught him when his sled bogged down on the bank where the trail hooked into the woods. But he had weight and upper body strength on her and rocked his machine free before she could pass him. The rest of the way back to the camp, she ate the snow fishtailing off his track, never quite able to get a clear sightline to a space where she could safely pass him. He was laughing when she slid to a stop beside him and his silent sled in front of the shed.

She turned off her sled, smiling, knowing she'd just had the most fun she'd had since…Dane had last been in her life.

Her good spirit faded, but she still teased him. "Glad you enjoyed beating me."

"Damn," he said. "I thought you were going to overtake me when we hit the woods. You're one scary chick on that thing."

Something akin to pride stirred in her chest. She shouldn't like that she had impressed him. But she did. Not that she'd let him know that. Still, she couldn't help but needle him a bit. "If I could have seen a way around you in the woods, I'd have overtaken you."

He stood and brushed away the remnants of snow her machine had kicked back at him during her brief period in the lead. "I don't think so. You saw for yourself that you couldn't overtake me on the flat."

She dismounted her sled and brushed from her shoulders the considerable amount of snow she'd taken off his tail. "I'd have outmaneuvered you through the woods," she said, striding over to him and eying the big snowmobile. "That sled is fast. But it's old and it's bulky. It shouldn't have been able to outrun mine. You modified it."

"Left the muffler off," he said.

"So I noticed," she said, lifting a smug smile at him.

"Muffler's there for a reason. We have a noise ordinance in these parts."

His smile crooked. "Uh oh. Looks like the Game Warden lady is about to ticket me. Or is the offense serious enough to cuff me and take me in?"

"Consider this a warning. Just get that muffler back on the sled."

"Actually, I'd like to make my future forays into the woods without the noise of any motors." He motioned for her to follow him into the shed.

It took her eyes a few minutes to adjust to the dimness—to see what he pointed at in the eaves.

"Those are cross-country skis," he said.

"Yeah."

"Any problem with me using them?"

"You know how to—" She stopped, shook her head. "Of course you know how to cross-country ski. You know everything."

The lift of his lips slipped. "I don't know why you're so angry with me, Kel."

The comment hit her like a punch in the gut. Still, she responded with as much calmness as she could muster. "I'm not angry with you."

"Seems that way."

Going for misdirection, she pointed at the skis above his head. "Those require boots with a toe binding. You'll never fit into Dad's boots." She moved deeper into the shed and pointed at a weathered pair of skis with leather bindings. "Those bindings work like snowshoe bindings but they're old and rotten."

"Snowshoes?"

She raised an eyebrow at him. "Mr. I've-done-it-all has never snowshoed?"

He ducked his head, his grin returning. "Looks like there's something else I don't know."

She smiled at his comment, but was thinking about what she preferred he not know—not figure out. As she saw it, better to give him occupation rather than time to think about the little girl with his eyes.

So she retrieved her dad's snowshoes from their wall mount in the cabin, and hers from the back of her truck…even though the lesson meant she'd have to spend more time with him. The important thing was to distract him.

## CHAPTER THIRTEEN

Dane tried to focus on Kelly's instructions about walking in snowshoes. But he was too busy doing mental backflips of joy.

Dragging out his visit with her dad until the old man dozed off and her mother excused herself to put the baby down for her nap hadn't paid off. He'd even waited another half hour in his truck for Kelly to show up without luck. But that visit had drawn her out—had gotten her to come to the camp to check on him.

Better yet, she was staying to give him snowshoeing lessons. The whole thing couldn't have worked out better if he'd planned it. So much for his siblings warnings about his impulsiveness. Looked to him like spontaneity worked as well as any plan.

"We'll start on the snowmobile trail where the going will be easier," she said, striding off past the end of the shed on her snowshoes.

He took two steps, the second landing one snowshoe overlapping with the other and sending him face-down in the snow. From the edge of the woods, she called back, "Wide stride."

He righted himself and untangled his snowshoes with the grace of a toddler taking his first steps. Was she laughing at him? She turned and headed into the woods before he could tell.

He headed after her, one awkward step at a time, every time he failed to remind himself to keep his strides wide, he planted one snowshoe on top the other and took a nosedive.

Meanwhile, she moved away from him with a steady grace. At one point, she even came loping back to him. Loping!

"You look like the abominable snowman," she said,

hands on her hips, her spread leg pose making her look like a super hero as she looked down on him wallowing in the snow.

"You're enjoying this, aren't you?" he stated more than asked as he righted himself and brushed snow from his clothes.

She gave a little shrug. "Can't help it. It's all that ego you carry around. It makes it fun to take you down a notch now and then."

He laughed, but there was a serious note to his words. "After all the phone calls, emails, and texts—after spending those ten days together, do you really still think I have such a huge ego?"

The cocky slant of her lips slipped. "You want to learn how to snowshoe or stand around jawing?"

Afraid choosing *jawing* over snowshoe lessons would mean a premature end to their being together, he followed her for the next half hour, silent for the most part. He picked up the rhythm of snowshoeing quickly enough. But it was hard work, making him sweat.

He opened his jacket to the weather, even removed his knit cap. He should have noted that she'd stripped off her heavy jacket before strapping on her snowshoes and left it back at the shed. But, then, he'd been preoccupied with his success at having kept her from running away from him. Now, he was sweaty and thirsty.

"Can we take a break?" he called.

She glanced over her shoulder at him, slowed, and stopped where the path hooked around a fallen tree. He scooped up some fresh snow and shoved it in his mouth.

"Thirsty?" she asked.

"Dry as a desert," he said.

She unhooked a canteen from her belt, unscrewed its lid, and handed it to him. "This'll better quench your thirst."

"Thanks," he said, accepting the canteen and taking a long drink before handing it back.

She took a swallow, stoppered the canteen, and

reattached it to her belt. "Ready to go?"

He leaned back against the deadfall, studying her. "Not quite." *Not when I've got a load of questions that need answering and we're far enough from any vehicles for you to make a speedy escape.*

"Kelly, I'm confused," he ventured. "I thought we were building something. If that just petered out, I could understand you being…cordial, indifferent, distant even. But, when we met in the Buck Inn parking lot—when you left me at the cabin, you were angry."

She gave him her profile and he could see her working to retain control. Before she hid behind her CO mask again, he pressed, "You also started distancing yourself from me long before that made-up engagement announcement. What did I do to hurt you so badly?"

"There's that ego," she said in a tone that could have been mistaken as teasing were it not for the barely contained emotion blazing in the hazel eyes she slanted his way. "You think everything is about you."

She snorted and stepped away from him with a flippant, "Enough lessons for one day. Time to head back to camp."

Outside the cabin, as she stowed her snowshoes in her truck. He invited her to stay for hot chocolate. She declined with a terse, "I've got work to do."

"Thanks for taking the time to give me lessons," he said, when he wanted to grab her and hold her until she told him what was bothering her.

"There's ibuprofen in the medicine cabinet," she said, turning to the cab of the truck.

Thrown by her comment, he asked as she opened the truck door, "Why are you telling me about the ibuprofen?"

"You'll know why in a couple hours," she said, climbing into her truck without looking at him and starting the engine.

He stepped back, lost for an idea of how to make her stay without going Neanderthal on her. Like manhandling her would have worked. He'd seen her take down a man twice as big as her. Hell, she'd flipped him that time they were fooling around in bed.

To his surprise, she powered down her window, adding, "You might also consider hot compresses."

He'd have pressed for why she was giving him all this pain-reducing information except he was too focused on how her gaze failed to meet his. Then she powered up the window, put the truck in gear, and backed it and the trailered snowmobile down the steep slope of the camp road.

He lay on the lower bunk where they'd once upon a time ago made amazing love. But making love wasn't what was on his mind. What he needed to figure out was how to get her to open up to him—share with him what he'd done wrong so he could fix it. If there was anything left to fix.

But what if the problem was the long-distance relationship? Bad news because their respective careers meant there'd always be the distance issue between them.

What if she couldn't handle the gossip too readily reported by the rags? Another issue he was helpless to rectify because she was the one who needed the confidence to get past jealousy.

What if what they'd shared was too badly broken to repair? This one scared him most of all because it would mean *they* were beyond repair.

A soft mattress, a sleepless night, and a morning full of fresh air conspired against Dane, and he was asleep before he could find the answers to his questions.

An hour later, a Charlie horse ripped up the inside of his right thigh and jerked him awake.

He rolled off the bed with a curse, hopping on one foot as he fought to stretch his spasming leg. His stockinged foot met the cold floor, draining away the spasm but leaving behind a deep ache. Then his left thigh went into spasm.

"Damn," he howled, hobbling over to the medicine cabinet for the ibuprofen.

He shook the standard two pill dose into his palm, then

doubled it and swallowed the pills without water. Staring at the bottle in his hand, a slow smile pulled across his lips. Kelly had known the over-use of seldom used muscles would take their toll on his body and she'd made sure he'd know where to find something to ease the pain. Oh, she definitely still cared for him.

And she cared big time or she wouldn't have come all the way up to the camp before dawn and tracked him into the woods to make sure he hadn't broken down or gotten himself hurt. He had his answer to his last, most troublesome question. They weren't broken beyond repair, not as long as Kelly still cared about him.

Not as long as she still had strong emotions towards him like anger.

Not as long as she could forget whatever it was that had gotten between them and enjoy his company as she had this morning, racing their sleds—teasing each other. She'd even hung around to give him snowshoeing lessons.

Things hadn't gone bad until he'd asked her point blank what he'd done to hurt her. So, directness scared her off. That meant he had to use a less straight forward approach to get to the bottom of what was going on with her. Which meant he needed to go against his instinct to be candid with Kelly. He wasn't keen on the idea. But, if it was the only way to get them back to the point where she would talk to him, then he'd do it.

Now all he had to do was figure out how to create contact between them.

#

Four days had passed since she'd come to check on him. He'd purposely not called her cell or the house phone, hoping she'd come back out to check on him. But she hadn't.

So here he was, plan B. His planning-obsessed brother, Roman, would be so proud of him.

Dane strode the half block from where he'd parked his SUV to the Jackson house. Like last time, Kelly's truck wasn't in the driveway. Like last time, Alma answered his knock. Unlike last time, she didn't act as nerved up as she had the first time he'd shown up unannounced on their doorstep. Still, he was quick to establish his misdirection.

"Frank up for some company?"

Alma actually smiled as she let him in. "I'll let Frank know you're here while you take your boots off."

Frank met him at the kitchen table with his cane and lopsided smile. Alma plopped two mugs of coffee on the table.

"Beer," Frank said.

Eyes lowered, Alma turned to the countertop saying, "Just brewed a fresh pot of coffee."

"Want beer." Frank looked at Dane. "Dane? Beer?"

He caught the sideward glance from Alma. There was that beer issue again. Then the woman said, "You can't drink alcohol with your meds, Frank. You know that."

Okay. That made sense, and Dane said, "Coffee sounds great to me."

Halfway through the mug, Dane brought up the reason he'd stopped by, at least the smokescreen reason. "Kelly tell you I got the sled running?"

Frank nodded.

"I promised you a ride if I got it going. You up for a run?"

Frank's eyes brightened. "You betcha."

Alma appeared at the top of the basement steps, laundry basket on her hip. "But Frank, you wouldn't even go up to the camp before your stroke."

He waved her off.

"I'll take good care of him," Dane said.

"He doesn't go out much." She glanced between Dane and Frank. "The drive to camp alone could tire him out."

Dane hadn't thought things through as thoroughly as he should have and he wasn't sure wearing Frank out was worth it for the sake of getting Kelly's attention. But, before he could withdraw his invitation, Frank waved his wife off with both hands this time.

Alma set the basket on a chair and nodded. "Okay. It'll be good for you to get out, even if it ends up just a ride to the camp."

"Underwear," Frank said, pushing himself up from the table and tapping his chest. "Shirt."

"Long johns and wool shirt," Alma said, heading through the front room for the stairs. "I'll bring them to your room."

By the time Alma came back down the stairs, Frank had gone into his bedroom off the kitchen and Dane had answered the gurgling call of their granddaughter in the dining room end of the front rooms. Alma slowed as she came off the steps toward where he and Angel were making faces at each other through the mesh of the playpen, laughing.

He glanced up at her when she didn't pass. "Hope you don't mind. I can't seem to resist the flirting of little girls. I blame it on my sister, Dixie. She's been a flirt all her life."

Alma patted his shoulder. "You need to know…"

He peered up at her. Alma looked from him, to Angel, to the archway between the front room and kitchen.

"What do I need to know, Alma?"

She looked at Angel, then shook her head.

"Alma. Is there something I should know about taking Frank out?"

Her shoulders sagged and she gave him a sad smile. "Sure. About Frank. After he got shot, he said his life was over. Nothing any of us said or did could get him back into the woods."

"He helped at the command center when that boy was lost."

"DNR business." Alma gave a little huff. "*That* motivates him. But, he hasn't been up to the camp since then."

"If I'm overstepping—"

She shook her head, cutting him off. "I don't know why he's willing to go now. But bless you, Dane."

#

The ride to camp had tired Frank. But, when Dane suggested they take a rest in the cabin before going snowmobiling, the old man had swung his cane and jabbered disjointed words from which Dane had deciphered "ride" and "now."

So Dane had driven the sled up to the passenger side of the truck to make transitioning from vehicle to sled easier for Frank. And they'd ridden, not too far, not too fast. Just far and fast enough to stretch Frank's lopsided grin about as wide as it would go.

When they returned to the camp, Frank had hobbled to the end of the cabin facing the point.

"Stupid o-old man," Frank said.

"Why would you say that?" Dane asked, stepping up beside him.

Frank shook his head. "St-stuboorn." He waved a weary hand at the snow-laden landscape beyond the point. "Stayed away. Too long."

It was then when Dane saw the tears in Frank's eyes as he looked out from Angel Point that he knew he'd done something right, even if it never got Kelly's attention.

But it did get her attention.

He was gathering wood from the shed when he heard her truck. He met her outside the cabin with an armload of firewood and a grin. But *she* wasn't smiling.

"What the hell do you think you're doing?" she demanded through clenched teeth, "taking my father snowmobiling. Just the ride up to camp was enough to exhaust him."

His grin faded. "Your mother said the same thing. But she also thought getting out would do him some good."

Kelly crossed her arms over her chest. "Did you even try to make him rest before going snowmobiling?"

"He wanted out in the woods on that sled and he wanted it as soon as he got here. I couldn't hold him back, Kel. You know your dad."

"He could have had another stroke. It could have killed

him."

He frowned. "If there was a real danger of that happening, wouldn't your mother have warned me?"

She grimaced as though she couldn't argue with his reasoning, but her voice still held its reproachful edge. "You two have been gone for hours."

"I called the house a half hour ago. Told your mom we were back at camp—that he was fine and taking a nap. You must have been there."

#

She'd been there alright. She'd been there at the house freaking out about her father being alone the whole afternoon with Dane, her father who *hadn't* promised to keep her secret. That was the real reason she'd raced up to the camp.

How selfish could she be?

And, now, seeing the confusion in Dane's eyes, knowing her worst fear had not materialized she could add shame to her guilt. *Damn.*

She pushed past Dane and went into the cabin. Her father was in his usual chair, the lone recliner in the camp, dozing. She pressed her fingertips to his wrist. His eyes fluttered open and he shook her off.

"What you doing, Girl?"

"Just checking on you, Daddy."

He shuddered. "C-creeps me out."

Dane dumped his armload of firewood in the wood box. Kelly glanced at him, caught the concern in the way he studied her. Her stomach churned. She didn't want his concern—couldn't afford his taking further interest in her. Not now, not when she was beginning to fear he could want custody of Angel...should he figure out he was her father...if he hadn't already.

Or maybe his concern was simply for her father's well-being. She had pretty much told him it would be his fault if her father had a stroke.

She rose from her father's side and met Dane's worried

gaze. "He's fine," she said with as much normalcy to her voice as she could muster. "But I should get him home."

Her father stirred. "No—not yet."

Dane glanced from her to her father and then back, his eyes so much like Angel's they brought tears scratching at the backs of her eyes.

"If he wants to stay longer," Dane said, "I'll drive him home."

*And the longer he's alone with you, the greater the chance he'll tell you about Angel.* She hated herself for her selfishness.

"Stay," her father said.

She rubbed his shoulder, glad to see him enthusiastic about the camp. He'd avoided it for too long. But, aside from her fears, all this activity really could be too much for him.

"I've got cocoa heating on the stove," Dane said. "The two of you could stay long enough for a cup at least."

"Beer," her father said, banging a fist on the arm of the chair.

"No beer," Dane said. "Beer doesn't mix with your meds, Frank."

Kelly eyed Dane. "Who told you that?"

He blinked at her. "Your mother. When your dad asked your mom for a couple of beers for us, she said alcohol didn't mix with his meds."

Confused, Kelly shook her head. "My mom's protective about him, but he can have a beer now and then."

Dane shrugged. Frank slapped the arm of the chair, demanding, "Beer."

"Sorry, Frank," Dane said. "I don't have any beer here."

She studied Dane, wondering if there was some truth to the gossip rags speculations that he had a drinking problem after all. He had said the isolation of the camp was just what *the doctor ordered.*

Though she'd never seen any indication of a drinking problem back when they were sharing wine and a bed. If he'd developed a drinking problem, it was one more reason to keep him out of Angel's life—out of her life.

Dane motioned toward the kitchen end of the camp. "I might be able to scare up some red wine. I'm sure there's enough left in the bottle for a couple glasses."

*Would an alcoholic leave a couple glasses worth of wine in a bottle?*

She didn't think so; and the real reason her mother, fan of all things written about celebrities, had refused to serve her dad and Dane beer almost made Kelly laugh.

"What?" Dane asked, her expression apparently giving her away.

She smiled at him. "Thanks for everything you did for my dad today."

He blinked at her, looking bewildered as he answered, "It was my pleasure."

Frank grumbled something unintelligible.

"Dad clearly had a great time, too. But I think he's done enough for his first day out like this. A cup of that hot chocolate and we'll hit the road."

"Sure," Dane said, stuffing his hands in his pockets and shrugging his shoulders. She'd loved his boyish gestures. She'd loved a lot about Dane St. John. Still did. But, to be a father, he needed to be a man, not a boy.

#

The reaction he'd gotten when Kelly had come to camp to get Frank hadn't entirely been the one he'd been going for. But, by the time she'd bundled Frank off, it was close. She had at least expressed appreciation for what he'd done for her father.

So, here he was, two days later back at the Jackson house. Having noticed award plaques for decoy carvings on the living room wall, Frank had ushered him into his first floor bedroom where shelves lined the walls, most filled with wood-carved waterfowl.

"This used to be his office," Alma said, bringing in a tray of coffee and chocolate chip cookies.

"The workmanship is amazing," Dane said, perusing

the shelves.

"Was," Frank said.

Dane squatted in front of a low shelf containing articulated fish carvings. "What are these?"

"Decoys."

Dane motioned to one of the fish decoys. "May I?"

Frank nodded.

Dane straightened with the articulated wood fish in hand and studied it. It didn't have the elaborate paint job the duck decoys had, but it interested him. "I didn't even know decoys were used to lure in fish?"

"Spearing," Frank said. "Through the ice."

Dane swam the decoy through the air.

"You should see it move through the water," said a familiar voice.

Dane turned toward the doorway, knowing who he'd find there. "Hi, Kelly."

She entered the small room and took another fish decoy from the shelf. "Dad won a big award for this one. Proud day for the whole family, huh, Dad?"

"One of the best," Frank said, his gaze intent on his daughter.

Kelly's eyes took on a watery sheen. She cleared her throat. "How about I fill the tub full of water and show him how they move?"

"No," Frank said. "Tub upstairs."

"And you want to be the one to show off your decoys, huh, Dad?"

"I'll take him spearing," Frank said.

"You don't even know if he wants to go spearing."

"I've never done spearing," Dane said. "I'd like to give it a try."

She looked at him, one hand on her hip. "It's cold. It's wet. You're out in the middle of a frozen lake."

He grinned at her. "And the downside is?"

She shook her head. "Of course. You're the guy who'll try anything that falls into his lap. I should have remembered."

Fact was, she had remembered. Another reason she couldn't chance Dane finding out about Angel's parentage. She wouldn't let her daughter be just another *thing* Dane St. John tried out.

"I better go change out of my work clothes," Kelly said, realizing she should have stuck to her usual routine of picking Angel up and nuzzling her first thing upon arriving home rather than let worry of what her father might be telling Dane draw her into his bedroom. Maybe if she hurried, she could scoop Angel up and flee up to her room where she could hide them both away from Dane.

But Dane followed her into the front room where Angel stretched her arms up for her usual motherly hug.

Kelly hesitated and Dane picked her up as he asked, "Do you think Frank can handle going out on the lake, spearing?"

Kelly stared at him cooing at Angel—his daughter—as he waited for her answer.

"What do you think, sweet Angel? Is your grampa up to some spearing through the ice?"

Angel smiled and patted Dane's chin. He sucked her fingers in between his lips, nibbling them playfully. She giggled, clearly connecting with Dane...as easily as Dane had connected with her. He was a natural with kids. She should tell him Angel was his. Give him his due.

Behind them, Carrie stepped into the room. Dane glanced at her then turned his attention back to Angel. "And here's your mama."

Kelly looked at Carrie, who stared back at her with a look of near-panic. Angel was beginning to put sounds together. So far, mama hadn't been one of them. Kelly uttered a silent prayer that now would not be the day Angel put that word together with her.

"Bet your mama's eager to say hello to you," Dane said, holding Angel out to Carrie.

Carrie took the child and murmured motherly sounds to her while all Kelly could do was stand there and watch, her heart aching. Was this what it would feel like if Dane found out Angel was his and took her away?

"So," he said. "Your dad? Spearing? You think he can do it?"

Thank goodness for Dane's penchant for trying all things new...and his boyish focus.

#

Kelly, Carrie, and Angel escaped to her bedroom where Carrie lectured her on confessing to Dane. As usual, she'd silenced her sister with her worst fear, that he'd take Angel away. When they went back downstairs, it was to find her father and Dane making spearing plans and her mother's announcement that Frank had invited Dane to stay for supper.

Kelly's stomach bottomed out. Snowmobiling, spearing, suppers with her family, and they weren't even halfway through his month-long stay. She needed to establish some boundaries for him.

Handing Angel off to Carrie, she said, "Dane, let's you and me run to the store for some wine."

He brightened. "Sure."

As she followed him to the mud room, her mother snagged her by the arm and mouthed *wine?*

"Chill, Mom. It'll be okay," she murmured back and followed Dane out the back door.

"Your dad's real excited about getting back to spearing," he said as they pulled out of the driveway.

"He certainly seems more interested in the things he used to be passionate about," Kelly said, steering the truck toward the main street, but having second thoughts about her intent to establish boundaries for Dane with her family.

"Your mom said he gave up on life after he got shot."

"Dad lived and breathed being a CO. The forced retirement all but killed him."

And here she was planning to take away from her dad one of his best motivations. She winced.

"Yet he's interested now after a stroke that physically disabled him far more," Dane said, his tone pensive.

"What happened?"

*Angel. You.*

Her instincts warning her to keep the focus off the granddaughter connection, she said, "Seems having another male figure around has renewed his interest in a lot of things. He's even working his strength-building weights again."

Dane grunted. "I don't know that I'm so much a motivation."

"That snowmobile ride you took him on perked him up big time."

"Sometimes it takes losing everything for a person to realize what they are *letting* slip away."

She glanced at Dane, his remark reminding her how much he'd experienced by being the kind of guy who'd try *anything that fell into his lap*, and that not all of it had been fun and games...like his Lithuanian friend who'd lost a leg fetching his soccer ball from a World War II mine field.

"Stubbornness," she murmured, pondering her own actions of the past year and a half.

"When we were at camp," Dane said, "your dad looked out over the valley and called himself *stubborn*. You think that's what he was referring to, his not doing what he could when he was able?"

"Maybe," she said, steering the truck into the Grocery Mart parking lot, wondering if she was letting stubbornness influence her choice not to tell Dane he was Angel's father.

They picked out a couple Merlots. But when they got up to the checkout, the checker looked at the bottles then at him, turned red and blurted, "I can't sell wine to you."

Standing in the line behind Dane, Kelly glanced up from the magazine rack as he responded, "Fine. Get whoever can ring it up."

"I-ah." The girl turned away from him and waved the checker from two aisles over to her.

Kelly scanned the headlines of the magazines and newsprint on the racks while the two checkers tried to dissuade Dane from buying the wine. He argued. Kelly took one of the rags from the rack, laid it facedown beside the wine bottles, and instructed the checker to ring up the order for her.

Outside, he said to her, "What the hell was that all about? They'd sell to you but not me?"

Nearing the truck, she handed the rolled up gossip rag to him. He opened it, its giant headlines unrolling before him.

### *Dane St. John in Rehab?*

He looked across the hood of the truck at her. "Are you saying they recognized me—think I'm an alcoholoic; and that was the reason why they wouldn't sell me the wine?"

"Yup."

"I thought I was safely hidden away up here," he said, climbing into the passenger seat.

Here was her chance to get rid of him. Just verify that his secret was out and he'd leave.

*He'd leave, wouldn't he?*

"Nobody here's going to blow your cover," she said, closing her door and keying on the ignition.

"But—"

"The residents of Copper Falls like their gossip magazines," she said, putting the truck in gear and pulling out of the parking space. "But they're also a tight-lipped bunch when it comes to protecting their own."

"And they think of me as one of their own?"

"You're the first movie star ever to come to our little town," she said, checking for traffic before exiting the parking lot. "I guess you could say Copper Falls claims you."

"So no one's going to call one of the rags on me?"
He studied the newspaper in his hand. "And because they believe I'm an alcoholic, they refuse to sell me wine to protect me?"

"You got it," she said, heading down the main

thoroughfare.

He snorted. "That explains a few things."

"Like my mother refusing to give you a beer and telling you alcohol didn't mix with Dad's meds?"

"That, and my attempt to buy beer. The cashier told me he couldn't sell beer on Sundays, that it was a county ordinance."

She laughed. He laughed. For a moment it was like old times when there'd been nothing between them but skin.

"I don't have a drinking problem, Kel," he said, his tone turning serious.

"I didn't think you did."

"There's been a lot of crap in the rags suggesting I did."

"I know," she said, turning off the main street toward home. "There was even a picture of you falling over a table."

He grunted. "I picked up an inner ear infection during the African shoot. It went undiagnosed for a while. Resulted in some balance issues. I even lost some weight."

Tabloid images of a gaunt Dane flashed behind her eyes and her mother's comments about that lost weight—his unhappy eyes, rang in her ears, and she murmured, " Easy fodder for the tabloids."

She caught the swing of his head in her direction. "You believe me, don't you, Kel?"

*She was the liar, not him.*

"I believe you, Dane."

But, she still faced the problem of hiding Angel's parentage from him, she realized as she pulled into the driveway at home. How long it would take before someone in her close-knit community would let it slip that he was Angel's father. She still didn't know if he'd reject his daughter or claim custody.

He reached for the passenger door. She caught him by the arm, stilled him. He looked at her.

"There is something I want to make clear with you before we go back inside," she said, justifying what she was about to do by reminding herself if he chose the latter, to claim custody of Angel, a lot more people would be hurt than just her.

"What's that?" he asked.

"If you're trying to reconnect with me by endearing yourself to my dad—my family, it won't work. I've moved on and I suggest you do likewise."

## CHAPTER FOURTEEN

Dane slumped on the camp couch, his feet on the coffee table in front of the fireplace, staring into the flames. In the week since Kelly had all but told him to stay away from her family, he'd done everything there was to do around the cabin twice over and snow-shoed just about every inch of the surrounding woods. Add in how the wind and snow battered the woods and cabin today, he was stuck inside with nothing to do but build a fire in the fireplace and think.

And all he could think about was it'd been seven days and he hadn't heard a word from her. Maybe she really meant it when she said she'd moved on.

But if that was the case, why the anger? If she really had moved on, why did she still harbor such strong emotions?

This was the one thing he couldn't get past—the one thing that nagged him night and day—that kept his instincts on high alert. If Kelly truly had moved on, she shouldn't be angry—she shouldn't be hurting.

And that was *the* thing, her hurt. Every sense he had told him, behind the anger, she was hurting; and *that* he couldn't bear.

He'd called Tess. Of all his family, his sister-in-law was the one who'd gotten to know Kelly best, the one most likely to know how to handle her. Tess agreed Kelly was hiding something. She had urged him to keep pushing—keep crowding her.

"But how do I push and crowd her when she won't even let me near her?" he'd asked.

"You've got to get her someplace where she can't escape you—can't run away from your questions."

But the days were slipping away and he was no closer to figuring out how to keep her someplace long enough to get some answers. He was beginning to think what he needed was divine intervention.

The grind of a truck in all-wheel drive climbing the grade to the cabin broke him from his commiserating. Hope surged through him before he tempered it with, "It's probably just Andi Johanson come to plow." Though, at the same time, he thought it odd Andi would show up before the storm ended.

Dane rose, crossed the room, and looked out the window at the truck pulling up beside his SUV. It didn't have a plow on it but it did have a DNR emblem on the door. He stepped into his boots, threw on his jacket, and bounded out the door before the truck had even come to a full stop.

He met Kelly as she dropped from the driver's side door, unable to hold back a grin. She, however, wasn't smiling.

"I tried calling you on the bag phone," she said in a tone that hit him with all the force of the gusting storm.

He ducked his head, realizing he hadn't given her his satellite phone number. Hell he hadn't even told her he had a satellite phone.

"I told you to keep it charged," she said in the same unforgiving tone. "You did keep it charged, didn't you?"

He grimaced, which apparently was enough of an answer for her.

"Dammit, Dane." She howled above the roar of the wind. "This storm's going to be a big one. Three more feet of snow predicted. You'll be snowed in for a couple days, if not longer. I was calling to make sure you were stocked up for it."

"Still worrying about me, huh, Bright Eyes?" he ventured.

She slammed the truck door shut, plowed through the five inches of snow that had already accumulated, and folded back her truck's bedcover, revealing bags of supplies. "I had to assume you hadn't thought to stock up for the storm and do it for you."

*A storm. Two to three feet of snow. Divine intervention?*

Dane raised his face into the falling snow and mouthed, *thank you.*

"Here," she said, shoving bags into his arms. "Help me unload so I can get out of here before I'm snowed in, too."

Dane peeked skyward, silently intoning, *help.*

"Move it," she snapped when he lagged.

She dumped her load on the kitchen table and turned for the door.

"Kelly, wait."

"I've got no time for waiting around," she said, jabbing a finger in his face. "Turn on your SUV and plug in that bag phone. I want it charged and available to receive calls."

She strode toward the door.

"I've got a satellite phone," he called after her.

She stopped, pivoted, and glared at him. "And you failed to tell me this why?"

"I didn't think you'd call me."

She threw up her hands and turned for the door, ordering over her shoulder, "Write down the number for me while I haul in the last load."

His chance to keep her here at the camp was fast slipping away.

"Think," he ordered himself. "What can I do?"

She banged her way back into the cabin with the remaining satchels of supplies and dropped them on the floor beside the table. "I had the propane tank filled before you came up here so you should have plenty to run the fridge, stove, and lights. I filled a gas can in case you need any for the SUV. I'll leave it outside the door. It'll be fine there or you can haul it into the shed yourself. Got that number for me?"

"I need to find some paper—"

She tore off a corner of a grocery bag and slapped it down on the table in front of him. "Need a pen?" she asked, reaching inside her jacket to her breast pocket.

He took the pen she held out to him and wrote his number on the scrap of grocery bag as he spoke. "We need to talk, Kel."

"We've done all the talking we're going to do," she said, snatching the paper with his number off the table, stuffing it into her pocket, and turning for the door.

"Kel, please." He caught her by the arm.

She glared at his hand on her arm, then at his face. "Let go of me."

"Please, Kel."

She shook her arm free and escaped out the door.

He followed, a wind gust slamming into him. He barely felt it even though his jacket hung open and his head and hands were bare.

"Get back inside before you freeze your ass off," she ordered, yanking open the driver's side door of her truck.

"Don't leave like this, Kel."

She climbed into the truck. He grabbed for the door handle. She locked the door, keyed on the ignition, and backed hard away from him, the light rear-end of her truck fishtailing into a turn that would send her front end first down the road away from him.

So much for divine intervention.

But, between her heated retreat and the snowfall obscuring where the road dropped off, she must have miscalculated. Helplessly, Dane watched as her truck lurched to one side into the ditch.

He raced up to the truck, the driver's side tilted forty-five degrees toward the leaden sky. He wrenched open her door and found her fumbling to release her seatbelt.

"You need to take the pressure off it," he said.

"I know," she shouted back.

"Grab onto me," he said already hauling her close with one arm while reaching around her for the buckle with the other and freeing her.

He set her on the ground, slow to let her go. She flat-handed him in the chest, shoving him off.

"Damn you, Dane. If I hadn't had to come up here…"

As badly as he wanted to keep her at the cabin with him, he had to offer, "Take my SUV."

Her glare could have melted the snowflakes falling between them. "I can't leave my work truck here."

"Then get your tow rigging," he shouted over the howling wind. "We'll hook the truck up to the SUV and I'll pull you out."

"That SUV doesn't have the power to pull the truck out, as badly stuck as it is," she called after him as he hoofed it over to the SUV, determined to play her hero.

And how right she was he realized as he tried to position the SUV downhill of the truck only to go into a skid that turned the SUV sideways across the narrow camp road. The SUV didn't even have power or weight enough to keep itself on the road.

After attempting a few maneuvers to free the vehicle, he climbed out the passenger door and up to where she waited for him, hands on hips.

"Sorry," he said as he strode past her, hands shoved in his pockets, bare head bowed into the wind, the last to hide his smile.

#

"You did that on purpose," she said, slamming the cabin door shut behind her.

He was holding his hands up to the fireplace, an eyebrow raised at her. "And just how did *I* put *you* in the ditch?"

She stomped the snow off her feet, muttering curses and pulling her satellite phone from an inside pocket. She should have called in from her truck radio, even if it meant doing gymnastics to reach it. At least she wouldn't be inside with Dane and his cocked eyebrow.

She called the office first, reporting her situation, and requesting help. But everybody was tied up doing *more important things* what with this storm. Besides, she was reminded, she was due for a pass day…just in case she couldn't get back to civilization by morning. In other words, she was going on the books as taking the rest of the day off…and possibly tomorrow as well.

Her second call was to Moody's Tow Service. But Moody was already swamped with calls to drag people out of ditches; and, besides, she was too far away for him to waste his time coming after her unless it was an emergency. Her third call was to home to tell them she was stuck at the camp and wouldn't be home for the night. Her mother assured Kelly she'd take good care of Angel.

She unzipped her jacket and rattled one of the bags on the table. "Some of this stuff is perishable. You might want to get it in the fridge."

"Yes ma'am," Dane said, looking way too pleased as he strode toward the bags of supplies.

"You should have given me your satellite phone number," she groused, needing to be anywhere but stuck in a cabin with the only man in the world she wanted.

"I know," he said, hefting two gallons of milk into the fridge with one hand. Damn him and his big, strong, skilled hands.

She pivoted away from him, went to the window overlooking the driveway and their two mired vehicles. Andi Johanson lived just a mile away. Her truck might not have the power to pull her buried truck from the ditch. But she should be able to drag the SUV around so it at least pointed down the road instead of across it. If she took it slow, she could handle the slippery track out to the highway. At least she wouldn't be trapped in the cabin with Dane.

She punched in Andi's number and got her answering machine. "Andi. It's Kelly. Call me when you get this," she said and supplied her phone number.

"That eager to get away from me, Bright Eyes?"

The fingers on her free hand balled up and those still holding the receiver tightened on it. Most definitely she was eager to get away from him, not that she was going to admit it to him.

She faced him. "I've got better things to do than sit out a storm out here with you."

He stood beside the fridge, a carton of eggs in his mitt of a hand. Why did she have to keep noticing his hands—remembering how they felt moving over her body?

"Good weather for poaching?" he asked, sounding far too smug.

"There're always fender-benders in this sort of weather. The troopers can use all the help they can get sorting them out. And power outages. Maybe even someone lost out in this."

He sobered, set the eggs on a wire shelf and closed the fridge door, murmuring, "Someone who needs your help more than a dumb ass actor who doesn't know his way around a snowstorm."

"Dammit, Dane. I need to be out there helping."

"Out there, or just anywhere but here with me?"

She paced the length of the cabin away from him. Bad choice as she ended up staring at the double bunks, particularly the lower one where they'd made glorious love. Three strides away from the beds and she was in front of the fireplace. It blasted her with heat, making her want to remove her jacket and hat—to curl up in front of its fire and doze off in the arms of...

She tore the cap from her head and strode to the hooks by the door, grousing, "I told you the wood stove would heat the cabin more efficiently."

"I thought a fire in the fireplace was more romantic," he said, giving her a mischievous half-grin.

#

She paced the cabin like a caged animal. She hadn't found his remark about a romantic fire amusing. So much for ice-breakers. Not a good lead into asking her questions—pushing her for answers.

Mid-afternoon, she climbed into the upper bunk and fell asleep. At least Dane assumed Kelly slept. He couldn't hear anything what with how the wind rattled the rafters and the icy snow pelted the windows. He knew only that he wanted to climb up in that bunk and wrap his body around hers and hold her until her rage drained away.

He thought his frying chicken would bring her down for supper. But it didn't.

Come nightfall, he closed the dampers on the fireplace, added a couple logs to the wood stove and climbed into his own bunk. Sleep was slow to come, though, given how the angry energy she'd brought into the cabin still crackled through the air. It didn't help, either, that she was just one thin mattress beyond his reach.

Sometime during the night, he woke to find her silhouetted in the open door of the wood stove as she added a couple logs. She was still dressed in her fatigues, though her shirt hung open over her insulated underwear.

She shuffled, stocking-footed into the kitchen and opened the refrigerator door where she stood chowing down a piece of chicken and drinking milk from the carton.

He smiled to himself. It was the sort of thing he and his brothers did. His mother had always scolded them for it. He wanted to tell her that. Two summers ago, the words would have come easy because she'd been so easy to talk to.

But now… Something told him to stay quiet and leave her to own devices.

#

Dane next woke to the smell of coffee, crawled out of his tangled sheets, and shuffled into the kitchen. She gave his long john clad body a once-over.

"You couldn't put something more decent on, St. John?"

"You've seen me in a lot less," he muttered as he snagged a mug from the cupboard, immediately regretting his words. His morning grumpiness was not conducive to conversation, especially not the kind he needed to have with her.

She took her mug to the couch where she curled up in

front of the wood stove. He cooked enough bacon and eggs for the two of them, unable to remember a time he woke at her side grumpy.

"Breakfast's on," he said, setting two plates on the table.

"Not hungry," she replied.

He sighed. "Don't tell me. You like your eggs cold and in the middle of the night, too."

Her head snapped in his direction. So now she knew her nighttime foray hadn't gone unnoticed.

She came to the kitchen table, picked up her plate, and returned to the couch where she ate. He ate his breakfast staring at the back of her head, not at all what he'd intended when he'd placed her dish across the table from his.

Not at all what he'd envisioned when he'd thought the storm and her truck getting stuck was divine intervention.

When she brought her empty plate and the kettle of hot water off the wood stove to the sink, he said, "This isn't good for you."

"Too much cholesterol?" she quipped without humor in clear reference to the eggs and bacon.

"I'm talking about all this tension," he said, moving to her side and adding his plate to hers in the sink, determined to get some sort of dialogue going between them.

She stoppered the drain and poured the hot water over a squirt of dish detergent.

"Kel, this anger isn't healthy for you."

"My health is none of your concern," she said, pumping cool water into the steaming suds.

"I care about you," Dane said, holding his ground even as she elbowed him aside for the dishrag.

"You aren't the same Kelly I—" He hesitated, not sure saying *fell in love with* wouldn't send her running out into the storm. "You're not the same Kelly I came to know two summers ago."

"Get used to it. This is the Kelly I am now," she muttered, seemingly focused on the dishrag she slopped in the sink.

"I don't buy that for a minute."

She slapped the dripping dishrag into his hands and strode back to the couch. Tossing aside the rag, he followed her.

"Talk to me, Kel."

She hugged her knees up against her chest. "If you don't leave me alone, I swear I'll go out in that storm and walk back to town."

Sighing, he returned to the kitchen sink. Silently, he cleaned their breakfast dishes.

Selecting a faded tome from the bookshelf under the window between the cook stove and wood stove, he joined her on the couch. She glowered at him. He held up the book. "Not much light by your dad's recliner."

Come lunch, she made two ham sandwiches and returned to the couch, muttering, "Yours is on the table."

Likewise, she ate her spaghetti supper on the couch. The tension wasn't proving any too healthy for him, either, given the tightness pulling across his shoulders. This time, when she brought her dirty dish to the sink, he stayed at the table but he didn't stay quiet.

"This is a small cabin, Kel. We can't avoid each other."

Without so much as a glance his way, she returned, "But we don't have to talk to each other." And headed toward the far end of the couch.

He cursed, rose, and went to the sink. The wood stove door creaked open. She was fueling the fire.

In more ways than she knew, Dane thought, pumping cold water over their dishes because, if he went to the wood stove right now for the pot of hot water, he wasn't sure he wouldn't take her in his arms and try kissing her attitude away.

The scrape of chair legs brought him around to the dining table to find her sitting in the chair nearest the door pulling on her boots.

"You can't go out in this weather," he said, sounding far more Neanderthal man than he intended.

Her head came up, her shoulders rigid.

"I didn't mean it the way it sounded," he said, taking a step toward her. "If it takes me not talking to keep you from going out in that storm, then I'll shut up."

She tied off her boot laces and rose without looking at him. "There's that ego of yours again, St. John. Still thinking this is all about you."

He skirted the table toward her. She threw on her jacket. He caught her by the arm.

"If it's not about me, then why won't you talk to me?"

She blinked up at him, surprise and anguish flashing across her eyes before she pulled up her CO cloak. "Jeese, St. John. I'm just going out to get more firewood."

Bewildered by what he'd seen in her eyes, his fingers were slow to release her. "I'll go with you."

"Don't need the help," she said, zipping up her jacket.

A blast of icy air hit him and she was gone, the door shut between them. She was independent. He knew that. She was sensitive about men seeing her as weak, at least her father and her fellow COs.

He moved from window to window, watching her plow through knee deep snow as she made her way around the cabin toward the shed, head lowered against the driving snow, pausing now and then and huddling against the wind. The hell she didn't need his help

He pulled his jeans on over his long johns, cinched his boots tight above his ankles, threw on his jacket, cap, and gloves and went after her. By the time he got to her, she was fighting to tug a toboggan full of firewood from the shed.

Reaching around her, he grabbed the rope handle and reefed the sled from the shed. She went down in the snow on her back.

"What the hell," she shouted, slapping away his hand as he reached for hers. "I told you I didn't need help."

"The hell you don't," he shouted back, hauling her to her feet in spite of her fighting him. "Now grab the rope and help me."

Even with the two of them, it took longer than expected to drag the heavy toboggan to the cabin door. Arms loaded with wood, they stumbled into the cabin to the wood bin where they collapsed, winded by their efforts.

"What…were…you…thinking," Dane panted out, "trying to haul a toboggan full of wood from the shed?"

"That…I…didn't want…to make the trip…twice," she managed to answer.

There'd been a time when he would have laughed at her stubbornness. But that was back when she'd have laughed with him.

With the snow melting into his jeans and the sweat seeping out through his insulated underwear, he shivered. "We better get out of these wet clothes."

"Speak for yourself, St. John," she said, climbing to her feet and giving his legs a pointed look. "I wasn't dumb enough to go out in this snow wearing only jeans."

"Those top-of-the-line DNR duds of yours keep you dry inside and out?" he asked, standing.

"Of course," she said, hanging up her jacket by the door.

He joined her at the table where they sat on kitchen chairs removing their boots. "So that's not a sweat staining back of your shirt?"

Ignoring the scowl she lifted at him, he dropped his boots on the boot tray, hung up his jacket, and headed to the bench at the foot of the bunks. By now, his jeans were sodden and removing them a chore.

"I could use some help here," he said, giving her what he thought was a plaintive look as she rounded the near end of the couch.

"That's lame even for you, St. John."

"It wasn't meant as a come-on," he said, weary of her undeserved disdain. "I was simply asking for help. Some of us aren't afraid to do that."

He wrangled the wet jeans off along with his soaked long johns, leaving them in a pile on the floor while he dug a pair of sweats from his duffle on top the dresser. Insulated top exchanged for a fresh sweatshirt, he hung his wet clothes on the fireplace mantle and built a fire in the fireplace.

He turned and caught her studying him. "I'll pay for the extra wood the fireplace eats up."

"Of course you will," she said, all curled up in her corner of the couch pretending her sweaty t-shirt wasn't growing colder by the minute, which he was certain it was.

He stalked into the kitchen end of the cabin where he poured milk and cocoa mix into a pot on the range. He stirred the mixture, thinking he should treat her the way she'd been treating him.

His shoulders hurt and his neck was stiff. Hell, he was renting this place and he couldn't even relax.

Tendrils of steam rose from the cocoa. He turned off the burner, frowning at the mix. He'd made enough for two. He should have made only enough for himself if he was going to play her game.

He filled two mugs and carried them to the couch. He held one out to her.

"No, thank you," she said, arms wrapped tightly around her torso.

He plunked the mug down on the coffee table in front of her and sat on the far end of the couch, feet propped on the table, his wool socks soaking in the heat from the fireplace. The first sip of his cocoa scalded his upper lip.

He cursed under his breath. He couldn't even drink cocoa around her without getting burned.

On the other end of the couch, Kelly shivered.

He scowled at her. "You sure you and Frank aren't blood kin?"

She blinked at him, eyes widening in confusion. "What?"

"You are as stubborn as he is. If I didn't know better, I'd

swear you were his daughter."

Her cheeks turned red. "I—what?"

"You're sitting there in wet clothes, shivering. If you don't still have some old clothes of your own in the dresser to change into—" The memory of the spread eagle tee she'd taken from that dresser and worn that one time she rode him to oblivion flashed through his mind, making his chest ache. "—at least put on one of my t-shirts and a pair of my sweats."

"Don't tell me what to do," she growled, the effect lost when her teeth chattered.

He slammed his mug down on the table and rose to his feet. "If you don't get yourself out of those wet clothes, Kelly, then I'm taking you out of them."

She jumped to her feet. "We're not lovers anymore, St. John. You don't get to see the goods."

"Is that your problem? You think I'm looking for a cheap peek?"

Her chin swept the air between them.

"You want me to step outside while you change?"

Her brow puckered and she shook her head. "Just turn your back. And keep it turned."

## CHAPTER FIFTEEN

He lay in his bunk, staring up at that thin mattress separating him from Kelly. She turned over, the bed springs above him creaking. It had been like that all night, her tossing and turning, him listening to her restlessness—staring into the darkness, at a loss as to what more he could do after their row.

And time was running out. The abating wind told him the storm was dying down and the grayness filling the windows marked a new day.

All he'd come up with through his sleepless night was her obstinacy had begun to remind him of how she'd treated him when she'd first met him—when she'd thought him no more than a Hollywood actor.

But it didn't fit. She knew him better. She had to.

"What happened with us, Kel?" he asked.

No answer. But her sudden stillness told him she'd heard him.

"Everything seemed good and then you stopped responding to my texts and emails. Why?"

Still no answer.

"I thought we'd built at least a friendship," he said

"Friendship?" She harrumphed. "More like friends with benefits."

"Is this really about sex? Is that what's wrong?"

No answer.

"Okay. We started out with an amazing attraction to each other. We started out with sex. But I thought there was also friendship."

Silence.

"I told you things I hadn't felt free to talk about with anyone outside my family. I trusted you with my private thoughts and you seemed to trust me with yours."

More silence.

"I really thought we were building something more through our correspondence."

She remained silent.

"Did I write something that hurt your feelings?"

Still no answer from the top bunk.

"If I wrote or said or did something wrong, tell me. Give me an opportunity to make things right between us."

"There is no *us*."

Her words were like a knife to his heart. "I guess the joke is on me, then. I thought there could have been. Thought there might have been some spark between us we might have built on."

"The spark was lust," she said, her tone almost harsh.

"If you believe that's all it was, why are you so upset with me?"

No answer.

"If sex is all there was between us… Is it because I didn't keep the relationship at a sexual level? Are you angry because I didn't jump your bones the moment I saw you? I wanted to. But—"

"But what?" Kelly shot back, forcing a hard edge into her voice. "Were you afraid I'd reject you, wound your ego?"

"You'd already rejected me. You rejected me when you stopped answering my emails."

The pain in his voice sliced through her. She badly wanted to reassure him he'd done nothing wrong, that she died a little with his every observation, his every plea. But she couldn't let herself feel for him. Because to feel for him was to set herself up for an even bigger hurt than the one she already suffered.

*Because*, if he found out Angel was his and she hadn't told him, he'd never forgive her. Or worse. He'd fight her for custody, maybe even take Angel away. She had to stop his probing, and if it took giving him some ridiculous reason for how she was reacting to him then she'd do it.

She swung down from her bunk under the guise of adding a log to the fire, flinging words at him. "What do you expect from me, Dane? I see you on screen making love. Those scenes look pretty damn real to me."

She turned to find him standing beside the bed, all bronze and gloriously naked in the firelight. In that instant, everything that magnificent body had ever done to her, everything good he'd ever made her feel slammed through her.

"They're supposed to look real, Kel," he said. "That's why it's called acting."

Tearing her gaze from him, she slammed the wood stove door shut. "I suppose you're going to tell me you were thinking of me all through those scenes."

"Actually, I couldn't," he said, taking a step toward her.

She turned away from him and headed for the kitchen end of the cabin before he could reach her—touch her. One touch and her resolve would crumble. But his voice kept pace with her steps.

"Whenever I'd think of you, the acting stopped because my body took over. That doesn't work for movie-making. When making love for a movie, an actor has to be aware of where the camera is and how the lighting is hitting him."

She yanked open a cupboard door, silently begging him to stop. But he kept talking—crowding her.

"The actor has to remember his angles. All that posing is for the audience."

She turned to the sink. He turned with her.

"And let's not forget the fact you're doing all these bedroom gymnastics on a soundstage full of cameramen, grips, make-up artists, hair-stylists, producers...a whole phalanx of people."

She pumped water into the glass she held, her hand shaking so badly the water spilled over her hand.

"Then there's the director yelling "cut" at moments an audience would find quite frustrating," he hammered on. "Not to mention the numerous reshoots to get the shot from a dozen different angles."

Leaving the glass in the bottom of the sink, she

wheeled at him. "Tough job, huh?"

"Dammit, Kel. When you and I were making love, do you think I could have stopped just because someone yelled cut?"

"There was that time Max interrupted us," she leveled as her heart was breaking.

"You were the one who stopped then," he said, moving closer, trapping her between the edge of the counter and him. "If you recall, even with that interruption, it took a while for my body to *settle down*."

She remembered all right. Her body still thrilled with the memory—itched for want to return to that day.

*Not for you, not if you want to spare yourself a whole lot more hurt.*

*Not if you want to free him.*

And there was yet another reason to make him give up on her…to set *him* free

She lifted her CO face at him. "You telling me in all that time we were apart you didn't once have sex with another woman?"

She saw the answer before he even spoke the words. Saw it in the way his shoulders dropped. Saw it in how he sank back on his heels. She wanted to weep.

"I hadn't gotten an email from you in over a month," he grumbled. "We'd gone from production of movie two to three without a break. I hadn't seen you in nearly a year."

She managed a contemptuous snort that was Academy Award worthy. "And of course making it with that other woman meant nothing."

His head lifted through the gray light coming in through the window, the hinge of his jaw popping. "It wasn't *making love*."

"And how often did you have to experience this meaningless sex?"

"Just that once. It was enough to show me another woman couldn't take your place."

She wanted to believe him. *Hell*, she did believe him. But this whole charade was about giving him a reason why there could be no *us*. To make him move on and not just for hers and Angel's sake.

Before she could slap him with another jealous sound bite, though, he shot a zinger of his own.

"What about you, Kel? Did you honor that unspoken commitment you seem to think we made?"

It cut deep to have the tables turned. But she'd pushed him there.

"Of course you did," he said, not waiting for her answer. "You weren't the one isolated from family and friends—stuck on a—"

"Movie set acting out love scenes?" she finished for him, her disdainful tone mean to push him away.

Instead, he stepped forward—pressed himself into her. "Feel that?"

She sucked a breath before she could stop herself.

"*That's* the real deal. *That* never happened on a movie set in any of those love scenes, which, by the way, there's only one of in each movie."

He stepped her—released back, and paced a half-circle away from her. "A hundred action scenes per movie and you fixate on the one and only love scene."

He faced her. "If we're going to have a chance together, Kel, you can't get jealous every time I kiss a woman in a film. It's part of my job. I'm still on that bloody Sexiest Man of the year list! Audiences want to see me doing romantic things. They want me to take my shirt off. They want me to kiss the girl."

*If we're going to have a chance together* echoed his words inside her skull.

Her heart shattered into a million pieces because she knew any chance they had to be together she'd destroyed by her lies—shattered that he still fought for what could never be. She shook her head when all she wanted to do was throw herself into his arms.

"There is no *us*. There never was," she managed to huff out.

"The hell there wasn't," he shot back. "From the moment you dabbed anti-sting sticks on my wasp bites, I started thinking there could be an *us*."

He shook his head. "All those long talks, the unspoken words in our kisses. I *wanted* them to mean more than what we shared in those moments. That's what I was working to find out before you stopped answering my emails—to see if we had more than wild chemistry going for us."

"The hell you did," she said, advancing on him, trying for all she was worth to cut off his offensive. "You wanted to get into my pants that day you got stung and you want the same thing now."

He shook his head, backing from her. "Kel, no."

She kept advancing, driving him back from her. "You want sex? You got it."

"That's not what I'm asking for."

She backed him through the cabin between the dining table and couch, all but purring, "You don't want me?"

"I want you more than breath itself, Kel. But not like this."

She peeled off her tee, bared her breasts to him. "How about like this?"

He groaned, the backs of his knees clipping the edge of the bed. "Kel, don't."

She slid her panties down her legs and stepped out of them toward him. "How about like this?"

"Geez, Kel. It's not about the sex, not for me."

"Maybe it *is* for me," she said, reason telling her she'd pushed him far enough, something else entirely making her reach down between them and close her fingers around his arousal.

He pulled in a breath. She yanked open the dresser drawer at her hip, the fingers of her free hand easily finding what they sought.

*What the hell did she think she was doing?*

He stroked her cheek, softly, gently, and shook his head.

Damn him for still caring—still being the man she wanted.

Taking a corner of the foil wrap between her teeth, she tore open the packet and held up the condom. "Shall I do the honors?"

"Kel, please."

"That's what I thought," she said, purposely misunderstanding him and pushing him back onto the bed. Faster than she could have believed herself capable, she sheathed and mounted him.

He groaned and caught her around the waist. Maybe he would push her away. He had every right to do so. She wasn't sure which she wanted him to do.

He circled his pelvis beneath her, and the reasons she'd pushed him to this point no longer mattered. Worse, she knew she would never stop wanting him and there was no way to keep him, not given how she'd lied to him.

Taking his mouth with hers, she silenced any words he'd have spoken—swallowed every moan he made, making the latter part of herself. And she rode him hard, memorizing the sensation each stroke sent through her body, memorizing the way his hands moved over her skin.

They came together in an explosive orgasm as the cabin filled with the golden light of a new day. She collapsed on top of him, their bodies wet with sweat, her face with tears because, even though the storm had passed, the issue of Angel still spread between them like a chasm.

"Ah, Kel," he murmured, hugging her to him.

She pressed her face into his shaggy hair, blotting her tears, fighting the pain the sad, gentle way he spoke her name caused her. For all her efforts, he still hadn't given up on *them.*

She rolled off him to the edge of the bed where she snagged her panties and tee off the floor, a coldness schooled into her voice. "Nice to see you can still get the job done, St. John."

Instantly, he was on his hip at her side. "That wasn't

just about sex for you, Bright Eyes."

She tugged the tee down over her head, fighting back the lump climbing into her throat. "Jeese, St. John. Get a grip on that ego of yours."

"Kel—"

"I've got no complaints," she said, standing and pulling up her panties.

"That was angry sex. Why?"

"Angry sex. Happy sex," she said with a flippancy she hoped hid her pain as she donned her fatigues. "Does it really make a difference?"

He climbed from the bed and followed her to the dining table where she sat, pulling on her boots. "It does if you're angry with me."

"There you go again, thinking it's all about you," she said, threading her arms into the sleeves of her jacket and turning to the door. "Get over it."

She closed her fingers around the doorknob.

His arm shot past her head, his hand flattening against the door, holding it shut. "Where are you going?"

"To dig myself out of the ditch," she muttered. "Let go of the door."

"Not until you tell me why you're angry with me."

"You preventing me from leaving is making me angry," she said through teeth clenched against the tears that wanted to fall.

She jerked at the door. He pressed harder.

"What did I do that hurt you so badly you'd throw *us* away?"

Heaven help her, she couldn't bear his pleading—couldn't bear him thinking her pain was his fault.

"You did nothing to hurt me," she growled to cover the huskiness of raw emotion in her voice.

"It can't be because I stopped corresponding, because I didn't," he said, through gnashing teeth. "You're the one who stopped writing."

His hand shifted from the door. She took advantage of it, reefed open the door, and escaped. Behind her, the door shut beneath the sound of a hand slamming into it.

Guilt twisted through her, but she didn't stop. She couldn't risk him wearing her down to the point that she confessed everything to him—couldn't face his reaction to learning Angel was his—his reaction to her lying to him....his rejecting them both.

She plowed through thigh deep snow to her truck, retrieved a shovel from the back, and went to where his SUV blocked the road. She hadn't cleared more than half a tire when he appeared at her side, a shovel in his hand and a soul deep pain in his eyes.

"If you're so damned determined to get away from me," he said, his voice husky, "the least I can do is help you get on your way."

Then he began to dig and she died a little more inside.

#

The sun was nearing its apex when Andi Johanson came pushing a path up the driveway through the snow. She stopped well short of the SUV, stepped out of her truck, and shook her head at the vehicle sitting crossways in the road.

"Looks like you need more than plowing out here," the lanky woman called.

Kelly planted her shovel in the snow, climbed the bank next to the truck she and Dane now worked at digging out, and joined Andi. Beyond suggesting a break to warm up, Kelly hadn't said anything to him since leaving the cabin. Even inside earlier warming themselves by the woodstove, the only talking she did was on the call to Andi, warning her the road was blocked and to not come up the camp road blazing guns.

Andi retrieved tow chains from the bed of her truck and Kelly crawled under the SUV and attached them. If he thought he'd be welcome, he'd have offered his help. But she'd made it clear she wanted nothing from him. So he returned to shoveling out the truck which, once freed, she'd use to drive out of his life.

With a little horse power from Andi's truck and Kelly's steering, they had the SUV straightened out. Dane sprinted over and disconnected the tow chains.

With a wave, Andi backed down the road, dragging her blade to give the SUV a clear path. When Kelly drove off with the SUV, it struck him she may not park it out of the way on the county road but keep going. The possibility tore at his gut.

Andi came back up the road, widening the path and pushing the snow past him and the cabin. She backed up, angled her truck toward Kelly's, dropped her blade, and dragged back the snow her pass had deposited.

"I'll turn her around so we got the best pulling angle," she called through her open window.

Heart aching, he nodded, crawled under the DNR truck, and attached the tow chains. When he emerged, Kelly was hoofing it up the road toward them and his heart skipped a beat. She hadn't left.

Not yet.

The three of them wedged boards under the tires giving the vehicle the best chance for grip and dusted the ground with wood ash for extra traction. Andi climbed into her truck and Kelly climbed into hers. He added his weight to the bed of Andi's truck, positioning himself over one of the rear tires. It wasn't much, but it beat standing beside the cabin just watching.

It took far fewer attempts to drag Kelly's truck from the ditch than it had taken him to lose her. While Andi stashed her tow chains, Dane watched Kelly drive off. By the time Andi climbed back into her truck, Dane had accepted Kelly wasn't coming back.

## CHAPTER SIXTEEN

Andi finished pushing snow back from the front of the cabin and Dane sent her on her way, shoveling what snow the plow couldn't reach away from the cabin. He needed physical work to distract him from the loss burrowing a hole his chest.

And when there was no more to shovel—when he realized he was drenched in sweat in spite of having tossed off his jacket, he went inside. He built a fire in the fireplace, shrugged off his wool shirt, and peeled off his tee. He was slipping a fresh tee on over his head when he felt a blast of cold air.

His head clearing the neck-hole of the tee, he found Kelly standing just inside the open door, her jacket unzipped, her gloves bunched in one hand, her eyes wet.

"You get stuck again?" he asked.

She shook her head and closed the door behind her.

"You forget something?"

She looked away, strode to the kitchen table, and fingered the back of the nearest chair, her voice, when she spoke quiet. "I guess you could say that."

This wasn't the same woman who'd silently dug out a truck and an SUV with him. This wasn't even the same woman who'd made mad, mindless sex with him mere hours go. Something had changed.

"There's something I need to tell you, Dane," she said in a tight voice.

Was she finally going to admit she was mad at him—reveal the reason why? He held his breath.

She glanced at him ever so briefly as though she couldn't bear to look too long upon him. "Something I should have told you a long time ago."

Suddenly, he was afraid of what she was about to confess.

"I've been keeping a secret from you, Dane."

"Is there someone else?" he asked, his mouth going dry.

A small sound escaped her, a cross between a laugh and a groan, and she shook her head.

His breath balled up in his chest. "Is it something medical? A...terminal illness?"

Her head snapped up at him. "No. Nothing like that."

He expelled the breath he'd been holding. "Just tell me there's still an *us*, Bright Eyes, and I can bear anything."

#

Kelly winced. There was the rub.

She'd gotten halfway to the highway before she knew she'd never outdistance that pained look he'd worn all the while he shoveled snow beside her—before she accepted that she couldn't leave him with that much hurt. He'd done nothing to deserve it. The onus was all on her.

Kelly closed her eyes as if closing off everything that was breaking inside her could be so easily denied, and she whispered, "I wish I could tell you that."

"What the hell did I do to fail you, Kel?"

"You did nothing wrong." She opened her eyes and looked at him. "What I'm trying to tell you, Dane, is *I* haven't been honest with you."

His brow puckered. "So, be honest with me now."

"I want to be. But I'm afraid."

He came to her and took her by the shoulders. "If there's anything you should know about me after those ten days we had together, Bright Eyes, it's that you can tell me anything."

She stood stiffly within his embrace, afraid to accept its comfort. "And if there's anything you should know about me by now, Dane, it's that I'm a suspicious person by nature. Always looking for the lie in others."

He tugged her closer, his thumbs stroking the crests of her shoulders. "Goes with being a CO, no?"

"It's an asset I use to do my job," she said, dying a little inside, knowing he'd surely never touch her with such affection again once he knew what she'd withheld from him. "A habit that's hard to turn off when I'm not on duty."

He frowned. "Is this about my being an actor? Are you afraid I use my acting even when I'm not working?"

She winced. "No. I've come to realize you differentiate between your job and the real world far better than I do. You are, as you once said of me, the real deal."

Confusion pulled at his mouth, at the corners of his eyes, and pinched a groove above the bridge of his nose.

"I'm not as real a deal as you think I am," Kelly said quietly.

His eyes narrowed at her. "I don't understand."

"I've kept a secret from you." She swallowed hard and forced herself to look him in the eye. "Angel isn't my niece. She's my daughter."

He blinked. She could almost see the calculating in his eyes—the adding up of months since that night they made love without protection and coming up with Angel's age.

"Yes," she said before he could even ask the question. "Angel is your daughter."

A myriad of emotions pulsed in his eyes, before settling on anger. His hands fell away from her and he backed away from her, his voice a hoarse whisper. "Angel is mine?"

"I don't expect anything from you," she said.

*Just your forgiveness, your acceptance, your love.*

*"You don't expect anything from me?"* Each enunciated syllable of his words struck her like buckshot. "Is that what you think, Kel, that I wouldn't want anything to do with my own—" the harshness of his voice gave way to a choked "—daughter?"

"I'm sorry. I didn't—"

"You had to know how I felt about family. I talked enough about mine. I wrote you endlessly about them all the time. And your family—"

He stopped short, his brow puckering a new emotion, one more akin to bafflement. "Your parents, do they know she's mine?"

"Yes."

"And your sister, playing along when I talked to her like Angel was hers. How could they not tell me she was mine?"

"They wanted to."

"Then why didn't they?" he all but howled.

She jumped. "They were trying to protect me."

"What about Angel? Didn't any of you think she had a right to know me—her father?"

"It's not that simple," she said. "I'd just found out I was pregnant when my father had his stroke and everything went crazy."

"There's nothing in this world that could have happened to merit not telling me I was her father, that... that little girl was—" Tears turned Dane's famous blue eyes liquid and when he finished, the words came out thick and husky. "—*is* mine."

He paced a circle between her and the cabinets. "I should have figured it out," he muttered. "Her age. Her eyes. That she was always at your house. The awkward moments with your sister. Your mother getting all nerved up the first time I showed up—when I asked to pick up Angel."

He ran his hands through his hair. "Her name!"

He stopped pacing and looked her hard in the eye. "Angel after Angel Point...where she was conceived. You named her the way my parents named me and my siblings."

His hands tightened into fists. His whole body shook. He spun away from her, and with one sweep of his arm, cleared the table of condiments and the ever present cribbage board and cards.

Then he grabbed his jacket and slammed the door shut behind him.

And she was left staring at the space where he had stood as she'd told him the extent to which she'd deceived him—where the man she loved had wept and railed. She had broken his heart.

For the first time in her life, Kelly realized she didn't truly know what a broken heart was until that moment.

When it finally registered with her that he'd driven away—that his destination could be no other than her parents' home—and Angel, she bolted out the door to her truck and went after him.

Fear sent her slipping down the narrow road off the bluff. Fear sent her skidding around an icy bend in the county road. Fear pressed her foot down on the accelerator, speeding her along the slippery highway. He must be trucking along himself because she hit town without catching up to him.

#

He didn't even knock. He just charged into the house and through the kitchen to the playpen in the sunny corner of the dining room.

"What's wrong?" her mom asked, having followed him from the kitchen.

He turned on her. "Where is she?"

"Kelly?"

"Angel."

A sound came out of Frank like a cry from the bowls of hell. Her mother backed toward the second floor stairway, keeping herself between him and the stairs.

"She's napping," she said.

He brushed past her, taking the stairs two and three at a time, not stopping until he was at the side of the crib in Kelly's room.

The baby was sleeping, all sweet innocence. He knew he should leave her be. But he needed to hold his daughter.

*His* daughter.

Carefully, he slipped his hands under her and lifted her. She stirred, blinked at him—blinked those St. John Blue eyes.

He hugged her against his chest—into the nest his open jacket created. She settled her head against his shoulder and tucked her tiny fist under his chin.

*His daughter. His Angel.*

"I'm your daddy," he said on an awed whisper.

Then hummed to her, rocked her side-to-side until her breath against his neck evened out and he knew she was once more asleep. Still, he didn't stop rocking her—holding her to him like the precious being she was. He'd missed nine months of her life. How many firsts in that time had he missed?

Her birth, of course. And the first time she opened those blue eyes.

The first time she rolled over. The first time she sat up.

Her first smile.

His legs went weak as though all the hurt and anger…and love…bearing down on him were more than they could hold. He made it to the rocker where he lowered himself as gently as he could so as not to jar Angel from her sleep. If it were within his power, he'd make sure her every nap, her every night's sleep would be as peaceful as this one. But that wasn't reality. Even he, with his charmed life, had managed only thirty-two blissful years.

#

She parked across the end of the driveway, blocking his SUV. He'd have to plow through the DNR truck to escape with her daughter.

She charged through the back door and the dining-living room. Her father was on his feet in front of his chair, his cane shaking under his grip. Her mother stood at the base of the stairway looking stricken.

"He knows, doesn't he?" her mother said as Kelly dashed past.

She wasn't sure what to expect when she stepped into the open doorway of her bedroom. Dane stuffing diapers into the diaper bag, wrapping her daughter up in blankets to take her away from her? A raging bull of a man?

She wasn't prepared to find Dane in the rocker hugging a dozing Angel against his chest, tears streaming down his cheeks, murmuring, "I'm your daddy."

"I'm sorry," she said in a voice barely more than a whisper.

"You should be," he said without looking up at her, his voice ominously low.

"I shouldn't have kept her a secret from you."

"No, you shouldn't have."

"I made a mistake."

"Yes, you did."

She swallowed hard. "Now what happens?"

He lifted angry eyes at her, his mouth tight. "Maybe I take her away from you for the next nine months. How'd you feel about that?"

Though not unexpected, his words hit her like an avalanche, knocking her back a step. She grabbed the frame of the door to steady herself. Angel stirred—fussed as though sensing the tension mounting around her. She lifted her head from Dane's shoulder.

"Hush," he cooed, one large, protective hand cupping the back of her head. "Hush, my little Angel."

Angel's tiny fingers curled over Dane's bottom lip. All curious little girl once more, distracted from the drama unfolding around her. When Dane gazed over his daughter's head at Kelly, a deep sadness lined his brow and crimped the edges of his anger-filled eyes. Kelly held her breath.

"But I wouldn't do that," he said. "I wouldn't take her away from her mother."

Kelly let out the breath she'd been holding. "Thank you."

"Not for your sake," he whispered almost harshly and dipped his chin at Angel. "For hers."

"Of course." Drained, Kelly moved to the side of the bed closest to the rocker and sat. "Everything we do from here on out has to be in her best interest."

"And it starts this minute," he said.

"Okay."

"It starts with me getting the time to bond with her."

"Okay."

"That means I won't be leaving her side."

"For how long?"

The lines in his forehead and around his mouth deepened and his voice rose. "As long as I see fit."

Kelly flinched. Angel's babbling took on a clipped, anxious note and she patted his lips with her tiny fingers. He brushed his lips against her brow, murmuring, "It's okay, my sweet Angel."

When he spoke again to Kelly, it was in a quiet, but determined voice. "I'll be staying the night in my daughter's room."

"But it's my room, too," Kelly said, struggling to keep her voice composed for Angel's sake.

His response came through tight lips. "Then be prepared to share that bed you're sitting on because I'll be sleeping in it."

#

She'd said she'd bunk with Carrie. That Kelly would rather share her sister's bed than one with him rankled him. Though why he couldn't fathom, not when he was madder at Kelly than he'd ever been with anyone in his life.

Besides, he had a daughter to think about.

A daughter.

His.

A sweet girl who gurgled away in the loop of his arms, her tiny fingers and hands exploring his ears, his nose, the buttons on his shirt. *His* daughter. He had so much to think about, so much to plan. His mind reeled.

Angel, on the other hand, had her own agenda. She wanted down. And when he didn't put her down, she squirmed and fussed.

From where she sat on the bed, an ever present sentry, Kelly said, "After her nap, she usually goes downstairs to play."

But he wasn't ready to share her and his words came out more peevish than he intended. "The rest of you have had her to yourselves for nine months. It's my turn now."

Kelly got up from the bed and walked out of the room. What the hell was she going to do, enlist the aid of her father? Frank couldn't even climb the stairs.

A twinge of guilt twisted through his gut. He knew how much Frank doted on his granddaughter. He knew he was denying Frank by not letting Angel play downstairs. But his emotions were too raw, his hurt too new. And he hurt like he never thought he could.

He should call Dixie or his mother or even Tess. A woman would know what to advise him to do at this moment.

Except he wasn't sure he wanted any advice right now. He just wanted his daughter...who was squirming to get out of his arms.

He eyed the braided rug in front of her crib and wondered if it was soft enough—sanitary enough for her to play on. Before he had to decide, though, Kelly reappeared in the doorway, a bundle in her arms that looked like a lumpy, mini comforter. When she spread it on the floor, he saw what the lumps were. Toys.

Without a word, without trying to take Angel from him and put her down amidst her toys, Kelly turned and left. She was giving him the space to be alone with his daughter as he'd demanded.

His first instinct was to thank her, but he was still too angry with her.

So he sat on the floor, his back to the doorframe where he watched Angel kick her little legs—where he could readily head off any crawling explorations into the hall leading to the stairway. Or he lay on his belly beside her, the two of them playing with soft puzzle toys that stimulated little minds.

Come suppertime, much as he wanted to keep her to himself, he joined the family at the kitchen table, taking the seat next to Angel's highchair, the seat her mother no doubt usually occupied. No one argued the point with him. Kelly even refused her mother's offer to change places with her so she could sit on the other side of the highchair.

She really was trying to give him his space with his daughter. She even silenced her family after a barrage of "You're feeding her too fast," and "That needs to be mashed more," and "Wipe her chin." She even stood guard in the bathroom doorway against her mother when he insisted on bathing Angel.

But Kelly watched over them, her only comment referencing her refusal to leave a quiet, "In her best interest."

Not that he was going to give Kelly any breaks. Not yet. But he was grateful for the back-up. Angel was a leave-no-prisoner-dry bather. As he dried her on Kelly's bed, wondering over her tiny, perfect toes and dimpled kneecaps, Kelly brought him one of her father's t-shirts.

"Thought you could use a dry one," she said.

He accepted it with a nod, not yet ready to even talk to her.

Even when he diapered Angel and picked her up only to have the diaper fall off, he said nothing as Kelly showed him how to diaper the baby properly. Having successfully dressed her in her pink onesy pajamas for the night, he glanced toward the doorway where he expected to see Kelly overseeing everything. But the doorway was empty. Only then did he realize he had a smile on his face.

Had he really been looking for Kelly's approval?

He shook off the sentiment and turned his attention back to Angel, tickling her, making her giggle. *His* daughter. The reality of it was still sinking in.

Yet, at the same time, this half a day of knowing she was his had tired him out more than a fourteen hour shoot. He lay down on the bed beside Angel, watching her explore his fingers, listening to her babble and giggle, engulfed in her fresh-bathed baby-smell.

A movement woke him. Kelly stood at the bedside, easing Angel out of his arms. He jerked into a sit.

She held up a silencing finger, whispering, "You can't sleep *with* her. You could roll over on her. She could roll off the bed."

"Sorry," he muttered, climbing off the bed and following Kelly to the crib. "I didn't mean to fall asleep with her on the bed. I know better. You have to believe I would never do anything intentional to hurt her."

Kelly laid the still sleeping Angel in her crib and covered her with a blanket. "I know you wouldn't."

Then she kissed her fingertips, pressed them against their daughter's forehead, turned and left the room.

#

He carried Angel into the kitchen the next morning, feeling anything but rested. Not Angel's fault. She'd slept the night through. But there'd been so many emotions, so many concerns rolling through him, he hadn't been able to sleep peacefully.

She'd awakened all happy gurgles. But, seeing her mother at the kitchen table, Angel brightened even more and reached for her. He didn't want to hand over his daughter but...

*For her good.*

Kelly hugged Angel to her, smiling, kissing her head, and cooing at her. Alma set a mug of hot coffee in front of the seat next to the highchair and asked him what kind of eggs he wanted. So they weren't ganging up to do battle against him.

"What's Angel usually eat?" he asked.

"Soft scrambled," Alma said.

"Then make mine the same," he said.

He sat around the corner from Kelly, the highchair between them. She was wearing her fatigues and looking no more rested than he.

"You working today?" he asked.

She nodded.

"You trust me that much with Angel?"

"She's your daughter," Kelly said. "Besides, you'll have the family here for back-up."

He grunted. "I half expected to find you in a sleeping

bag outside Angel's bedroom this morning, making sure I didn't try skipping out in the night with her."

She bounced Angel on her knee, but spoke to him. "You said you wouldn't take her away."

"I could have been lying."

She looked him in the eye. "I'm the liar here. Not you."

Then she rose, placed Angel in the highchair, gave her a good-bye kiss, and headed into the mudroom where she grabbed her jacket, but paused. "I called Andi last night. Had her go over to the camp and drain the pump so it wouldn't freeze when the fire died out. You want me to pick up your things and bring them here?"

#

He hadn't known what to tell Kelly when she asked if he wanted her to bring in his things from camp. He hadn't thought that far ahead. In the end, he'd muttered a, "yes." By the end of the second day, though, he knew moving into her house had been a mistake.

When Kelly returned from work, he beckoned her to follow him upstairs, leaving Angel happily ensconced on her grampa's lap.

Closed in Kelly's bedroom, he started with, "Everybody here keeps jumping in to take over Angel's care."

"They're used to taking care of her," she said. "It's a natural response for them. It's nothing personal."

"But *I* need for her to bond with me; and I don't know how else to make that happen than to take care of her and that's not going to happen when everyone here is getting in the way?"

"It'll take time."

"Easy for you to say. Everyone else has had nine months to build a bond with her, eighteen if you count…" He glanced down at her stomach.

She spread a hand across her mid-section. Of their own volition, his hands cupped the air between them and it hit him how badly he'd have liked to have felt their daughter moving inside Kelly's belly. Both Roman and Sam had told him how amazing the experience had been for them.

Hell, there was even a picture of Dixie and Michael, her first husband, living that moment; and it made him ache for all he'd missed.

"Dammit, Kelly," he said, emotion driving up the volume of his voice. "I can't fight my way through your parents every day for a chance to hold her—care for her. If she's going to come to know me as her father, I need alone time with her."

The color drained from Kelly's face. "You said you wouldn't take her away from me."

"I don't want to."

"And where do you propose to have this alone time?" she asked, her voice likewise rising. "Dixie's, where the paparazzi are sure to descend on you? Have you thought out how scary that kind of environment could be for a baby who's been separated from everything and everybody she knows?"

"That's not—"

"You said you'd make decisions based on what was best for Angel."

"That's why—"

"I won't allow you to turn her into some story on the front page of the tabloids. I won't let you put her through that kind of hell."

He caught her by the shoulders, stilling her. "I wouldn't do that to her, either, Kel."

She stared at him through tear glazed eyes.

"There is a place I could take her where there will be no paparazzi. The camp."

She stepped back from him, breaking from his hold, the expression in her eyes shifting from apprehension to pain and protectiveness. "But she'd still be without anything or anyone familiar."

"Not if you come with us."

## CHAPTER SEVENTEEN

She followed Dane in her truck, Angel's car-seat safely secured in the backseat of Dane's SUV. Her truck had an extended cab which would have kept Angel just as safe. But, he wanted alone time with his daughter and a thirty minute ride with a nine-month old babbling nonstop could be quite the bonding experience.

And if she cried through the whole trip?

Then thirty minutes of incessant tears would test Dane's commitment.

Kelly winced. The idea of her daughter weeping inconsolably tore at her motherly instincts.

But, the way Angel's little head tipped this way and that reassured her the baby was in adventure mode and not crying her heart out. And, the movement of Dane's mouth caught in his driver's side mirror suggested he was carrying on a conversation with a child who hadn't yet put together any intelligible words.

Still, heaven help him if Angel turned out to be just another passing fancy. If he created a bond with Angel and then walked out of her life...

For an instant, all the old feelings of being rejected by her own father slammed through Kelly.

But, Dane wouldn't do that. She was counting on him not doing that—counting on the fact he had strong family values—that family was important to him. Counting on the strength of his reaction to learning he had a daughter.

He took the rough road into camp slow, for which she was grateful. Seeing a thick plume of smoke rising from the woods above the location of the camp, she added a silent thank you to Andi for setting a fire in the wood stove so the cabin would be warm for Angel.

By the time she'd unloaded the Angel's gear from the back of the truck and joined Dane and Angel in the cabin, he had her snowsuit off and was carrying her around the one room building, pointing out things to her. He was a natural with babies. But then Angel was an easy baby, good-natured and out-going. How well would he handle the inconsolable sobbing that came with cutting a new tooth?

Kelly set up Angel's playpen-crib combo in crib mode and placed it beside the double bunks, stationed her highchair by the table, put her baby walker by the couch, and position a baby-barrier around the woodstove. That last Dane had purchased, his foresight in seeing she'd need protection from the hot stove boding well for his father-sense. That and the fact he recognized Angel would need someone she knew with her even as he demanded his *alone time* with her spoke volumes to Dane's commitment to *for the good of Angel*. For that above all, Kelly was grateful.

Not that she should have been surprised. Even two summers ago as a *Sexiest Man* in the making, he'd demonstrated a groundedness she hadn't expected.

"And that one," Dane was saying to Angel as he pointed out the perfectly symmetrical eight-point rack of antlers above the fireplace, "is your mommy's."

She'd done him a great disservice by not involving him in his daughter's birth—in her first nine months of life. She'd seen that the moment she'd found him rocking their daughter in her bedroom, tears on his cheeks.

That's why she'd played the hands-off parent as much as she could bear in the days since. Which, no doubt, was the reason he'd felt comfortable about choosing her to be Angel's anchor, the familiar tie to the world she knew.

Dane stood in front of the mirror next to the window over the sink, Angel held high in the crook of his arm. He pointed at her image in the mirror.

"That's Angel. That's you."

Then he pointed at his own image. "And that's me. That's your daddy."

And so it went throughout the rest of the day and into

the next. Dane carrying his daughter about the cabin identifying things for her—identifying himself as her father every chance he got, playing with her on the bottom bunk, feeding her, changing her diapers, watching over her as she slept while Kelly watched over them both should either need her, and aching to be part of their interplay. But she'd promised this time to Dane and she owed it to him to keep her promise.

The payoff, for Dane, came their third morning and it was a big one.

He was playing the *who's-in-the-mirror* game with Angel when her babbling took the form of a word, her first.

"Da-da."

"Yes," he said. "That's your Da-Da."

Kelly turned from the stove where she was making scrambled eggs. Angel looked from the mirror to Dane, her tiny fingers grabbing his chin as she repeated, "Da-da."

"Yes, I'm your Da-Da," he said, his voice husky, his blue eyes shimmering with unshed tears; and he looked at Kelly grinning. "Did you hear her?"

She nodded, tears welling in her own eyes. She could have told him babies usually discovered the hard consonants before the softer ones like the *mmmms* as in mama—that she probably didn't grasp the concept of daddy yet. But Kelly would have died before she took this first from him. He'd missed so many.

"Her first word," Kelly said, beaming at father and daughter. She should never have doubted him.

But then, she'd never before seen a man so happily interact with a baby the way Dane did.

#

They'd shared Angel's first word, him and Kelly. And it felt good, right. It felt like something he wanted more of.

But she hadn't shared.

Not the first nine months of Angel's life. Not all the months before while she was carrying his daughter...their daughter.

Angel gurgled up at him from her crib and smiled.

"You little flirt," he said, chucking her under the chin.

Angel giggled.

"Hard to take a nap when the room's so bright, hey my sweet Angel?"

She yawned but waved her tiny fists in the air, fighting sleep. It reminded him what a fighter her mother was.

His smile slipped. Whatever his feelings for Kelly, they would always be bound together by this child.

He looked to where Kelly was wiping down the table after their macaroni and cheese lunch. Even angry with her, the sight of her made his chest ache.

Maybe he wasn't so angry with her anymore. After all, she'd consented to his taking her—his daughter to a camp where there was no electricity or hot, running water. She'd kept herself as much out of the way as possible in the one room cabin so he could bond with Angel.

He stroked his daughter's silky hair. She blinked up at him with sleepy eyes.

"How come, the last two days I put you down for your afternoon nap you were asleep almost before your head hit the mattress? Did all that exploring we've been doing tire you out? You all acclimated to the place now?"

"Da-da, Da-Da, Da-Da."

Angel had been trying on that word ever since first saying it this morning. The sound of it still brought a lump to his throat.

He slid his fingers away from her head. "Daddy will fix it."

By the time he rigged a drape around the crib of a blanket strung from the bunk post to Frank's repositioned recliner, he knew he had something more to fix for his daughter than an overly bright sleep-space.

#

Dishes washed, Kelly wrung out the dishrag, hung it up, and drained the sink. When she turned around, Dane sat at the table, a mug of coffee in front of him and another across from him.

"Sit with me," he said.

Her heart leapt in her chest. For the most part, he'd ignored her presence since coming to the camp; and that he now wanted her company...

She slid into the seat opposite him, warning herself he probably wanted to talk logistics of sharing parenthood when they lived so far apart.

He sipped his coffee, staring over her shoulder toward the drape she'd seen him rig around Angel's crib. This was definitely going to be about Angel.

She wrapped her hands around the hot mug, breath held, the silence stretching. When his gaze finally shifted to her, his eyes were somber but no longer full of anger and, when he spoke, it was with a quiet solemnness.

"Why didn't you tell me you were pregnant?"

The breath shuddered from her. "I was going to."

"What stopped you?" he asked almost gently.

She stared into the dark liquid shimmering in the cup between her hands. "When I told my dad, he had a stroke. One disastrous reaction was more than I could handle."

"So you knew when you called me from the hospital," he said, only the faintest hint of censure in his tone.

She looked up at him. "Everything was crazy that night. I thought my dad was going to die and it was my fault."

His gaze slid toward Angel's enclosure before coming back to her. "And in the days following...when he did survive, after he came home, why didn't you tell me then?"

Though his tone didn't accuse, she felt the full weight of her guilt. "I was afraid to."

"That I'd do to Angel what your biological father did to you?"

So he remembered what she'd confessed to him in their closest moments so very long ago. She grimaced. "I thought I could protect her against the pain of growing up, knowing she'd been rejected by her father."

"After all I told you about how I felt about family, you still thought I'd abandon her?"

She stared into her full mug. "Your career was just taking off. You were having the time of your life."

"I remember telling you I wanted a family."

She met his gaze, looked into his wounded eyes. "You also said *someday.*"

"So I did." He sipped at his coffee, his pupils pulsing with thought. When he put his mug down, he asked, "What were you going to tell Angel when she was old enough to ask about me—her father?"

"That I didn't tell him—you about her."

His brow wrinkled in bewilderment. "And you thought that would be less painful for her?"

"You don't know what it feels like to be rejected by someone that important to you."

"Maybe not," he said, his voice tight. "But I know what it's like to live for texts and emails from someone you love only for them to stop coming."

She blinked at him. *Love?*

"After the director forbid me from bringing my cell to the shoots, I'd race back to my trailer at every break just to see if you'd sent me a text. The first full day I went without getting anything from you worried me."

"You were in love with me?" she asked, stunned, hopeful.

He glanced toward where Angel slept and drew a deep breath. "I think I began falling for you when you ordered me to drop my pants so you could dab sting stop on my ass, Kel. Maybe even before then. That stiff handshake you gave me when we met at the ranger station piqued my curiosity."

She thought she understood and some of her hope died. "I challenged you."

"Okay, you were a challenge," he conceded. "But when we made love the first time, I felt something I'd never felt with another woman. It was like a seed of something greater was being planted in me."

"A seed definitely was planted in me that first time,"

she said, a bittersweet smile pulling at her lips.

He glanced toward the drape strung from the bed where they'd made love. She wanted it to have been love. But, even if it was, she'd destroyed it.

There was a great sadness in his voice when he spoke again.

"Your messages came pretty sporadically after that. For a long time I believed it was because you were dealing with your dad's situation. Then, one evening, sitting in my trailer sweeping through a week's list of texts, I realized there were none from you."

He looked at her through sad eyes. "That's when it hit me. You'd been distancing yourself from me for months."

"I couldn't keep lying to you, not telling you I was pregnant. Given how your career was flourishing, given what I feared your reaction would be, I thought it was for the best."

"You never thought to give me a chance?"

"I vacillated. I came close to having my mother call you the night I went into labor. But a nurse walked into the labor room with the latest tabloid paper and there, splashed across the front page was a picture of you with some beautiful starlet, the headline reading, *The Hawke Engaged.*"

"It wasn't true, Kel. Those rags—"

She reached across the table, her fingers against the back of his hand stopping him. "I know. But at the time—"

"So you figured it would be better for Angel to grow up believing in a fairytale, that if only her father knew about her he'd come to her like some shining knight?" He shook his head. "Didn't you see that, when she found out you never told him—me, she'd blame you for not having a father?"

Kelly pulled her hand back and swallowed against the lump in her throat. "I thought it would be better if she hated me for keeping her father from her, than for her to live with the hurt of his not wanting her. I thought, better if she had someone tangible to vent on."

Pain pinched at the corners of his eyes, reminding her of the tabloid pictures her mother had shown her in the months after they'd stopped corresponding and her mother's comments about how sad he looked in those pictures. She'd seen it, too, the smile for the cameras that didn't reach his eyes. The sadness she saw in his eyes now went even deeper.

"I'm sorry I didn't tell you," she whispered. "I really am."

Accusation melded with the sadness in his eyes. "And when I came back, when I showed up at your house, held Angel right there in front of you, why didn't you tell me then?"

Coffee sloshed from the mug between her hands and her stomach bottomed out. "I was afraid you'd take her away from me."

He shifted back in his chair and drew a deep breath. "I can relate to that one."

"I'm sorry, Dane."

He held up a hand and flexed a woeful grin. "Maybe that's how it had to be. I've lived a charmed life, everything falling into my lap. Maybe I needed to know what it was like to lose something I was pursuing—something precious in order for me to learn what's really important."

"You always knew family was important," she said, believing she knew what the important thing was that he was talking about.

He nodded. "I *knew* it. But I'm not so sure I *felt* the full force of its importance, not until I realized how close I came to losing my own family."

He closed his eyes, his brow puckering. He shook his head. She thought she knew what he was thinking, that she'd nearly succeeded in keeping his daughter from him.

Then he looked at her and put it all into words.

"Can we at least be friends for her sake?" he asked.

*Friends.*

"Of course," she said, her heart breaking.

#

Dane had been so angry—so focused on how he'd been wronged—on what he'd missed out on that he hadn't even considered what all this had done—was doing to Kelly. He hadn't even asked her why, halfway through the first night at the camp, she'd climbed down from the upper bunk and had slept on the couch ever since.

But now he knew why she'd excluded him—understood that her avoiding—rejecting him since his return was more of a pre-emptive strike.

Had he done the same thing that afternoon by suggesting they be friends after telling her he loved her; or, more accurately, *had* loved her? Was his not telling her he still loved her to punish her, or just his way of protecting himself? Truth of it was he didn't know how she really felt about him.

"Ready," she said, drying her hands and stepping away from the sink where she'd been mixing hot water from the stove with cold from the pump for Angel's bath.

All he knew for certain was friendship would never be enough—that he wanted a complete family. As he carried Angel toward the sink, he motioned for Kelly to join them.

"We're a family, whether we want to be or not," he said. "Time we get used to doing things together."

So the two of them crowded around the kitchen sink to bathe their daughter, Kelly's hoarse, "Thank you," making him feel like a heal.

Why'd he add that *whether we want to be or not* part onto his invitation?

Because he was an idiot. Because he was impulsive and this was an instance of that impulsiveness biting him in the ass.

Because it still hurt that Kelly had let him go.

Plus, he was a coward. If she didn't feel for him the way he felt for her…

Bath done, he wrapped Angel in a big towel and carried her back to his bunk, inviting Kelly to help him dry their daughter. They sat on either side of the baby, making a game of rubbing her with the soft towel—making her giggle which in turn made both him and Kelly laugh. He looked over at Kelly, her face aglow with love.

She glanced up and caught him watching her. The glow faded and the love... He swore it didn't fade. It just ducked behind that bruised look in her eyes before she glanced away. Maybe she hadn't let go of *them* as easily—as completely as he feared.

At one point, Angel clutched Kelly's finger in one tiny fist and one of his fingers in her other fist. It was as if Angel understood their link—that they belonged together. When he looked at Kelly, he saw the tears in the corners of her eyes even as she laughed and cooed over their daughter. Had she, too, seen the same hope in that innocent gesture?

Later, arms folded on the side-rail of her crib, he and Kelly watched their daughter until she fell asleep. How easy it would be to slip an arm around Kelly's shoulders—how natural the notion seemed.

But Kelly straightened before he could act. She stretched her neck side-to-side and he heard the popping.

"That doesn't sound good," he said.

"That old couch isn't the best for sleeping," she said.

"Why are you sleeping on it then?"

"Too hot in the upper bunk," she said, gathering her pillow and a blanket from the bench at the foot of the bunks.

"We can cut back on the fire some," he said.

She shook her head as she headed for the couch. "Have to keep the place toasty for our little angel."

He snagged her by the wrist, not entirely sure why he stopped her until he positioned himself behind her and placed his hands on her shoulders.

"Let's see if I can loosen up those muscles," he said, ignoring her momentary tensing.

When she sank into the rotation of his fingers, Dane

said, "I think I misspoke earlier when I suggested we be friends for Angel's sake."

She tensed again.

"Relax," he said, deepening the pressure of his kneading fingers. "I'm just saying…we should try to be a family."

Her muscles went rigid. "Whether we want to be or not, right?"

"I didn't mean it the way it came out. I was just trying to say we *are* a family."

"And you'll do anything for Angel's happiness," she said in a tone rife with resignation.

"She's my daughter. I want her happy," he said.

*Just as I want you and me happy.*

"I understand your need to make sure Angel is part of your family," she said, her muscles like bands of steel beneath his fingers. "But you don't need to make me part of the package. I'll never try to keep her away from you again."

"I'm making a real mess of this," he said, softening the stroke of his fingers. "I'm not talking about just Angel. I'm saying I want to find out if we can be a family, *all three of us*."

"Okay," she said, her shoulders easing a tad. "How do you suggest we go about doing that."

"For starters, you and I stop sleeping apart."

## CHAPTER EIGHTEEN

Kelly lie in the bottom bunk facing the wall, her back to Dane. What madness had made her agree to his plan?

She knew this experiment of his wouldn't work. Hell, she'd known it the moment she'd crawled into his bed and he'd turned his back to her. She knew, because she couldn't bear sharing his bed and not touching him.

The tears came silently at first. But they wouldn't stop—wouldn't stay quiet. She stuffed the corner of her pillow into her mouth to stifle the sobs—curled her body away from his so he wouldn't feel the quaking of hers. Even in this, she failed.

"Kelly, what's wrong?" he asked, suddenly hovering over her.

He touched her shoulder and she shrank from him, sobbing out, "I can't lie next to you, pretending everything is normal, not touching."

"Do you want me to touch you, Kel?"

She swallowed a sob. "You love Angel so much you'll do anything for her, even try and find some way to reconcile some sort of relationship with me. I respect that. But it hurts too much to know you're only pretending with me."

He gathered her in his arms and drew her across his lap as he sat back against the headboard and rocked her.

"Don't," she sobbed against his chest.

"Ah, Kelly. I didn't mean to hurt you."

"I deserve to be hurt."

"Never."

She shook her head. "My not telling you about Angel wasn't all that altruistic. I didn't tell you because I was afraid of-of—"

"Being rejected by yet another man who should love you?"

She cried all the harder and he hugged her closer. "Aren't we a pair? You willing to sacrifice yourself to save your daughter the kind of pain you've suffered, and me willing to sacrifice the love of my life over a fit of temper."

She peeked up at him, her sobs giving way to hiccups. "The love of your life. That's Angel, right?"

He kissed her brow and murmured, "In this case, Bright Eyes, I was talking about you. I love you every bit as much as I love that little girl we made together."

"You're not just saying that for Angel's sake?"

"Not for Angel's sake," he said, meeting her gaze. "For mine."

"How can you love me after what I've done?"

He shook his head. "Ah, Kel, we hit a rough spot. That's all."

She slumped against him. "That's putting it mildly."

He stroked her hair. "A big rough spot. And now we're talking about it. I know I wasn't talking or listening all that well when I first found out Angel was mine."

"You were angry and had every right to be."

"Yes, I was and I did. But I've gotten past that."

"Meaning?"

"Meaning we can survive this."

She lifted her head from his chest and peered into his eyes. "How?"

"We start by not being afraid to love each other." He swiped the tears from her face. "I start by saying I love you, Bright Eyes. I knew it that first night we made love." He shook his head. "I'd never before forgotten to use protection. I think the Fates knew they had to bind us together some way."

"Really?"

"Cross my heart and hope to die. Now tell me you love me, too, Bright Eyes, so I can propose to you and make us a proper family."

She hesitated just long enough to absorb what he'd just said, then threw her arms around his neck. "I love you,

Dane St. John. You are *my* hero."

He held her and stroked her back, kissing her hair, his tone when he spoke full of teasing. "Didn't you once say heroes are just ordinary people who do extraordinary things?"

"Yes," she said, easing back in his arms so she could see his face and he hers.

"I haven't done anything extraordinary," he said.

"You came back."

"I needed a place to hide."

"When you found out Angel was yours, you didn't run," she said

"Nothing extraordinary in that, not for a real father."

"You never let go of *us*—of *me.*"

"I love you, Bright Eyes. There's not a single extraordinary thing about that."

"It's extraordinary to me," she said, stroking his cheek.

He caught her hand and pressed a kiss to her palm. "That better not be about you feeling unworthy of being loved, because you are anything but unworthy."

She smiled up at him. "I think I've gotten past that."

He smiled back at her. "To be on the safe side, I promise I'll spend the rest of my life trying to do extraordinary things for you, and only you."

"And Angel?"

He tucked her hand against his chest above his heart, vowing, "Angel, too…and every other little angel we make."

"And I promise to love you to the ends of the earth, Dane," she said and kissed him long and hard.

When their lips parted, he said, "That jealousy thing…"

"Just a tactic to throw you off," she said. "Now make like the hero you are and kiss me again."

## EPILOGUE

No one had dared count on Plan A...except the groom. Mid-February in Michigan's Upper Peninsula was unpredictable snowfalls and fluctuating temperatures, mostly on the low end of the thermometer. Definitely not outdoor wedding weather.

But Valentine's Day had dawned with a landscape glistening with a dusting of fresh snow beneath a cloudless, blue sky with temps in the rosy-cheek range.

In front of the intimate gathering of their families on Angel Point, Dane accepted Kelly's white-gloved hand from her father, grinning as he murmured below the hearing of those gathered to witness the nuptials, "Told you the weather would be perfect for us."

"You lead a charmed life, Dane St. John," she said, her heart bursting with joy.

"And I'm glad I do or I'd never have found you," he said, the love in his eyes making her knees go weak.

She wobbled. He slipped an arm around her, steadying her—crushing her white, velvet cloak to her. It didn't matter, that last part. Dane had taught her the importance of support, especially from a life partner...even for a strong, capable woman.

And he'd shown her his support almost from the moment they'd met—shown it most definitely the minute she'd said "yes" to his proposal nearly a month ago in the bottom bunk at the camp where they'd discovered there was nothing that could ever keep them apart.

"What kind of wedding do you want?" he'd asked.

"A justice of the peace at the courthouse will suit me just fine," she'd said.

To which he'd shaken his head. "Not good enough for you, Bright Eyes."

"I don't want some big splashy Hollywood bash," she'd shot back, terrified that's where he was heading.

He'd smiled, drawn her close, and whispered in her ear, "Neither do I. Just family. But soon. I want us married soon. Before I'm due back on set the end of February."

She'd gasped. "February! Not much time for more than a Justice at the courthouse."

He'd just brushed his lips across hers, promising her a fairytale wedding.

And here they were, Dane having arranged for a Judge to perform the ceremony at the very place where they'd fallen in love.

The official welcomed the little group gathered between the overlook of Angel Point and the cabin, then requested the happy couple join hands.

Kelly handed her fur muff off to her Maid of Honor, her sister Carrie, the two exchanging warm smiles. They'd grown close over their father's illness and closer still over Angel's birth.

Facing Dane, they took each other's hands and looked deep into each other's eyes. Whatever the Judge said about the sanctity of marriage didn't matter. The two of them already knew how precious forever love was…and how to survive the tough spots every relationship encountered.

Then it was time for them to share the vows they'd written, promises more personal and meaningful to them than any pledges a Judge could have had them recite. Kelly spoke first.

"You are good for me, Dane St. John. You showed me I was worthy of love—taught me to leave the past behind me."

Between the loving way he looked at her and how he gave her fingers a squeeze, her throat tightened.

"You taught me," she continued, her voice thick with emotion, "to believe in myself and not let the opinions of others drag me down."

Tess cleared her throat and Kelly gave her bridesmaid an acknowledging glance. She'd all but burst into tears when Tess had unzipped the over-sized garment bag and revealed the cloak with the fur trimmed hood and satin gown Dane had chosen for her. She would have worn a dress out of her closet to get married in. But he'd said he wanted something for her that would remind her of the woman he knew she was—the woman she'd too long hidden behind a DNR uniform. It had been the only moment since agreeing to marry him she'd questioned if she was the right woman for him. After all, his was a high profile life and hers...

Thankfully, classy, sophisticated Tess had insisted the movie crowd would be green with envy over her perfect skin and fabulous bone structure. Tess, perfection personified in her crimson bridesmaid gown, had also bolstered Kelly when she'd frowned at the made-up bridal version of herself in a full-length mirror back at the house, worrying aloud she didn't look like herself.

"You look like a polished you," Tess had said, giving Kelly's shoulders a reassuring squeeze.

"But I'll need to look *polished* whenever I go out in the world with Dane. How do I accomplish that?" Kelly had demurred. "I don't want to embarrass him."

Tess had pinned Kelly's gaze in the mirror then. "You could never embarrass Dane. He loves you; and my guess is he loves the au natural you even better than the polished one. But if it will make you feel more confident, I'll teach you how to use make-up."

Kelly returned her gaze to Dane. "Though I might still need a little help on the confidence front," she continued. "But I'll always have you beside me to reassure me, if not physically then in spirit."

"Always," he crooned, his eyes full of promise.

If he kept looking at her like that, she was going to throw herself into his arms and soak the front of his wool coat with her tears, so she varied a tad from her planned vows and smiled widely. "You make me laugh."

"And cry," he said, releasing her hand long enough to wipe a tear from the corner of her eye.

"You take care of me," she pressed on.

"Hopefully as well as you have taken care of me," he said, his fingertips lingering on her cheek.

She cuffed him on the arm, good-naturedly grousing, "Stop interrupting me."

Laughter murmured from their loved ones. His grin returned tenfold. She shook her head.

"You're such a shit," she said to more laughter. "But I love that about you, too."

He wagged his eyebrows. "Good because I'm not likely to change."

"I don't want you to change," she said, totally off script. "Never change. I love you just as you are, Dane St. John. You are the man I want our daughter to grow up knowing. You are my hero."

He drew her gloved hands up and pressed his lips to the backs of her knuckles before offering her his vows.

"I promise to do everything in my power to live up to your opinion of me, Bright Eyes. Every day of the rest of my life, you will be my first thought when I wake and my last before I sleep."

She chuckled. "You have much yet to learn about fatherhood."

Snickers waffled through the gathering, none louder than Best Man Roman's. Even unattached baby brother and groomsman Renn snickered as though he understood what it was to have a baby in his life. But Dane didn't laugh.

"Thank you for my daughter," he said with such heartfelt earnestness it might have shot guilt through her. Okay, it did. But just a twinge. She'd made progress in adopting Dane's attitude of leaving the past in the past as he'd urged her to do.

"Thank you for protecting her so well through the hard times," he went on, "and for understanding my needs when I discovered her."

"For the good of Angel," she said barely above a whisper.

"For the good of *our* family," he retorted, drew a deep breath, and continued. "I love that you love me, Kelly Jackson, because I love you with every cell of my being. I love that you are the woman I need, because you are the woman I want. I pledge to be, today and forever, your hero."

And so on a sunny February morning on Angel Point overlooking a valley of frosted trees that shimmered in the sunlight like diamonds and with all their family as witness, particularly one special rosy-cheeked *angel,* Kelly Jackson married the hero of her dreams and became Kelly St. John; and Dane St. John gained his own family…a little sooner than he'd expected, but with the greatest of joy.

the end

## Excerpt from FOREVER KNIGHT: St. John Sibling Series, Book 4 by Barbara Raffin

Light glinted off the long blade slicing the air toward Renn St. John's head—the same blade that had already driven him to one knee in the sand. With the flat of his own broadsword, he blocked the blow, sending his attacker staggering backward.

Taking advantage of the opposing knight's imbalance, Renn leapt to his feet and lunged at him, their clashing blades ringing throughout the arena. With practiced, unrelenting blows, Renn drove the knight back until he stumbled and fell to the sand, disarmed, Renn's blade at his throat.

Lifting his blade and sheathing it, Renn handed the new recruit off the ground, "Perfect. Once you unseated me in the joust, you drove me well away from the rail where the fight could be seen from every seat in the house. Do it just like that tonight during the show."

"Got it," said the former squire now The Joust's newest addition to its stable of stunt riders, his grin about as wide as the Rio Grande.

Though only a few years older than the newby, Renn cuffed the new rider on the shoulder. "Now go after your horse and make sure he knows he did a good job for you."

A smile stretched across Renn's lips as he watched the kid trot off toward one of the end openings in the arena the horses were trained to exit once they'd lost their rider in the joust. Barely three years ago he'd been the one facing his first show as a knight at The Joust. He still remembered the excitement he'd felt that night.

Hell, he still felt the excitement every time he suited up for a show. Damn, he loved this job.

Turning for the opposite exit through which his mount had left, his gaze caught sight of another of the Knight brigade, this one still mounted and hugging the stadium wall. Concerned there was a problem with the horse, Renn headed toward horse and rider.

But, closing on them, he saw the attraction...at least what held the *knight's* attention. On the far side of the wall dividing arena from viewing area, a serving wench was laying out dinnerware for the night's show.

Her thick mane of black hair hung midway down her back and her off-the-shoulder peasant blouse costume bared a lovely expanse of skin. Something he noted as he strode toward her and Dugan, the mounted knight.

He likewise noted hers was a figure his boss and owner of The Joust would call buxom. Though, she had a narrow waist and, judging by what he could see above the dividing wall, gently flaring hips.

Unencumbered by the chainmail and knight's regalia worn during shows, Renn easily vaulted onto the ledge separating spectators from jousters. Yup, nothing overly done about the hips under the long skirt she wore. He wasn't surprised. Dugan was a man of discerning taste.

Dugan's roving eye also tended to wreak havoc among the younger of the female staff. Renn wouldn't be surprised if the high turnover rate of clerks, ticket takers, and serving wenches wasn't in part due to Dugan's entanglements. Something Renn intended to head off with this latest hire.

But, when the girl in serving wench costume turned from Dugan to him, he amended girl to woman. Deep brown eyes regarded him with a dark glance. No, this one wasn't the usual college co-ed hired to play one of The Joust's serving wenches.

In spite of a sense that this one could handle herself with the likes of Dugan, he gave her a crooked smile with a nod in the direction of the seated rider. "I should warn you, fair maiden, Dugan here has a way with the ladies, lad*ies* being the operative word here."

Her dark eyes appraised him. "And you, do you likewise have *a way* with the lad*ies?"*

Dugan chuckled and his horse nudged Renn's chest with its muzzle. Cradling the horse's head and scratching his ears, Renn answered, "I fear I have more of a way with horses than ladies."

The wench's eyes narrowed.

Giving the chestnut gelding's ear a final rub, Renn met Dugan's gaze. "Shouldn't you be riding Tyke around the arena, getting him accustomed to it—bonding with him?"

The humor drained from Dugan's eyes as he held Renn's gaze a couple seconds too long. Challenge duly noted. Then, with a half-bow to the serving girl, he heeled the horse away from the wall.

Renn kept a watchful eye on Dugan and Tyke for a few more seconds before turning his attention back to the raven–haired beauty who'd attracted Dugan's attention. He half expected her to have gone on about her job of setting out faux-pewter plates and mugs. Instead, he found her watching Dugan put Tyke through his paces.

"You're new," Renn said, his seat on the divider ledge putting him eye level with her as she stood in the aisle in front of the first tier of plank tables.

"I am," she said without taking her eyes off horse and rider. "And that's a quarter horse."

"That it is," Renn answered, his chest spontaneously puffing with pride.

She looked him in the eye. "An American made breed in a medieval times setting. A bit anachronistic isn't it?"

He'd have been impressed with her knowledge. But everybody in Texas knew quarter horses were American made. Then again, no wench before this one had ever bothered to point out the fact. Even though her comment deflated him a bit, he had to admit he was at least a little impressed.

She raised one finely arched eyebrow at him, reminding him she waited for an answer. Add assertive to the budding list of reasons to be impressed by this woman.

He grinned. "You haven't seen a quarter horse run the

joust yet, have you?"

"That's not the point," she said, not a hint of a smile on her full lips.

"Ah, but it is," he said, oddly tempted to kiss some of the sternness from those ripe lips glossed a deep shade of red. "A quarter horse is faster off the mark than any other breed; and, being they can outdistance a Thoroughbred race horse in the quarter mile—" He smiled crookedly. "Makes for quite a show."

Bracing her tray of dinnerware with both hands to her midsection, she faced him full on. "I know how speedy a quarter horse is in the short run. That doesn't make him any more suitable a mount for a medieval knight than would a Shetland pony."

Going for humor, he retorted, "Actually, as old a breed as Shetland ponies are, who's to say they weren't used by a medieval knight or two?"

With what could only be described as an exasperated sigh, she turned back to her task of laying out plates and cups.

"Some of those knights of old could be rather small," he called after her as he rose and strode along the ledge of the divider after her, determined to get at least a smile out of her.

"If you're trying to impress me with your wit," she tossed over her shoulder, "save it for some naïve girl."

"I'm not trying to impress you, just get a smile out of you."

"I'll smile at the patrons I serve tonight during the performance," she said, efficiently laying out dinnerware along the long tables.

"That'd be *my* performance," he said in a bemused tone. "The one where I dazzle our patrons with a lightning fast ride toward the point of lance…astride a quarter horse."

She huffed and moved to the second tier of tables.

"They won't give a fig what I'm riding," he pressed, pivoting on the narrow ledge to keep up with her path.

"Quarter horses are anachronistic," she repeated,

slapping down a mug a little too hard.

What was this woman's problem? Was she some history teacher who'd lost her job due to budget cuts? Maybe an historian unable to find a job in her field?

"Look, lady," he called up to her. "We're just about having fun here."

She wheeled at him, her skirt swirling against the backs of the first row of bench seats, the mugs on her tray swaying. "Fun. That's the be all and end all with you guys, isn't it?"

The vehemence of her question drew him up. "You got a problem with fun?"

"When it gets in the way of responsibility, I do."

He hooked his thumbs in his jeans pockets and cocked his head to one side, studying her. He wanted to ask her why she thought fun and responsibility were mutually exclusive. What came out was, "Maybe The Joust isn't a good fit for you."

The corners of her mouth lifted into something more akin to smugness than a smile. "Are you threatening to have me fired?"

He held her gaze, noting a glint in her eyes that matched the smug line of her mouth. He didn't know who'd hired her. But, clearly, she didn't know that he had the power to fire her.

Good thing for her he wasn't a man given to rash decisions. Besides, something about this obstinate, raven-haired beauty intrigued him—made him want to prove to her fun and responsibility could go hand-in-hand.

Giving her a courtly bow, he turned and hopped off the rail back into the sands of the arena, the fun area of his job.

## About the Author

An obsessive writer who'd rather write than breathe, Barbara Raffin wrote her first novel at age twelve in retaliation to the lack of female leads in the adventure stories she loved reading. But it was a love of playing with words, exploring the human psyche, and telling stories that kept her writing.

This award-winning author lives on the Michigan-Wisconsin border with her Keeshond dogs Katie and Slippers and her avid outdoorsman husband who has always supported her love affair with reading and writing. Learn more about Barbara Raffin and her books, or contact her through her web site at www.BarbaraRaffin.com

LINK TO MY WEB SITE:
http://barbararaffin.com/
LINK TO MY BLOG:
http://barbararaffin.com/barbsblog/


Be sure to check out:

Stacey Joy Netzel's
**Romancing Wisconsin Series**

*To everything there is a season...*

Love finds a way during the four seasons in the **Romancing Wisconsin Series** Starting with

Christmas/Winter, then moving on to Autumn, check out the first six books in this bestselling, heartwarming series set in small town Wisconsin, where hope springs eternal for each happily ever after. Meet the Rileys, the Walshes, and best of all, Butch...a.k.a. *Santa* Butch. The mischievous matchmaker makes a cameo in each story—adding a touch of magic to the lives of everyone he loves, and even those he's just met.

Romancing Wisconsin Series
*Mistletoe Mischief*, #1
*Mistletoe Magic*, #2
*Mistletoe Match-Up*, #3
*Autumn Wish*, #4
*Autumn Bliss*, #5
*Autumn Kiss*, #6

"The Romancing Wisconsin series is fantastic. The characters are amazing and the plot makes you want to keep reading straight through to the end." Debbie ~ Amazon reviewer

Sneak peak at AUTUMN WISH

Nikki Rowen desires a family of her own—but first comes love, then comes marriage. She thought she had the former, until the moment she mentioned the latter and her boyfriend left her with nothing but a broken heart. Just as she's beginning to doubt she'll ever have a *'til death do us part* Happily Ever After, she meets her new neighbor in the most unexpected way.

In Sam Mallin's experience, the word *family* is synonymous with abandonment; he's more than content on his own. Yet, in less than a week, he finds himself caring for an infant dropped on his doorstep, and playing house with his beautiful next-door-neighbor. When his feelings for Nikki deepen, he fears he's nothing more than the ready-made family she so desperately wishes for. How can a self-proclaimed loner hold onto the two females most important to him without history repeating itself in a world of heartbreak?

EXCERPT:

He'd just reached into the refrigerator for a beer when the doorbell chimed. The cheery summons grated across his nerves, making him cringe. Could he ignore this unwanted visitor who appeared to have practically been waiting in the bushes for him?

A glance over his shoulder gave him the answer. Nope. His bare windows, glaring lights, and the volume of the TV made it impossible to pretend he wasn't home. Curtains and blinds seemed a great investment right about now.

Kicking the fridge shut, he twisted the cap from the bottle. The doorbell went off again, twice as long as before, as if the person on the other side held it down. Damn it. If this was another married woman bringing him pie, he was going to—

*Smile, and say, "Thank you."* That's what neighbors did, right?

He took a long, fortifying pull off his beer, then thumped it on the counter on his way to answer the door. Too bad his neighbor right next door hadn't been one of those pie-wielding visitors. He'd have invited her inside.

Then he got a glimpse through the window...of *her* standing on his front porch.

"Well, whaddaya know," he murmured with a sudden grin of anticipation. Maybe she'd come in and watch the game with him. Hell, he wouldn't even care if she held a pie in her hands.

He swung the door open and smiled his welcome at the pretty blond. His gaze dropped, then froze. Where he would've preferred a pie, she held a baby carrier—

complete with baby.

Damn, she had a kid. After what his mother put him and his sister through, he didn't do women with kids.

"Samuel Mallin?"

He lifted his gaze up from all that pink to a pair of guarded blue eyes. Forcing his lips to maintain their upward curve, he answered, "I prefer Sam. And you're Nicole, right?"

"Nikki." She frowned. "How'd you—"

"I had some of your mail in my box yesterday," he admitted.

"Ah."

Her wry smile was appealing enough to make him forget about the baby. But it faded fast as she took a breath, shifted her stance, then extended her arms, carrier and all.

"Sam, this is yours."

There was a crumpled envelope clutched between the fingers of her right hand. Tilting his head, he read his name in the crinkled address field and removed it from her grasp with a laugh. He liked that she'd chosen to bring his mail over personally. If he'd been thinking, he'd have done it first—and found out about the kid.

"Thanks," he said as her baby began to fuss. "I just put your stuff in your mailbox."

Nikki lifted the carrier higher with an exasperated huff. "You don't understand. *She* is yours."

In the middle of stuffing the folded envelope into his back pocket, his gaze dropped to the baby. Blue eyes, just like her momma. It took his brain a moment to make the connection, and then his pulse jumped as his eyebrows shot skyward. "Uh...I don't think so."

The baby sucked hard on a pacifier, her eyes shifting back and forth as she squirmed in the confined seat. *Oh, hell no.* He lifted his gaze once more, taking note of the woman's curves on the way up. Yeah, she was pretty, but not worth this level of crazy. He'd have much preferred another pie.

"May I come in?"

"No," he stated. "She's not mine."

He fumbled for the edge of the door. The woman stepped forward as he began to shut her out.

Her chin lifted and those blue eyes of hers glittered with determination. "Her name is Ella. She's three and a half months old."

"I haven't—"

He broke off as she shouldered her way past, into his living room. Sam closed the door and followed her to the couch where she set the carrier and an overflowing diaper bag. He glanced toward the kitchen, searching out his cell phone on the counter. Was he going to have to call the cops to get rid of her?

The baby started to cry, so Nikki picked her up and rocked her while speaking in a soft, crooning voice. The gentle sound soothed his nerves until common sense returned with a vengeance.

Denial shook his head as he moved to stand in front of her. "Listen, I don't know what you think you're going to get out of this, but we've never met before, much less done what we would've needed to do to create that baby."

~~~

BUY AUTUMN WISH HERE:

Amazon US UK CA DE, BN, Apple, Kobo, ARe, SW

Stacey Joy Netzel Newsletter signup:
http://bit.ly/SJNnewsletter
(New release info. only)

Website and Blog: http://www.StaceyJoyNetzel.com
Facebook: Facebook.com/StaceyJoyNetzel
Twitter: http://twitter.com/StaceyJoyNetzel

Made in the USA
Charleston, SC
11 December 2014